WHO SHALL DIE

CAROLYN GEDULD

Black Rose Writing | Texas

ISBN: 978-1-68513-077-0
PUBLISHED BY BLACK ROSE WRITING
www.blackrosewriting.com

Printed in the United States of America
Suggested Retail Price (SRP) $21.95

Who Shall Die is printed in Book Antiqua

*As a planet-friendly publisher, Black Rose Writing does its best to eliminate unnecessary waste to reduce paper usage and energy costs, while never compromising the reading experience. As a result, the final word count vs. page count may not meet common expectations.

For my parents, Howard and Helen Taft, of blessed memory.

ACKNOWLEDGEMENTS

With gratitude to those who encouraged me, including Didi Kerler, Sue Swartz, Michael Taft, and the staff of Black Rose Writing.

This is the ritual law that the Lord has commanded:...bring a red cow without blemish, in which there is no defect...It shall be taken outside the camp and slaughtered...The cow shall be burned...A man who is clean shall gather up the ashes of the cow...to be kept for water of lustration for the Israelite community. It is for cleansing.
Numbers: 18

WHO SHALL DIE

CHAPTER 1
AZURA

In 2040, five years after she entered the forest to have her baby, Azura emerged with her daughter, Noam, at dusk. The small community of older women who lived in the forest and supported Azura died, one by one. There was no choice but to move back to town.

She held Noam's hand in her left fist and a small bundle of belongings in her right as she walked to what had been the state park entrance with its long-abandoned guard shack. A night's journey lay ahead, on the neglected road to town, the same road Azura's great-grandmother travelled when she took Azura's mother to the forest at the beginning of the century, before the plague and the change in the weather. Now, the heat softened the pavement, making it too hot and uncomfortable to trudge along during the day.

She waited for a full moon, which provided just enough light to see a few feet into the dark stretch ahead. A kitchen knife held in her belt provided her only protection against the dog packs that hunted at the edge of the forest and the unsavory humans who might drift along the open road. Another advantage of traveling at night was that both dogs and humans might be asleep in their dens and residences.

"I'm hungry, Mama."

There was not enough to feed the child after the forest fires devoured the edible plants and small mammals living in the woods. Azura hoped there would be more resources in town. Noam's skin stretched over her ribs and her belly protruded, the beginning signs of starvation. Her large, dark eyes bulged from her tiny face. Azura was in no better shape.

She remembered the crops growing near the side of the road during her first trip to town. The area was turning to desert. Still, the land might be farmed. Feeling along the edge, she found a few stunted ears of sweet corn, which she shucked and gave to her child. They had to be eaten raw. If she made a fire to cook them, it might attract attention. Azura intended to stake out whatever lay ahead before making herself or Noam known to the townspeople.

Neither she nor the child wore shoes with thick soles. They struggled to walk on the sticky pavement, as if the road itself wished to delay their progress, rather than on the cool loam they were accustomed to. Night hoots from owls and scurrying sounds of raccoons were familiar, but the baying of coyotes was unnerving. Azura touched the knife handle to make sure it was still with her. Soon, it would be chilly, and she would wrap herself and Noam in shawls she brought in her bag.

"I don't wanna walk, Mama. Carry me."

Azura squatted to allow Noam to climb onto her back. The child could be a handful. The older women of the forest said she took after Azura's mother, who was strong willed even as a toddler. But on this strange and dangerous journey, she must have sensed Azura's anxiety. She rode on her mother's back with none of her usual squirming or demands.

Azura's feet knew the way. The road was straight. If she put one foot ahead of the other, she would get to the place where streetlights would lead her to the center of town. Until then, darkness smothered them. The elders in the forest had visions in the night. Memory fragments besieged Azura, flashing by like images on the monitors and screens in town. Running through the woods as a young child, swinging on vines, climbing trees. Going to the town to find her father. Living in the beehive-style rehab unit the government provided. Returning to the forest to give birth to Noam.

It had been five years since she saw a monitor. She heard no news in that period, nor any inkling of world events, nor knowledge of how townspeople lived. She only knew what she saw with her own eyes. The forest drying and igniting. The lack of rain. The unseasonable cold and heat. Plants sprouting and birds hatching at the wrong time.

Hunters shooting most of the deer and trapping the rabbits. When these were gone, they came for the squirrels and groundhogs. She and the elder women fled deeper into the woods.

She still owned her old iPhoneXR and its cable. When she got settled, she would find out if it would charge. Until then, she had no way of telling the time. She would keep forging ahead until she reached the lit area of town or until dawn arrived, whichever came first. The child grew heavier when her sleep became sounder. Azura hoisted her up as she slid down her back. If only she could doze for a few minutes, too. But she was alone in the world, with no one to help her or offer her a bed. A bed. Her best town memory. No matter what kind of nest she constructed in the forest, nothing was as comfortable as a bed with a pillow, cotton sheets, and a quilt.

It struck her as unusual that no traffic passed. At one time, the road was well-travelled, as townspeople came to the state park for picnics and camping, even at night. She imagined hiding on the shoulder as cars whizzed by. But none came in either direction. Maybe it was because the authorities closed the park and the campgrounds.

There was a candle and flint in her bundle. When they came to a dark patch, where the trees obscured the moon, the dim candlelight guided her, keeping her from stumbling into the potholes. The road was in disrepair, which was a surprise. She could not afford to fall and hurt the child or herself. If she twisted an ankle, how would she make it to town?

Memories continued to invade her mind, distracting her from the potential dangers of the night. The long, dark braid of her mother, Eva, piled on the top of her head. Reading to her blind great-grandmother, called Great Mother, from "The Book of Roots," a recipe book using ingredients found in the forest, stored in Azura's bundle. Her father, Isaac, taking hallucinogenics to foster religious experiences. Her occasional lover, Larry, the father of Noam. All dead from the plague that ripped through the forest and, she assumed, the town. Of the forest dwellers, only she and her child survived. Would anyone be alive in the town?

She made sure of survival by taking Noam to different parts of the forest as the elders sickened. They themselves encouraged her to abandon them against her will. No one took care of them in their dying moments. There was no way to take care of them. Not even "The Book of Roots" had a remedy. Guilt haunted her, although it would have been worse if she lost her daughter.

The girl was growing up with no children to play with. She never saw another child. For the past year, Azura had been her sole companion. Although she talked to her daughter, the child's language skills suffered from a lack of practice with others. And poor nutrition for the past months might affect her development in other ways. It was imperative for Azura to get her food and companionship before she started school somewhere, perhaps in town, when she was six. If they were there that long. Azura would not have minded living off the grid in the forest if the absence of a community did no harm to Noam.

And what if the plague took Azura? Noam was too young to be on her own. Horrible images assailed Azura of her daughter crying in a panic over her mother's dead body, terrified, with no one to care for her or even know she existed, no Amber Alert, no ranger patrol to rescue her, until the poor girl succumbed to starvation or, even worse, a predator. Whatever the conditions in town, at least there would be other people who might save her.

Azura felt sure she should pass farm houses by now. Just up the road where the scattered houses that preceded the more compact town residences. There should have been lights in windows or on porches here and there. Perhaps the electricity failed. She could think of no other explanation.

Her anxiety increased. Something changed in the past five years. Everyone may have died from the plague or the town might have ceased to exist. If it still existed, the townspeople might not be friendly, even hostile. Would she and Noam be additional mouths to feed during a famine? Would the town be fenced off, not admitting strangers? Would the authorities grab her child but not allow Azura in? The closer she got, the more insecurity tore through her.

The dim glow that foreshadows sunrise finally came. Birds began chirping. The silhouettes of trees were visible against the navy blue sky. Danger from predators was greatest at this hour. Besides coyotes, the people of the woods had reported sightings of black bears, mountain lions, and wolves, animals that had not inhabited Indiana for over a hundred years. Azura touched her knife again, straining her eyes to make out what lurked in the underbrush.

Dawn arrived just as she crossed the first intersection that marked the town boundary. Noam stirred. Azura squatted to allow her daughter to slide off her back. Her first words of the day were the ones she expected.

"Mama, I'm hungry."

"Let's keep going until we find you food."

She thought of knocking on the first door they came to and begging for something for the child to eat. But all she saw was rubble where houses had been, some with standing door frames, cement stairs leading to collapsed front decks, and intact brick chimneys. Sandy soil replaced the mowed lawns of the past. There were no foundation plants or flower beds of roses and peonies. Had they entered a ghost town or had a tornado decimated the area?

On high alert, she took Noam's hand and kept walking up the road toward the center of town. They passed the remains of the high school, shopping strips, gas stations, churches. The thought crossed her mind that there had been a war, and the enemy had defeated America. But she quickly rejected that idea. America was the strongest nation on earth. Nothing could bring it to ruin, could it?

She took a deep breath to calm herself and led the child ahead for another half mile. To her relief, she saw the beehive buildings that housed the homeless when she lived in town. These were still inhabited. People were about, entering and leaving the buildings, sitting on benches, or stumbling ahead to unknown destinations. Many were thin and bent, like elders, but with younger faces.

She pointed to a building.

"That's where I used to live, before you were born."

As they neared, it puzzled her when people stared at her and Noam, even stopping in their tracks, craning their necks to watch them. Their rough clothing, snarled hair, and worn shoes attracted attention, Azura thought. This was not what she wanted.

Just then, an official vehicle pulled up next to them. The window rolled down, and an officer spoke.

"Stop right there, Miss, and stay put."

He got out, and another officer emerged from the passenger side. Both stood gaping at Azura and her child. She trembled with fright. Would they arrest her? Then one officer spoke into a phone-like device smaller than the iPhoneXR.

"I have two Caucasians, a woman and a female child. Both underweight but able to walk."

Azura did not hear the response.

"Please get into the back seat," he said to her.

The driver opened the back door of the vehicle. Azura noted the "please." It did not seem like an order.

"My child is hungry."

She meant she would only get in the vehicle if the officers promised food.

"Don't worry. You'll have plenty of food. The bosses will take excellent care of both of you."

Without knowing where it would take her, Azura lifted Noam into the vehicle, not understanding what happened or what would happen next.

CHAPTER 2
THE PURE HOUSE

The vehicle moved at a fast clip, going around the beehive buildings to another road containing enormous buildings with smokestacks. Factories. There had only been one when Azura left. They travelled along this road, passing many more factories and beehive residences, more than Azura remembered from the last time she lived in town. Their residences were constructed from gray cement blocks with a number above each entrance—3700, 3800, 3900. There was no landscaping, just raw earth, no trees, no bushes.

When she was younger, the town had an attractive mix of houses, stores, schools, and parks. No longer. It was an ugly, utilitarian place, with nothing appealing or interesting to soften the stern environment.

She saw people looking out of the windows. They had to be on their knees. If the units were the same inside as Azura remembered, each was four feet tall by six feet wide for single people and eight feet for couples. The ceiling was too low for standing. These were sleeping cells. After work, people crawled in through half-sized doors straight onto beds. The next day, they crawled out again. They were expected to leave in the early morning, although many stayed who were jobless.

Neither of the officers said anything to their two passengers. Noam kept giving her mother wide-eyed looks. Azura squeezed the girl to her side to reassure her. But her own rapid breathing did not convey reassurance. Noam pressed her face against her mother's sleeve.

The vehicle reached a river that divided the town and crossed the bridge. When had the old boulevard been flooded? On the other side, which used to contain neighborhoods of small houses, there also had been a transformation. All the houses had vanished. In its place was an extensive park or formal garden with a green canopy created by tall trees leading to a large modern structure surrounded by a fence. At the gate, a sign read "The Pure House." When the driver murmured something into his device, and the gate opened.

Several people in lab coats waited at the entrance. The officer on the passenger side jumped out and opened the back door.

"Please get out," he said.

Again, Azura noted the word "please." But the closed gate behind her said otherwise. She kept her arm tight around Noam while they exited the vehicle. She still had her bundle in her right hand.

A blond woman in a lab coat with short, slicked-back hair, about twenty years her senior, stepped forward, all smiles.

"Welcome to The Pure House," she said. "I'm Constance."

She noticed Azura's bundle.

"May I take that for you?" She held out her hand.

Azura did not know whether she had a choice. Her grip tightened, then loosened. She wound up giving the bundle to Constance, who took it gingerly and handed it to another lab-coated individual.

"We'll take good care of your belongings for you."

Constance and the others kept smiling, looking at their two guests with interest. Noam still hid her face on her mother's arm, unable to tell if she should be frightened.

"Thank you, officer. That will be all," Constance said.

He re-entered the passenger seat. The car u-turned, the gate opened, and the vehicle disappeared.

"Now, let's go inside and get you two a good meal. But this is a weapon free building. You can't take your knife in. You can give it to Martin, and he'll put it in the locker with your bundle until you leave."

She wasn't being forced. She was being bribed. Food for the knife. Azura debated. Even if these people turned out to be dangerous, they outnumbered her. And the child had to eat. She gave the knife to the man who held out his hand. Martin. A muscular man, like a security guard.

Inside, in a four-story white marble lobby, the lab people surrounded Azura and Noam, as if protecting them from others who strode about, entering and leaving through doors, riding escalators, or waiting for elevators, as in any busy office building. Many of these also halted mid-step, swiveling their heads to glimpse the newcomers.

"Word spreads fast," Constance said to the other lab people, whose smiles changed to smirks. "We should go to a private dining area."

She turned to her guests.

"We'll take the executive elevator so you don't have to wait with the others. You don't want them gawking at you."

"I'm sorry about our clothes."

It was the first words Azura said since entering town.

"Not to worry. You and your daughter will have plenty of new clothing here."

The food kiosk in the lobby distracted Azura. She thought she would faint. Martin grabbed her arm. She and the child were being taken to a corner of the lobby, away from the kiosk, to the executive elevator. There was only room in it for Constance and Martin among the lab people. Martin still held her up, unless he was making sure she would not escape. They left behind the others, who sang out "Nice meeting you" and "Good luck!" Why would Azura need luck, she wondered?

"We're going to the top floor. That's where the private dining rooms are located. Of course, to reach the bosses, you would have to transfer to another elevator to get to the pent-house. We won't be going there, today."

The private dining room had been outfitted like an expensive restaurant, with a single mahogany table seating eight. A small door at tabletop height stood closed in the wall, possibly a dumbwaiter. There would be plenty of room between the four occupants, but Martin guided Noam and her mother to two seats next to each other. Constance and Martin sat opposite them. A large window looked out at a green vista from what had to be the back of the building. None of the beehive dwellings or factories were visible. Neither was any other sign of human habitation.

There were no menus.

9

"Bring an array. We want our guests to choose whatever they like. And drinks a child might prefer, like milk, coke, and juice," Constance said into a device on the table.

It was hard to concentrate while waiting for the food. The aromas of cooking wafted into the room. Constance said something. Azura forced herself to pay attention. Hunger made her both alert and lightheaded at the same time.

"Eat slowly if you haven't had food for a while. The server will bring a lot, but just have a sample. Your systems may not tolerate large amounts. In case you think this will be all you'll get, don't worry. More food will always be available to you and your daughter around the clock."

"Okay."

Azura did not want to say much until she knew what was happening. She wondered if she should thank Constance. She would if it turned out to be necessary. Never hearing Noam complain about hunger again was a wild dream.

The small door opened, and platters of food came to the table on a conveyor belt. Soups, entrees, bread, salads, fruit, and the drinks Constance had ordered for the child. Coffee for the adults. Azura had not had coffee for five years. It was one of the things she missed the most after leaving the town. She propped herself up on her elbows to keep from fainting from the tantalizing smells. Such an amazing amount of food. Such variety. Even when she lived in town and went to restaurants, she had never experienced such a magnificent spread.

"May I suggest the soups? They will be lightest on your stomachs. When your systems permit it in a couple of days, I recommend beef. You're both very pale. We have to determine if you're iron deficient or if this is your natural color."

A couple of days. Azura and her daughter had at least two days of free food. Some of her tension eased, and she focused on the soup which a server ladled into four bowls. Constance directed the server to make a plate of single spoonfuls from the array on the platters for the two guests. She and Martin helped themselves to larger portions.

Azura swallowed too fast to taste the soup. She stopped to help Noam, spooning soup into her mouth, which opened like a baby bird's. She whispered to her daughter, naming the strange items on her plate, never seen in the forest—peas, pasta, salmon, a piece of a dinner roll, urging her to take a bite. The child favored what looked most familiar to her—salad, potatoes, raw carrots, berries.

When Azura slowed down, Constance made her first request.

"Please tell me your names."

There was the polite "please" again. She had another choice. Perhaps a fake one, like the others. Azura debated. She could refuse to give her name or her daughter's. But food might be denied if she did. She could give false names. But that would confuse Noam. She had broken no law by moving away from town. She did not think she broke any by returning. No one arrested her or said she couldn't leave. Constance did not act like she was in trouble. It seemed safe to give their actual names and withhold other information until asked.

"Azura. My daughter is Noam."

"Martin. Please make a note. Azura and Noam. Unusual names."

Constance asked nothing else, which was strange. Did she already know they came from the forest, or was she just uninterested? Perhaps she knew she could only require so much of her already overwhelmed guests on their first day.

After the meal, Constance led them out of the dining room.

"I'll take you to your quarters. It's not far, right on this floor. You must be tired."

A short walk through a maze of hallways took them to a door with a sign reading "8097."

Martin had the key. Inside was a large bedroom containing a king-sized bed, just like the one Azura dreamed of, with several pillows and a puffy quilt. A table next to the window, with the same green view, contained a tray of fruit, breadsticks, and cookies, as well as thermal pitchers of milk and coffee. The promised available food.

"Don't eat yet. Give your stomach time," Constance said, noticing them staring at the table.

She opened a closet door. There was enough clothing inside for a year in the forest. And shoes, precious shoes, several pairs.

"The staff guessed your sizes. If nothing fits, they'll exchange everything."

Next, she opened the drawers of a dresser. Underwear. T-shirts. Socks. Treasures.

"Unless you have questions, we'll leave you to rest."

Azura had a thousand questions, but she was already on the bed with Noam. As soon as her exhausted head sank into the cloud-like pillow, she dozed. Even so, she heard the key turn when the door closed. They were locked in.

CHAPTER 3
THE MEDICAL EXAM

When Azura awoke, she did not see Noam in the bed. She shot up, afraid they took the girl or let her wander off. Noam did not appear to be anywhere in the room. Then Azura heard a moan coming from under the table. She squatted down and raised the cloth. Her daughter lay there, holding her stomach.

"What's wrong?"

"My tummy hurts."

"Come on out, and let me see what's wrong."

The child rolled onto all fours and crawled out. Azura helped her stand.

"I ate too many of those," she said, pointing at an empty spot on the tray of food left on the table.

All the cookies had vanished.

"Those were cookies. You ate all of them?"

Noam nodded, frowning.

"Why did you do that? It's too much for your tummy."

"I liked them."

If only Azura had the book in her bundle, "Roots of the Woods." It might contain a remedy. But Azura had no access to the forest, where the ingredients for the remedy would be growing. She sighed. The child had indigestion. Nothing serious.

"Lie in the bed. You'll feel better soon. No more eating until you do."

One thing was clear. It was permissible to take food from the table. No one entered the room to scold Noam for eating the cookies. But

Azura was cautious. She lifted the coffee pot an inch and put it down again, waiting for a buzzer or alarm to alert someone. Nothing sounded. Next, she poured the drink into a cup. Still nothing.

Hot coffee, a pleasure she was not sure she should have, without knowing the rules of this place, The Pure House. What was pure about it? She wondered. She went to the door, tried the knob, and found she had not been dreaming when the key turned from the outside. They locked them in.

She should phone someone. Who? She remembered her iPhoneXR, stowed in her bundle, somewhere in a locker. She noticed an object on the nightstand next to the bed, a phone, smaller and slimmer than an XR. When she picked it up, it rattled. She dropped it. It fell to the carpeted floor. What if she broke it? She had no way of paying to replace it. It seemed to work when she picked it up and opened it. A banner alerted her to a text message. There was a single one in Messages from Constance.

I hope you enjoy your new iPhone. You can no longer update an older model. May I suggest you and your daughter take advantage of the bathing facilities in your quarters and your new clothes? If there's anything else you need, text me. Otherwise, see you later.

The phone was hers. The new clothing, too. Azura was suspicious. She was nothing special, just a former addict with no education or connection with anyone in town. Why did they treat her and Noam like princesses?

Unable to figure out what no one told her, she inspected the bathroom—the "bathing facilities." It was beyond luxurious. The white tile room gleamed. Thick white towels lay folded on a shelf. Two terrycloth bathrobes, one for an adult, the other for a child, hung on hooks. All the appliances were white, including a spa-sized bathtub, with expensive-looking soaps, lotions, and shampoos along the edge.

She turned on the hot water tap. Noam only had a hot bath when Azura heated pond water on a wood stove in the forest. She helped the child out of her clothing, undressed herself, and deposited everything in a basket labelled "Laundry." Then she lifted the child into the tub and climbed in after her.

When she lived in town, Azura washed herself every day. That had not been possible in the forest, especially in the winter, when the creek froze and had to be axed just to get drinking water. In the summer, sometimes the creek dried. The waterfall was dependable, but it was three miles away from the place where they lived with the elders. Every time they moved deeper into the woods, a new water source had to be found. Sometimes she found one nearby, sometimes far away. At times, bathing was impossible for weeks.

That was their condition before coming to town. Layers of dirt fell off them in the bathtub. Azura drained the water and refilled the tub several times. Even then, a gray scum discolored the walls of the tub when they finished. She scrubbed it off with a towel, fearing to take too much advantage of hospitality she did not understand.

"I like the bath, Mommy."

Noam looked radiant in the terry robe, and then in a dress from the closet, a white one with tiny embroidered off-white roses. Her blond curls glistened. Azura noticed that most of the child's clothing and all the adult clothing were white, some with accents of ivory or cream. There was a lot of clothing, but little choice. A white T-shirt and white jeans were fine with her, more than fine. White was impossible in the forest. Not only would it be unable to be cleaned, it could attract predators — human or animal.

They were both hungry again and helped themselves to the breadsticks and fruit. A thermal pitcher contained milk. Noam had not had milk in two years, since the last of the elder's goats died. Cow's milk would have a different taste. But milk was strange to her. She shook her head after one sip.

"I want the fizzy brown drink I had in the food place."

She meant the private dining room.

"That's a coke. I'll ask for some when the staff comes."

"I don't like yucky milk."

While Azura worried about their situation and the locked door, Noam babbled about food, the only topic of interest to a food deprived child, about how the cookies hurt her tummy, about liking the fizzy brown drink, about all the things to eat in the food place, about the raw corn she ate on the road.

Azura's thoughts, too, centered on food—-what she had given up to get it, her bundle of belongings, her knife, maybe her freedom. She had seen the beehive residences and the factories. Hundreds of townspeople lived and worked there. Why were she and her daughter exceptions?

She considered her choices. Beat on the door and see if someone would let her out. Get Constance to tell her more about her situation, then decide whether to accept it or leave. Say nothing until Noam reached a healthy weight. Perhaps, she was kidding herself. As long as they stowed her possessions and locked in her, she had no choices. Constance decided for her.

The phone rattled again. Another text from Constance appeared.

It 's time for your medical examination. We have to take care of any health problems you and Noam may have. Martin will be there in a few minutes to take you.

Azura froze in place. She would refuse the exam. They could not force her. Yet, it might be a good idea. Noam had never been to a doctor. She had no vaccinations. That was fine in the forest, where she did not come in contact with other humans who might be diseased. A general exam would not hurt. She could use one, too.

There was a knock on the door and the sound of a key turning. She opened it to find Martin without the white coat, in street clothes that emphasized bulging muscles.

"Please follow me," he said.

She became accustomed to the word "please." It did not seem to mean anything. Taking Noam's hand, she left with Martin, who attempted to hold her arm before she yanked it away. He kept silent while they walked back to the executive elevator, then down several floors. They exited into a space like a hospital reception area. Martin handed a clipboard he had been carrying to a lab-coated woman, who stood near the elevator door, expecting them. She read the paperwork while glancing at the two patients.

Then she turned to them, smiling, as Constance did when they arrived.

"Welcome to the medical floor of The Pure House. I'm the Nurse. I'll be your medical guide today. And you are Azura and Noam? Hello, sweetheart."

She bent to greet Noam.

"Is there anything I can get you before we begin?"

"The brown fizzy drink."

"She means a coke."

The Nurse's smile broadened. "How about we get you a coke after the exam? I promise."

Noam was being bribed to cooperate. Azura's mouth dried, not knowing what was in store for them.

"Now Azura, you wait here while I take Noam for her exam."

Azura scooped her daughter up and held her tight.

"No! We won't be separated."

She panted. The Nurse kept smiling, nodding her head.

"There's nothing to fear. Of course you can stay with Noam if you prefer."

Azura carried the child after the Nurse, worried someone would grab her if she put her down. The exam room looked like a small operating theater, with incomprehensible machines both overhead and surrounding the exam table. One wall of the room was composed of a large mirror, a one-way window, Azura suspected. Noam stiffened.

A man entered.

"I'm the Radiologist," he said. "Please put the child on the table."

"No!" Noam screamed when Azura tried to sit her there.

"Don't worry. I'm staying right here with you," Azura whispered to her. "I won't let anyone hurt you."

"No part of the exam causes pain. It's all done remotely. The medical equipment is aimed in the patient's direction. It doesn't touch the patient," the Radiologist said.

"Should I take her clothes off?"

"There's no need."

Azura lay her daughter on the table, still holding her hand. The Radiologist adjusted the equipment, aiming it toward Noam's mid-section. This was unlike a conventional exam, in which a doctor puts a stethoscope on an undressed patient's chest and looks in their ears with a little light. It was too unfamiliar for Azura's comfort or the child's, whose eyes widened with fright.

"Now, if you'll let go of your mommy's hand, and if you'll be a big girl and lie still, I'll get you a coke," the Nurse said.

Tears formed in the corners of Noam's eyes, but she lay still. Soft, whirling sounds began, although nothing touched Noam. In minutes, the exam finished. The child sat up, and Azura stepped forward again to hold her.

There was a knock on the exam door, and a tray with a bottle of coke was waiting on the floor just outside, the same kind of bottle Azura remembered from the past. At least that had not changed.

"We can stay in this room for your exam, Azura, if the child will wait in the chair. Please lie on the table," the Radiologist said.

After her exam, the Radiologist left the room. The child asked for a second coke. The Nurse followed the Radiologist to get another bottle. Azura noticed a curtain sectioning off part of the area. It might have been for a second exam bed. A woman peeked out and spoke in a hushed tone.

"Is he gone?"

"The Radiologist? He should be back in a minute, I think. The Nurse is getting my daughter a coke."

"Are you a resident?"

The woman kept looking toward the door with anxious eyes.

"No. Just a guest for a couple of days."

"Don't let them fool you. If you're unhealthy, they may let you go, but never your daughter."

Azura's heart skipped.

"What do you mean?"

"Tell me, when they brought you here, did you see other children?"

The Nurse returned with the second coke. The other patient disappeared behind the curtain. On the way back to their quarters, with Martin leading the way, Azura tried to make sense of the warning. Come to think of it, she had seen no schools, no playgrounds, no daycare centers, and no children on the drive through town to The Pure House. Was Noam the only child left?

CHAPTER 4

The next day, Constance sent a text setting up a meeting. The Radiologist would tell Azura the results of the medical exams.

Not a doctor? She replied.

They 're for sore throats and sewing up cuts. Not for this kind of remote diagnosis.

Once again, there was a knock on the door and a request by Martin to "please" follow him. She took Noam's hand, not willing to leave her in the room by herself, and obeyed, even though she did not want the child hearing about any illness either of them might have. He escorted them to a small lounge on the medical floor. Constance and the Radiologist waited, both wearing Hazmat suits.

"Please take a seat, Azura. Noam can sit next to you or on your lap. You'll want to hear the findings of the tests," Constance said.

Noam climbed onto her lap and put her thumb in her mouth. Constance and the Radiologist both still had the same wide grin.

"I have good news. You are both in fine condition. Both blood screens are within normal limits. You're dehydrated and underweight, but we'll clear that up if you keep eating and drinking."

"That's not serious?"

"No. Life in the forest did you no harm," the Radiologist said.

"How did you know we lived there?" Azura shifted Noam on her lap.

"We observed you coming into town from the direction of the forest. That's why the officers picked you up before you could be exposed to any of the townspeople," Constance said.

"Observed?"

"Yes. There are cameras."

"Exposed to what?"

Constance stopped smiling.

"COVID-35. You haven't been infected if you and your daughter have isolated yourselves for the past five years in the forest."

Azura's eyebrows rose.

"You look puzzled," she said.

"I knew about COVID-19 and all the variants. It started before my birth. There was a vaccine for it the last time I lived in town, when I was still a teen."

"Then you know nothing about COVID-35, the plague that started in 2035?"

Azura shook her head.

"Well, there's more good news. All of your organs and Noam's are intact and normal," the Radiologist said.

"Why wouldn't they be?"

"COVID-35 attacks every organ system, including the brain and blood."

Azura's mind fogged with confusion. She and Noam were not infected. But maybe they were in danger. As if reading her mind, Constance spoke up.

"The Pure House will protect you. We will keep you away from all sources of infection here."

"Can't you vaccinate us?"

"There is no vaccine," the Radiologist said. "But the limited number of staff you will encounter here—Martin, Constance, and me—are screened daily or, like us, wear Hazmat suits to avoid transmitting the virus. No one who can compromise your health will be permitted near you. They're unlikely to be allowed into The Pure House, anyway."

Azura recalled the ride to The Pure House, passing jobless people staring out the windows, others outside the beehive residences looking thin and frail. Now it made sense. They had the virus. She put protective arms around Noam and drew her closer.

She remembered the other patient asking if she had seen other children.

"What about children?" She asked.

Constance glanced at Noam. She addressed the child, holding out her hand.

"Sweetheart, let's go into the next room and get you a coke. We'll leave the door open, so you can see your mommy."

Despite her apprehension, Azura let her daughter go, ready to jump up if Constance took her out of sight. Once Noam was settled, the Radiologist drew a chair near to Azura..

"I didn't think you'd want Noam to hear this. It could scare her. COVID-35 targets children. It's fatal for them, but not for most adults. Most of us lost offspring. Constance has an adult daughter who survived, but lost teenage twin boys. And a grandchild. I have no children of my own, but my nieces and nephews perished."

It was hard to take in. An entire town, perhaps all the towns and cities, too, without children. And parents, both grief-stricken and infected. Constance and the Radiologist hiding their pain and smiling. It dawned on her. Neither smiled at her. They smiled at her daughter, delighted to see a rare five-year-old.

"How does everyone stand it?"

She would kill herself if Noam died.

"We can't. But we've had five years to learn that the world must go on. People must be fed. There are jobs that must be done. We have to find ways to re-populate the earth."

"So COVID-35 is worldwide?"

The Radiologist nodded.

"And most of the children in the world died?"

"Babies are being born. The repopulation movement is starting. It'll be slow. Losing their children has caused people to become depressed, and that reduces libido. No sex, no children. Some won't have children without a vaccine to protect them. And many have been too sick or have damaged reproductive organs."

Noam sat in the next room, drinking coke. Azura's heart sank. She was one of the lucky ones, enjoying her daughter while the rest of the world grieved. She did not think of herself as special. Everything about her was average—her looks, her intelligence, her morals. A cloak of guilt descended on her. She had what Constance and the Radiologist did not have, and she had done nothing to deserve it.

The Radiologist glanced at the door, then leaned closer and spoke in a quiet voice.

"You're very pretty."

He took his glove off and put the tip of his index finger on Azura's cheek.

"So fair."

Azura turned her head away. No one had flirted with her for the past five years. The last one, Noam's father, had been too handsome to resist. Azura was not attracted to the Radiologist. He was too old, and his lab coat strained across his middle.

In the forest, she had lived with three senior women, the elders, one of them her great-grandmother. She had not encountered a man in all those years, or a person her own age. Her sexuality had gone into a state of suspension. The men she glimpsed in town were sickly. Some of the staff in The Pure House had to be male, although all but Martin and the Radiologist avoided her.

"Is Noam the only child here?" She asked.

"Now that she has medical clearance, she can meet the others. There's only a handful. All girls, of course."

"Why all girls?"

The Radiologist's index finger approached again. Azura pushed her chair back until it bumped against the wall.

"We selected for girls. For repopulation."

He touched Azura's arm, stroking the skin near her wrist.

"Extraordinary. If only...."

Just then, Noam bounced back in and stood next to her mother. The Radiologist withdrew his hand, putting his glove on again. Constance returned.

"I hope you will consider becoming a permanent resident of The Pure House."

"You mean I have a choice? I'm not a prisoner?"

"Of course not," Constance said.

"Then why have you locked us in?"

Constance's broad smile returned.

"This building's an absolute maze. We didn't want you to get lost."

It made sense, somewhat. The building had a complex floor plan. But Azura wasn't sure. They may have locked her in to prevent escape.

"I can leave anytime?"

"It would be very dangerous. The townspeople would infect you. You could die. And even if you survived to reach the forest, you'd starve," the Radiologist said.

Noam understood.

"Mommy, I don't want to leave. I like all the food and the big soft bed. And the bathtub, too."

"Let me think it over."

"Take your time. You both need to gain weight. Might as well stay until you do, since there will be no opportunity if you leave," Constance said.

Back in their quarters, the table was covered with enticing food, as if there had been instructions to tempt Azura to stay. Protein-rich entrees in covered plates on heating trays, meaty soups, buttered vegetables, breads, and alluring desserts. Several kinds of hot and cold drinks, including their favorites—coffee and coke. There were fresh linens on the bed, toys for Noam. The bathroom sparkled.

Azura surfed through the channels on the TV on top of the dresser. TVs still existed. They were limited to children's programming and one adult station featuring older soap operas. There were no news channels on the TV or on her phone. She wondered if the staff of news channels died, or if she was being restricted from knowing what was happening outside of The Pure House.

For the rest of the day, they left them alone. Azura helped herself and her daughter to plates of food. When she lifted the coffee pot, it surprised her to see a small piece of folded paper beneath. She glanced around the room, as if someone would object if she touched it. There was no one. After replacing the pitcher, she unfolded the paper.

Get out while you can.

She reread the message several times. Her mind whirled. At first, she thought it had to be a mistake, a message meant for someone else, inadvertently picked up with the pitcher and left on the table. She remembered the other patient, who gave her a warning after her medical exam. There were people in The Pure House sending her secret signals, warning her of some sort of danger, but not spelling it out.

Constance and the Radiologist told her about the dangers of town, where she and Noam might die from COVID-35. It targeted children. And they might both starve in the forest. Someone was trying to convey to her that The Pure House was dangerous, too. Who should she believe?

Meanwhile, she had to decide whether to stay. Each time she lay in the bed, or soaked in the tub, or ate, the temptation to stay strengthened in her and the child. It became harder to imagine going back to the hard life in the forest, carrying buckets of water, sometimes for miles, keeping the wood stove going day and night, hours foraging for food, more hours preparing it, freezing in the winter and overheating in the summer, predators, pests, poisonous plants.

And loneliness. That was the hardest to admit to herself because she was not sure of the name of the feeling. Constance, as old as she was, twice her age, was the youngest adult she had spoken with in five years. The elders were four, five times her age. Her parents died years before. And for Noam, it was worse. A future alone. Azura couldn't let that happen to her.

Constance said there were a handful of girls in The Pure House. They might be playmates for Noam. As for herself, she hoped there was a group closer to her age. The other patient in the exam room seemed to be in her twenties. Azura was not the only young person in The Pure House, even if there were only the two of them.

But the locked door and the warnings bothered her. Despite what Constance said about not wanting her to get lost if the door was unlocked, she was a prisoner. She prized her freedom and would choose it, but she had to put her child's safety first.

Her head spun from overthinking. If Constance gave her more information, deciding might be easier.

She sent her a text.

Just checking. We're free to go, right?

A reply came without a wait.

You are free to go, but we can't allow you to take Noam. She would die from COVID-35 or starvation. Child Welfare Services won't let that happen.

Azura fell on the bed.

"Mommy! Are you sick?"

She sat up, not wanting to scare the child.

"I'm not sick. I just lost my balance for a second."

If she couldn't take her daughter, she was a prisoner. But her choice was about to get worse.

CHAPTER 5
CONSTANCE

Constance returned to her quarters in The Pure House after her meeting with that idiot Radiologist and the new woman. She slept in one of the beehive units in the east wing. It was fortunate they did not assign her one of the upper cells, accessed by climbing a ladder. Her strength ebbed. She did not know if she would be able to pull herself up. After unlocking her lower door, she crawled in.

Her phone rattled. A message from her daughter, Molly, arrived. She read it while lying on her back.

Can U come over? Not doing well.

Constance replied.

After I rest. Had to work this a.m.

She waited for Molly to text just the sort of reply that always filled her with guilt.

I 'll try to make it for the next couple of hours until U have recouped.

One sentence with much unsaid. "Try to" meant Molly would do all she could to resist suicide. "Couple of hours" suggested that was the limit Constance might expect her to hold out. "Recouped" implied Constance put her own selfish needs ahead of her daughter.

Molly was all the family Constance had left, and she would do anything to keep her alive. But as soon as she put down her phone, she dozed off. Before the deepest sleep arrived, the thought came to her that Molly would also need to rest after the exertion of texting.

They were both in the Recovered group, suffering from post-COVID fatigue. No one in their group worked for more than a two-hour stretch. Factories had four shifts per day, and none at night.

27

Production was low, with the greatest amount produced being delivered to The Pure House, while the Recovered buildings, such as the one in which Molly lived, only received the basics. The COVID buildings, where those with active cases lived, had most of the medical equipment being produced. Ventilators. Oxygen. Syringes.

They isolated the Spreaders on an island. Constance guessed they fended for themselves. Only the handful of Pures, like the few uninfected children, were allowed luxuries — large quarters, TV, more than a couple of items of clothing, and plentiful food. Even during the drought, they took baths.

The new woman and her child were being tested for purity. The results showed promise, so far. A wait was necessary to see if they developed COVID. They remained in a Preliminary unit, with their exposure limited, waiting for two weeks to see if they would develop symptoms. If not, they would be moved to their permanent quarters.

When she awoke, Constance grabbed her ID, left her cell, and headed out of The Pure House. She would need the ID, stamped with her Recovered status, to return. She could visit Molly because they permitted Recovereds to mingle, but only outside. No one knew which of the Recovereds might be Spreaders, so indoor meetings were forbidden. Adult Pures might be Spreaders, too, but as long as that was unknown, they could briefly associate with one or two others of the same status.

What else could the bosses do, other than quarantine every Pure? That would destroy the mental health of the children, some too young to take care of themselves. They took the risk of hiring a few child care workers who were Recovereds. They tested them every day, since no one could tell who was a Spreader. Nothing stopped a Pure from getting the virus if exposed.

Constance used one of the motorized bicycles to get to Molly's residence, since public transportation was in lockdown. When she arrived at their meeting bench, she had an hour and forty-five minutes before she would need to sleep again. An hour-and-a half with Molly and fifteen minutes to return to The Pure House.

"I've been waiting for you." Molly looked at her mother with sulking eyes.

"I came as fast as possible on the bike. Work was a bitch this morning. I broke the news to a possible Pure that we wouldn't be allowing her daughter to leave with her. It knocked me out."

Molly's eyes moistened, although not for the Pures.

"Say something to stop the pain."

Tears dripped down Molly's face, dropping off her chin. The pain came from grief. Her infant son died of COVID a short time after birth. The virus infected him in the womb. Unless she also cried because of the death of her younger twin brothers. Both of them. A terrible blow for Constance, more so than the infant boy she never even held.

COVID obliterated empathy. Everyone lost someone they loved. The entire population of Recovereds was numb, traumatized, and exhausted. They survived an illness that almost killed them, too, and they might get it again, if they were exposed. They might not be lucky the next time.

What should Constance say to her daughter that she had not already said?

"Time heals all wounds, they say. It might be true."

In an instant, Molly fumed with rage. Her eyes seared into her mother.

"Don't you get it? I don't want to heal. That would mean forgetting my baby. He was a human being, and I killed him. It would be like... like... he never existed if I forgot him."

"You didn't kill him. The virus killed him, and you too, almost."

Now Molly's rage changed to sorrow and guilt. She sobbed, wringing her hands.

"I didn't take enough precautions, *Sob*. Let myself get close to some Spreader, *Sob*. Why didn't I die, *Sob*?"

Molly's shifting emotions exhausted Constance, and she had only been with her daughter for five minutes. At least she did not have to save Molly from a suicide attempt. Not this time. As tiring as Molly's dramatizing nature was, her emotionality meant she had the energy to live. When numbness overtook her, Constance sensed the most danger.

She would try distracting Molly by telling her about the new possible Pure.

"The woman I met with this morning. She has a five-year-old daughter. It seems they have both been living isolated in the forest since the daughter's birth. The mother lived in town before that."

Molly nodded, a sign of mild interest. It encouraged Constance.

"She and her daughter were both tested. No genetic defects. They're half-starved. We're feeding them around the clock. But neither had the virus. The mother never even heard of COVID-35."

Molly snorted. "Sounds like they lived in the forest under a rock."

"More or less, I guess. We know little about them."

Molly's eyes glinted in a way Constance observed before the death of her newborn. To herself, she called it an "evil eye." Did her daughter have evil tendencies or just selfish ones?

"If the adult turns out to be a Pure, you'll switch her with me, won't you?"

"I'll try. I don't have control."

"You'll figure out how, Mom. You keep saying I'm all you've got, and you want me to live. Prove it."

Later, back in her cell, worn out by her demanding daughter, Constance wondered for the thousandth time if Molly would kill herself or just keep manipulating her mother with the threat. She had been controlling Constance ever since the birth of her sweet baby brothers, dividing Constance's attention from them with crying fits and faked illness. But the virus and the losses had been genuine enough. Even if Molly took advantage of her, switching a Pure with her daughter was like an insurance policy. Whether she needed it would be a matter of fate.

She remembered Gary, her deceased husband, saying that Molly was spoiled. Perhaps time does heal, since she seldom thought of Gary. There had been so many other deaths since his death. He was one of the first ones to get ill, in early 2035, before they knew that COVID-35 was a more lethal variant of COVID-19. During this pandemic, unlike the last, the bosses had a tight grip on the population. No more individuals deciding to wear masks or not or whether to get a vaccine. This time, the virus infected everyone, and the majority died. It terrified people. If they survived, they were sick and terrified. The bosses promised an end to disorder, and they were voted in. No one wanted the chaos of the 2020s again.

In the earlier pandemic, only the long-haulers, as they were called, suffered the effects for many months, including lethargy, depression, and clouded thinking. Now, almost everyone among the Recovereds was a long-hauler, and the haul was longer than before, lasting years if not a lifetime.

When Constance awoke from her second long nap of the day, she typed a report of the morning's meeting with the new woman and her daughter, then prepared to join Martin and the Radiologist for the evening meal in the executive dining room. They were the "G Team," and they ate alone, not with the other teams, to limit contact with Spreaders while they were in charge of possible Pures. Nine teams rotated with the discovery of new possible Pures. Most of the new ones came from the forest, where they lived without awareness of each other.

Being with teammates was supposed to be relaxing, or as relaxing as it could be when interacting. At least none of them had to assume fake smiles. That used energy, as did eating, talking, and any type of movement. Everything except sleeping had a cost-benefit ratio. Standing cost more than sitting, but standing was a prelude to moving from place to place. Smiling put newcomers at ease. Listening was easier than talking.

In the dining room, an array of food arrived by conveyor belt. It relieved the teammates of having to use energy to make menu decisions and of the excruciating tasks of shopping and cooking. It was the end of the day, a low point for all three. That did not stop a hostile exchange between the Radiologist and Martin, which turned a relaxing meal into a stressful one.

"The new people didn't turn out to be much trouble, outside of the girl's constant requests for coke," Constance said.

The two men jammed large forkfuls of plant-based meat into their mouths, as if cutting the food into smaller bites took too much effort. Their irritable mouths chewed while they concentrated on the hard business of swallowing, neglecting to answer Constance.

Finally, Martin spoke to the Radiologist.

"You're an asshole, you know that?"

"Fuck you," the Radiologist said.

"You're a dick."

"Stop it, you two," Constance said. "What's the matter this time?"

Neither answered, but each gave the other contemptuous looks.

Constance hit the table with her palm, not slamming it down as she would have liked.

"I don't care. Figure out a way to work together or the bosses will break up the team. I don't intend to be sent to work in a factory because of you two, so knock it off."

Annoyance curdled her tired mind. She left the room without finishing her meal. It was hard to get a job in The Pure House, as well as a sleeping cell. She paid bribes to several people, using up her inheritance from Gary, to land this advantageous post, and she would not let the guys spoil it.

Back in her cell for the night, she obsessed about her daughter. Did she say the right thing or the wrong thing? Would Molly still be alive the next day?

Then her thoughts drifted to the new woman, Azura, living in the forest for the past five years, until climate change dried everything up. At one time, she thought of taking the twins and her daughter to live in the forest, off the grid, home schooling, fishing, collecting berries. The boys would have thrived, but Molly would have complained from day one. No TV. No Wi-Fi. *Borrrring*. It would have been intolerable.

But the death of all the boys, the twins and Molly's newborn, was even more intolerable. Her exhausted thoughts circled, with no respite, until her anxieties found an outlet in her dreams.

CHAPTER 6
AZURA

It was a week after their medical exam. They had left Azura and her daughter alone in their quarters, with the door locked, for fourteen days. Noam delighted in the food, baths, TV, and her new toys. But Azura waited, while her stomach twisted with anxiety, for whatever would happen next. As long as there was no way of leaving their quarters, she was helpless.

Finally, a brief text from Constance arrived.

Meet today at 1 p.m.

At that precise hour, the lock clicked, and Martin stood on the threshold, saying the usual.

"Please follow me."

Again, he escorted them to the meeting room on the medical floor. Only Constance was there in her Hazmat suit to greet them with her broad grin. Azura recalled learning that heartfelt smiles produce wrinkles in the corners of the eyes. The skin around Constance's eyes was smooth. Her grin was a fake.

"Where's the Radiologist?" Azura asked after Martin left, closing the door behind him.

"Not available right now. Please sit."

Azura took a seat, pulling Noam onto her lap.

"I've put a few toys over there for Noam."

She pointed to a box in the corner.

"Can I play with the toys, Mommy?"

Azura released her.

"You've both passed the medical tests. You have no congenital defects. You're gaining weight. And you haven't contracted the virus. If you had, you would've been symptomatic by now."

"Then, we can leave?"

"What I told you two weeks ago is still true. We can't allow you to endanger Noam. Without the protection offered by The Pure House, you'd both become infected. And even if you reached the forest, what would you do there for food? The forest is dying. The trees are blighted, and the heat from climate change is turning the landscape into desert."

"Then, we can't leave?"

Constance stopped smiling. Her facial expression became serious.

"It's complicated. You're not breaking a law by being healthy. But there are regulations instituted by the bosses to keep the virus from spreading. Lockdowns, isolating those with active cases, mass testing. The only ones detained against their will are Spreaders. They're active cases without symptoms."

"But Noam and I aren't Spreaders."

"Anyone can be a Spreader. They don't wear signs announcing what they are. They don't even know themselves. We discover them when their contacts become infected. Contact tracing is initiated whenever there is an active case."

"They tried that with COVID-19."

"Not successfully."

"Noam and I had no contacts besides you, the Radiologist, the Nurse, Martin, and the officers who picked us up."

Noam ran to her mother.

"Mommy, look. It's a doll. I'm giving her a name. Blondie, because she has blond hair, like me."

Azura had fashioned crude dolls for her daughter in the forest, made of woodland materials.

"Can I keep her?"

"Of course," Constance said, crinkling her eyes with an honest smile.

"Go back to the box and see what else is in there," Azura said.

"Okay, Mommy."

34

As soon as Noam left her mother's side, Constance spoke again.

"You and your daughter are what we call Pures. There aren't many as healthy as you two. Pures are the hope for the future of humanity. That's why you're allowed to live in safety in The Pure House. Only Pures and the few Recovereds who serve them live here."

"Recovereds? Is that what you are? You can't leave?"

"Recovereds had the virus and survived. We can leave for limited periods to visit family members. No one would work here if they weren't allowed to do that. I visit my daughter, for example. But we're tested when we return and again before we interact with a Pure. They tested me just before our meeting. Martin, too."

Azura knitted her distrusting brows.

"You said Pures are the hope for the future of humanity. Meaning what?"

Constance's fake smile returned.

"If you enter our repopulation program, they will grant you extra privileges. Recovered women with intact ovaries can become pregnant, but they have low energy. They're put on bed rest until their due date. After delivery, they're too exhausted to care for their newborns, who are placed in nurseries, where infection rates are high. Still, many try, and some succeed. Pures have a greater chance for successful deliveries, and they take care of their own infants, not exposing them to child care providers who might be Spreaders."

It was a lot for Azura to take in. Constance had to repeat the information several times. What sank into Azura's churning mind was that she was a Pure, that privileges came with getting pregnant, and that she would have the stamina to care for any babies she might have. Any other choice meant that she might lose Noam and die from COVID.

"But I don't have a boyfriend or husband. I'm not attracted to anyone. I can't have sex without being attracted."

A disquieting thought that they would force her to have sex with the Radiologist came to her. Constance put her at ease.

"If you join the program, they would impregnate you by *in vitro* fertilization. The sperm would come from a male Pure or, more precisely, from his frozen ejaculate. They would select female embryos to hasten the repopulation."

"Why females?"

"Think about it. One male Pure could, in theory, impregnate many females. That wouldn't be ideal, but it'd be a last resort."

Azura cast a worried look in Noam's direction. The girl was sitting on the floor with her back to the two women, absorbed with her playthings.

"We're in a race against time," Constance said. "The virus might sprout a stronger variant that would kill all us Recovereds. Protected Pures would be the only ones left, and they would die, too, if they weren't isolated from Spreaders."

"What if I refuse to get pregnant?"

"They'd release you to take your chances in town or back in the forest."

"Without Noam."

"Without Noam."

Back in their quarters, Noam played with her doll, trying to get her mother to join in. But Azura focused on her conflicting thoughts. There was a virus in town fatal to children and many others. The forest was dying, too. The only safe place was The Pure House. But she had to get pregnant to stay.

Did she want more children? Maybe. Someday. She never intended her single sexual encounter with Larry to result in pregnancy, but her initial panic was transformed into excitement when the fetus grew inside her, once she decided not to get an abortion. And she had three wise elders supporting her, helping with the delivery and with infant care. Despite primitive forest life, conditions were ideal. Noam could not have been born into a better environment.

Now, they pressured her to give birth for the good of society. Her only support so far was Constance, a fake; the Radiologist, an obnoxious flirt; and Martin, a polite thug. There was invisible help from whoever left the note.

Get out while you can.

Not without her daughter, she wouldn't.

Just then, another thought intruded. What Constance said made little sense. How did the off-chance that the virus had not infected her or her daughter make them "pure"? What did it mean to be "pure"? And how did her purity protect her — if it did — from being infected by a secret Spreader, who might be one of the other Pures? At most, she was a temporary Pure, just as everyone had been before the virus infected them.

What if she became pregnant and then contracted the virus, perhaps from Constance, who visited her daughter? If her daughter caught it, Constance might catch it and give it to her. Would they kick her out of The Pure House, carrying a doomed fetus? There was something she had not been told.

As the questions formed in her mind, she texted them to Constance, sending them after the child was asleep.

If you agree to enter the repopulation program, there would be another week's wait to see if you developed symptoms. If you didn't, you would receive the implant. At that point, all human contact would stop. Noam would go to daycare with the other Pure girls. Anyone interacting with you, like medical staff, would wear Hazmat suits, including during the delivery. It would be a hard nine months. The benefit would be that you and your two children would live.

How dare they separate her from Noam! The cruelty of the repopulation program appalled her. A five-year-old, taken from her mother, cared for by strangers. It was unthinkable, abusive, like the Holocaust. She seldom thought of her Jewish roots. Now she remembered them, and her hair stood up on the back of her neck. She had to give up her child to save her.

Her next question to Constance combined hope and, if the answer was the one she expected, despair. Would Noam be able to rejoin her and her new sister after the birth?

If Noam didn't test positive, the three of you would be permitted to be together until you wean the new baby. Then you'd be impregnated again and separated from your daughters in order to stay in the program.

The full horror of her situation came to her. To remain a permanent resident of The Pure House and to protect her daughters meant continuing to have children and continuing to give them up for as long as the repopulation program lasted, or until her body and soul gave out.

She lay on the bed — the kind she dreamed of in the forest — and let spells of quiet weeping, not loud enough to awaken Noam, alternate with spells of numb shaking. Intense emotions racked her. Those she named were panic, fury, sadness, and desperation. If only Larry or her father were alive. They would have helped her. Now there was no one except whoever left the note.

You said I'd meet other Pures.

We'll allow that for one day, then your isolation begins for the week before the implantation. It's a risk the bosses, out of their kindness, are willing for the Pure women to take. As long as you're willing to take the risk yourself. There's a slim chance that one of the others is a Spreader. That's why we'll only let you meet one of them, outdoors, where it's safer.

Kindness? It was more like a bribe. One day of socialization for nine months of isolation. The bosses knew she might walk away if they offered anything less.

How would separation from Noam work?

You'd be given a day to prepare her. Tell her she'd have toys and friends her age, other girls. You'd still see each other every day using devices. And the other girls she'd be with would be separated from their mothers, too. She wouldn't be the only one. The Recovereds who care for them are very loving.

One day to prepare Noam, then one day of socialization to prepare herself for nine grinding months of loneliness, worse than anything in the forest. Two days to save Noam. Saving Noam to save her future children. Or, and she did not hide the hideousness of the idea from herself, giving up Noam and her own life, if she died from the virus, to prevent future children from being born and undergoing the same fate.

Through the night, Azura agonized. She remembered going to Larry's bunker on the edge of the woods to tell him she was pregnant and that he was the father. He tried to convince her to sell the child to a wealthy couple who could not conceive, saying she could have another child, but her first one would live in luxury, and she would earn a good sum to support a second one herself. Somehow, she knew he would convince her to become a baby factory, selling all her newborns to others. She escaped to the forest to keep her child.

Now she was in the same predicament and could not escape, as she did with Larry, by walking away from his bunker. There might not be an escape this time.

CHAPTER 7
MARTIN

At 10 p.m., the hour Martin talked to his daughter, Penny, on his device, he lay in bed in his cell. He adjusted the monitor, which swung out on an arm attached to the wall. The pillows behind his head had to be adjusted as well, or he would get a crick in his neck. He had just finished doing his nightly pushups in the small area between his bed and the wall. He made space by pulling the dresser to the far end of the cell and stacking his belongings on its top until they brushed the four-foot ceiling.

As a Recovered, he had limited physical power. By nightfall, he had exhausted himself. But his job was security, and he had to keep his muscles toned. That did not reveal how deficient in strength he was. He would not have the energy to put someone in a hold or chase them if he had to. Many Recovereds faked their way through jobs with tasks they found too tiring to do. Like Constance, always smiling while putting new Pures at ease, despite the heartbreak in her life. Even that asshole Radiologist took sick days at least twice a week.

The monitor flickered, and Penny's head filled the screen. Tattoos covered her stern face. As always, Martin asked himself what happened to his sweet baby girl, now in her twenties. He knew the answer. The death of her mother, his wife, from the virus. Penny's status as a Spreader and the likely cause of her mother's infection. And her confinement on the island for the past five years.

Like most Spreaders, she objected. Every time they communicated, she demanded his help to get released, as if he had the connections or the will to do that.

"You're a Spreader, Honey. Stay where you belong."

"There's nothing wrong with me, Dad. I'm one hundred percent healthy. No symptoms. I'm healthier than you."

It was typical for a Spreader to believe their illness was not real or that it did not pose a danger to others.

"Sweetheart, you have the virus, a mild case. You don't feel sick, but you are. And you can infect others. That's the truth."

"*Pfft*. You blame me for Mom getting the virus, right?"

"Not on purpose. But all your contacts got the disease."

"They could've from each other."

They always wound up having the same argument. Martin felt both frustrated and saddened. He wanted to hit his head on the monitor, or stand and beat it against the wall. His daughter made her mother ill. He wanted her to see that, and he knew it would destroy her if she did.

That was the insidious nature of a contagious disease. People exposed and infected their own loved ones. Illness, grief, and guilt afflicted the entire population, although Spreaders were in denial. He survived, and his wife did not. His duty was to protect his family, giving his life for them. Instead, one lost her life, the other her freedom while he survived.

"You think the Pure ones are pure. They're just people waiting to get sick. We so-called Spreaders are the actual pure ones. We don't get sick, even if we're exposed."

The tattoos, horizontal stripes running across Penny's face, identified her as a Spreader and accentuated her expressions. When she gave him her wry, confident smile, the stripes travelled upward to the edge of her cheekbones before plummeting back down toward her earlobe.

"Yet, we're the ones they punish, while the Pures are in The Pure House, living in luxury in rooms with eight-foot ceilings," she said.

"You're not being punished. You did nothing wrong. None of us did. The bosses have to do what they can to give humans a chance to avoid extinction. You don't realize it, but you are just as sick and contagious as those hospitalized with active cases. That's why they don't consider you medically purer than the Recovereds."

"Just show me where I have a defect, inside or out."

He used a gentle tone when answering her.

"Can you reproduce?"

He did not say "get pregnant." She said nothing. It was well known that female Spreaders had atrophied ovaries.

"Show me children on the island, and I might believe you."

There were no children on the island. Some Recovereds got pregnant, but Spreaders let the virus run its course. By the time their silent disease was diagnosed, it had made its way to their reproductive organs, where it did its only actual damage.

Martin saw bits of the Spreader dormitory behind her and a small window overlooking a view of the ranch. Penny changed the subject.

"We had a birth yesterday."

She was not referring to a human birth. It was the craziness about red cows.

"The calf is too young to be sure, but we're getting closer."

She referred to the island's red heifer project. Many groups across the globe vied to produce a red cow without a single white or black hair. The belief, going back to Biblical times, was that the ashes of a pure red heifer would cleanse the population of disease. In the past, the motives had included starting Armageddon or the Messianic age and sending the heifer to Israel to instigate the building of the third temple. Since COVID-35 began, the idea was to use the ashes to stop the plague. How that was supposed to happen was beyond Martin's imagination.

"For Pete's sake, Penny."

He wished he could reach into the screen and shake her.

"The science is fascinating, Dad. We breed cattle with pure traits. That's what they're called — pure. It means the traits appear on both chromosomes of the animal. When the animal reproduces with another with the same pure traits, they call the resulting offspring purebred. See? There's that word pure again. Our effort is to produce a purebred heifer that is pure in a second way, with only red hairs."

"I guess that's difficult."

"Very. And we'd need two to produce a herd that would protect all of us. Then a repopulation program using Pures wouldn't be

42

necessary. There'd be no COVID. We Spreaders would come off the island with no one fearing us. Boom! Every woman who wanted to get pregnant would, just like that."

She snapped her fingers.

Martin sighed. How many times had he heard this? He had yet to connect the dots the way Penny did. Why would a hundred percent red heifer have magical properties when a hundred percent white one didn't? The only magic that would stop the disease was the development of a vaccine or herd immunity — everyone dead except the Pures.

He changed the subject.

"A couple of new ones showed up. They'd been living in the forest. A mother and five-year-old daughter."

"I'm guessing you took them to be Pures because they didn't seem sick."

"Only under-nourished. Thin as rails. But not coughing or feverish. As soon as the officers picked them up, they brought them to The Pure House for testing. They're not active cases or Recovereds. They've been off the grid in the forest since the child's birth."

"Now you'll force the mother to sign up for the repopulation program, right?"

"Not force."

"Ha!"

He did not fool Penny.

"Persuade."

"Dad, you're operating in a fascist system. The bosses are autocrats."

Another topic Penny brought up almost every time they talked.

"Would it be better if humans went extinct?"

"Yes."

From an early age, COVID-35 and climate change concerned Penny. She blamed human behavior for the ills of the planet, then for the pandemic that threatened the continuation of humanity. When there was no political will for changing the addiction to fossil fuels, meat-based diets, or a refusal to wear masks, Penny slid into pseudoscientific thinking, pursuing astrology, reincarnation, and now the idiocy about the red heifer.

From toddlerhood on, she was strong-willed, nearing fanaticism in whatever she believed. The difference now is that other Spreaders, who supported each other in their denial of their disease and its mysterious cure by their breeding program, reinforced her beliefs.

When they had exhausted the topics that pushed them apart, Penny reversed course to pull them back together.

"At least you get to keep your job as long as new ones keep arriving. You won't be kicked out of The Pure House into some factory."

"I could manage a two-hour shift."

"Are you sure, Dad? Factory jobs are harder than escorting the new ones here and there. I'd worry about you. You're the only parent I have."

Tears welled in her eyes. They shared so much sadness. It was easier to channel their feelings into arguments. How ridiculous to be fighting over damn cows! They should be grateful to have each other. Many had no one left. But gratitude was scarce when life was so difficult, so unrewarding. Martin remembered the three-bedroom house he shared with his wife when Penny was born. His big complaint was having to mow the lawn. When had he last seen a lawn? All the yards turned to dust before people stopped being able to maintain houses and moved into the beehive buildings. Some lived in squalor before being forced out. The bosses would not allow rodent-infested residences to spread even more disease.

Martin's eyes moistened, too. He might never share a meal or an in-person conversation with his daughter again. They could not exchange birthday gifts or hugs. He would not receive a phone call from her, saying, "I have news. I'm pregnant" or hold a grandbaby in his arms. She would not invite him over for Thanksgiving dinner or to hear the weird grinding sound her car made when she sped up or to see her new kitten. When he was old enough for assisted living, he would not wait for her Sunday visits or outings with her to baseball games.

Like Penny, he had contempt for the Pures, but for different reasons. It was not fair to favor them above all others because of their disease status. Prior to COVID-35, upper class white people had been the privileged ones. Skin color and financial assets determined social rank. Now, Pures were a diverse group. The pandemic was a racial and financial equalizer. Money did not buy health.

Those who had escaped the virus by staying in the forest or isolating themselves for years seemed, to Martin, to have cheated their way into the best current life could offer. Standing room in their quarters, for one. All the Pure women had to do was endure pregnancy, something Recovered women and Spreaders wished for. And when they were given that one condition, the Pures wept and complained. Martin had no sympathy for them. They were spoiled, the lot of them. He ground his teeth in frustration.

During his shift, he remained professional, speaking to the Pures in a civil manner, never saying more than was necessary. The bosses would never see him act in an inappropriate way, like that asshole Radiologist did. Martin did not reveal that his daughter was a Spreader engaged in the red heifer scheme. He did not speak about his personal life to his team. He did not speak about it to anybody.

Martin always tried to end their conversations with warmth, hoping she would receive that way.

"Take care of yourself, sweetheart. Know I'm thinking of you."

"I miss you, Dad. I love you."

That was a surprise. Penny almost never said the "L" word. As he shoved the monitor back against the wall, Martin wondered if his daughter was in trouble.

CHAPTER 8
AZURA

The day after Azura agreed to *in vitro* fertilization, Constance took her to an outdoor courtyard with a nearby playground. Noam would be there, within sight, minded by Constance. Another woman in a long white dress was seated on a bench, surrounded by blooming yellow rose bushes, sitting still, as if posing for a French oil painting.

"Azura, this is Marie. She's a Pure, like you," Constance said.

Marie stood up and took Azura's hand in hers.

"Hello, Azura. I'm so happy you're one of us."

Even her name sounded French, although she had no accent.

"I'll leave you two to get acquainted. I'll be at the playground." Constance walked away.

"Even when we are outside, Recovereds never stay among us for long," Marie said. She had a high, melodic voice, like Cinderella in the Disney movie.

"Why not?"

"In case. Shall we sit?"

Marie sat on the bench again, and Azura joined her.

"Azura. Such a pretty name."

"My mother's name was Eva. In the Bible, Eve's daughter is Azura, and her granddaughter is Noam. That's what I named my daughter."

They had met moments ago. Azura was not sure why she said any of this, other than she was glad to speak with someone her age and to make the most of their time together. One day. Perhaps Marie had answers to her questions.

"That's so romantic. They named me in the ordinary way, after my mother. All the women's names in my family are variations of Mary — Marie, Maria, Mary, Marsha."

Birds chirped. A brook or small waterfall gurgled. The air was scented. Like The Pure House itself, everything was luxurious and strange. Constance's smile. The abundance of food. And now this opulent garden and a woman in a long white dress. It reminded Azura of paintings in museums she visited when she lived in town before Noam's birth.

"I'm like you, between pregnancies," Marie said, with her hand on her flat stomach.

"How many pregnancies have you had?"

"We try for one a year. I've had four successful deliveries."

"Four?"

"Yes, four opportunities to save humanity."

Marie's smile was not forced like Constance's. She was not saying the polite thing like Martin. She meant the crazy thing she said.

"I'm guessing you had four daughters. Do you see them?"

"I see the ones who I have weaned once in a while. On their birthdays and holidays. I'm careful not to get attached."

"How do you avoid getting attached?"

Marie turned and pulled a rose toward her face, inhaling its fragrance.

"Oops," she said, holding up her hand, "a thorn has pricked me."

A drop of blood welled up on her fingertip. She licked it.

"Can't let that go to waste."

Azura stared, not knowing whether to be repulsed or curious.

"To answer your question, I avoid attachment by reminding myself of the goal of the repopulation program. The daughters I produce belong to society, not to me. I give them the gift of life, Pure life. Recovereds will raise them, and when they mature, they will give that gift to the next generation of Pures."

"Why can't you raise them?"

"Four babies a year apart? Not even a Pure has the stamina for that. I need to reserve my energy for the next pregnancy. We must have as many successful deliveries as possible. Four. Ten. Twenty. But we can't mother that many. Others have to help."

"I wouldn't give up Noam."

"What's the alternative, Azura? Isolating her with you for nine months at a time? How would she get an education or play with friends?"

Azura's stomach churned at the thought of relinquishing her daughter. Even if it was in the child's best interest, it would be like ripping out her arm or amputating her leg. The pain would be unbearable. She would spend the rest of her life weeping. The loss lay beyond her imagination.

"What about your babies? Don't they become attached to you?"

"They're weaned early, before they become too attached. Besides, I leave them in their bassinets between feedings. It's better that way."

Her melodic voice tinkled, as if she referred to fairies and elves instead of admitting to neglect.

"If you keep your mind on the greater purpose, any sacrifice is possible," Marie said.

"But… It's your children. It can't be that easy."

Marie smiled in her genuine way again, with crinkles in the corners of her eyes.

"It is that easy. All you have to do is realize the only purpose of the individual is serving the greater interest of the collective. What you or I suffer is immaterial, Azura. Even if our children cry for us, it's immaterial. Feelings don't matter. Not when survival is at stake."

There was no answer in the face of Marie's brute logic. Azura stayed silent.

"Take the active cases. They put some on ventilators, a procedure so uncomfortable they have to be sedated. Their suffering is worse, but it's done to save them. It's the only chance they have."

"You're saying that giving up our children is the only chance they have."

"Yes. It is. Otherwise everyone dies."

Tears ballooned in Azura's eyes.

"Don't cry. Try to accept what's asked of you and Noam as an honor."

When the tears rolled down Azura's face, Marie gave her a sly look.

"They will treat you and Noam as honored ones — lots of food and the best quarters. Toys for Noam. TV. Books. None of the Recovered have those things. We're the lucky ones."

Noam ran to her mother.

"Push me on the swing, Mommy."

"Ask Constance to push you."

Noam skipped back to the playground. Azura could see her talking to Constance, who remained sitting on a low wall.

"What you're saying, that we must sacrifice the individual, sounds like North Korea back in the 2020s or something."

Marie's melodic voice became squeaky.

"Oh, no. The sacrifice then was for the betterment of their leader, not of humanity."

"But Marie, all dictators say that. Even genocide was supposed to be for the betterment of the majority."

"This time it's true. And the virus is responsible for genocide, not us."

Her voice was shrill, like fingernails on a blackboard. Azura shivered from the sound. Marie shifted closer, as if to pressure Azura by closing the gap between them. Noam ran back.

"The lady can't push me. She's too tired."

"I'll be there in a minute. Go to the swings and wait for me."

She turned back to Marie.

"If a Recovered can't push a child on a swing, how can we trust them to take care of our babies?"

Without waiting for an answer, she stood. "I have to go. Noam needs me."

Marie stood, too. She reached for Azura's hand and held it in a firm grip. Then she kissed Azura lightly on the lips, released her hand, and returned to her pose on the bench.

"I'm waiting, Mommy," Noam called.

In a daze of confusion, Azura headed to the swings. What had just happened?

The next day, back in their quarters, was the time Azura had to prepare her daughter for their separation. She was not thinking of the good of humanity. She was thinking she had no alternative after a desperate night of no sleep, trying to think of some way to keep Noam.

The only plan that occurred to her was to tell the child the separation was temporary. That was Azura's intention. Somehow, she and Noam would be reunited, for the good of Noam, not humanity. Her child must not grow up to be sacrificed for a post-COVID society. Her decision about what to do with her life must be hers alone. That's what Azura would teach her when they were together again. If they were together again.

She set about her grim task, telling Noam in a matter-of-fact way, the way Constance might do it. The child cried and pleaded, then became enraged, pounding her mother with her fists, then sobbed and clutched at her. It broke Azura's heart. By nightfall, they were both weeping and clinging in the big, soft bed that was the wonder of their first time in The Pure House.

The next morning was worse. Constance unlocked the door. Martin stood there with her. Without ceremony, he scooped up the screaming child and carried her out the door. Constance locked it without saying a word to Azura. Noam's cries grew fainter as they carried her further away, until they must have reached the elevator, and the sound stopped. The silence was even more horrible.

In her mind, she could still hear her child calling.

"Mommy! Mommy!"

For the long, lonely week before the procedure, locked into her lavish quarters, with no visitors, she paced, wailed, yanking her hair, ripping her clothes, smashing plates, yelling curses at the ceiling and walls, hoping the bosses in their penthouse heard her. When she stopped eating, a note arrived with the next meal threatening to force feed her if she lost weight. Was Noam being threatened, too? The note added she could communicate with her daughter on her phone when her week was up, after the procedure.

Seven days passed. The lock clicked, and Martin appeared in a Hazmat suit.

"Please follow me."

Would he carry her off if she refused, as he had Noam? She looked at him with hate-filled eyes, saying nothing. She loathed all of them — Martin, Constance, the Radiologist, Marie. They took her child.

It did not surprise her to be led to the medical floor. Where else would *in vitro* fertilization take place? Constance waited. She was also suited up. Her fake smile was visible through the plastic in the helmet. Martin left, having done his duty.

"I'm not doing anything until I see Noam," Azura said.

"She would have to wear a suit."

"Why?"

"To avoid infecting you if she's a Spreader. From now on, no one comes near you without a suit."

"Noam couldn't have become a Spreader in a week."

"Well, she could have, although we take every precaution."

This was no comfort.

"I must see my child."

Constance sighed. "Only for a few minutes. Wait here."

She left. Azura noticed the curtain. Would the other patient she had seen the first day be behind it? She pushed it aside. No one was there. The medical machines hovered, birds of prey waiting to sink invisible talons into whoever lay on the exam table. A sound like chuckling started. It had to be the air conditioning cycling on. The room was cold. Azura waited, chilled.

The door opened, and Constance entered with Noam in a Hazmat suit that swam on her. It must have been the smallest size they had. She ran into her mother's arms.

"Mommy. Mommy. I missed you."

"My darling, I missed you, too."

"I can't feel you with this clothing."

"Tell me about your new room."

"There are two other girls. Ju and Sandy. Ju is Chinese. Her name means Daisy."

"What about Sandy?"

"She's like me. Only darker. She's nice."

It was a relief that Noam had friends. She wasn't alone, like Azura was.

"What else is your room like."

"There're toys and TV and three beds. They're smaller than our bed."

She meant the bed in Azura's quarters.

"Do you like it?"

"Yes, but when can I be with you?"

"Soon. While you are waiting, you can play with Sandy and Ju and all the toys."

"I want to be with you, but not in the forest."

"Okay." What could she say?

Constance stepped forward.

"It's time for you to say goodbye to your Mommy. When you get back to your room, you can take off that itchy suit."

"Bye, Mommy."

She wasn't crying. It surprised Azura. After giving her a tight hug, she let her go. Constance guided her out the door.

"I'll be back soon," she said. "You can take everything off from the waist down and put on one of the medical gowns on the exam table."

Constance had done what Azura demanded by allowing her to see Noam for a brief time. Now Azura had no way of not complying with the procedure. Her sadness at seeing Noam leave shifted to numbness. A syringe would impregnate her.

CHAPTER 9
THE RADIOLOGIST

He needed to stretch his legs when his two-hour shift ended, despite the shortness of breath that plagued him after work. The phlebotomy machine had miscalculated during the new Pure's ovarian reserve test and had to be re-done. By the time the ovarian ultrasound began, the subject, Azura, was in tears and had to be calmed by that bitch, Constance, anyone's last choice for soothing. Obstetrics examined the results, sent remotely, to determine the effectiveness of fertility medication. Irritated by the demands to re-do one image, the complaints of Constance, the puzzling phlebotomy machine error, and the itchiness of the Hazmat suit, the Radiologist walked off the stress.

The sun blistered his scalp. He dragged himself from the shade of one tree to another in The Pure House garden. It was only June, yet the temperature topped a hundred. The heat stabbed at his bare arms and his face, penetrating like x-rays. Except they were UVA and UVB rays, not producing images, instead causing deadly melanomas and other skin cancers, not that x-rays were harmless. He should have worn sunscreen. "Never go out without sunscreen." The bosses drilled that into the public. He was a radiologist. He should know. Yet, like the public, some ignorant part of his mind held fast to the notion that "what you can't see won't hurt you."

He also neglected to wear a hat. The top of his head received the full blast of the overhead furnace, the midday sun without a shielding ozone layer. Baldness ran in his family among the men. Many who survived COVID now made regular appointments with a dermatologist to have lesions removed. He used a hand mirror to examine his scalp for abnormalities, purple blotches with irregular edges. So far, so good for that one.

He sat on a bench to rest before dragging himself back indoors. The border between the leaf canopy and the bleached walkway was outlined at this hour, as if a giant concrete block pancaked the garden into two dimensions. The Radiologist sat hunched under the weight of the heat. With his head bent, he stared at the Astro Turf and artificial flowers. Only scrubby desert plants grew in the dust that covered the region, once home to vast stretches of prairie grass, later to acres of corn and soybeans. That was before. This was after.

A slight breeze, like the heat waves from a ticking car motor, did little more than kick the finer dust particles into the air, coating his nasal passages and eyes, but without being visible on his white lab coat, worn with the sleeves pushed up above his elbows. He would have to cough and sneeze to clear his lungs, already damaged from the virus.

The sound of the COVID cough protested the lack of space as the virus ravaged the air sacs which transported oxygen into circulation systems, like passengers jamming themselves into a train car that had no room for them. He gasped for breath along with the other active cases. They heard each other through the walls of the beehive residence reserved for them, coughing and wheezing, without the breath to call for help or say over three words if help arrived. He also heard cots being wheeled through the hallway, unaccompanied by the sound of wheezing or coughing. Everyone knew what that meant.

He survived, a Recovered now, waiting to be reinfected. As his energy returned, he could work the short shift before his brain fogged and his eyelids plunged downward, insisting on sleep.

"I can't keep my eyes open" had become a reality for Recovereds.

Despite his nap requirements, as his energy increased, his libido returned. He mustered a soft erection with effort. His dick was no longer a useless bump, shrunk into his balls. It was coming to life, trailing the rest of him after weeks of illness. He had crawled out of his cell with just enough stamina to reach the communal showers. But his sperm count had to be low to non-existent.

That did not bother him. He wanted to fuck, not make babies. Punishment for a Recovered fucking a Pure was harsh, yet the Radiologist dreamed of it, now that he could dream once more instead of spending weeks turned on his stomach, hoping to die. Pure women were the virgins of the mid-twenty-first century, just as prized as sexual virgins were for thousands of years before COVID-35.

Lying on his bed in his cell, the Radiologist's thoughts centered on the new woman, Azura, and all he might do to her if she lay crammed next to him on the narrow cot or in some town alley, on the ground, covered in dust, pleading, frightened. How much better if she was frightened. He touched himself. Half-hard.

Tomorrow, he would guide the Sonohysterography Machine into her, to inject fluid through the cervix into the uterus. No doubt that would frighten her. Then an internal ultrasound to create images of her uterine cavity. Obstetrics would use the findings to determine the thickness of her uterine lining before starting IVF. He would be professional, reserving his ardor for his return to his cell.

Girls like Azura no longer had families to protect them. Few people had families since COVID-35. It decimated his own family, taking his mother, father, sister, nieces and nephew. He was the only one left. Not that his circumstance was unusual. Most Recovereds were the only ones they had left. They could have caught the virus from one of their own family members, then they were left with the guilt of survivors. Survivor's guilt. Most Recovereds dealt with it by refusing to think about it. Therapists, the few that remained, advised facing it and grieving. That took too much energy.

The distraction of work was more helpful. So far, there had been a steady stream of new Pures, picked up in town and driven to The Pure House as dust billowed behind the vehicle's tires. Too many would overwhelm the resources of the staff, but too few meant fewer hours, more time without distractions.

If Azura's tests passed the requirements of Obstetrics, he would give her a luteinizing hormone by injection to stimulate her ovaries and chorionic gonadotropin to help them mature. Then he would not see her for a week or two until her eggs were ready for retrieval. They would determine that by another vaginal ultrasound, his favorite.

Someone from Obstetrics would do the egg retrieval and the embryo transfer. They did not train him to do that skilled work, which needed the delicate hands of a doctor versed in the procedure. Although in the old days a doctor did the whole shebang, now they limited the Pure's exposure. The more he did, the more it was limited. Advanced technology also kept human contact to a minimum.

Maybe that was the reason a Pure woman enticed him. Touching them for any but a medical reason was taboo. He was the one who had the most intimate contact with them. He positioned the machinery, hovering it over their pelvic section or guiding it into their cunts. With their feet in stirrups and their raised legs spread wide, they could not see what he did, although he explained every step, following protocol. They did not know about the extra seconds he took to look and memorize, the extra breaths he took to learn their scent. Not even Constance, who sat in the room lost in thought, realized.

In the Bible, God created Adam from dust. But He made Eve from bone, a hard substance with rich softness inside. In the days before they forced everyone to eat a plant-based diet, he would buy soup bones and suck out the marrow. Delicious. That's what he would do to a Pure, if he ever had an opportunity.

The only way would be to find one who escaped from The Pure House and offer to be her protector. He would need a safe place to take her. Sometimes, in his cell, he read through the rentals on Craig's List. There still were some, although ninety percent of the town lived in the beehives. On occasion, a remote place would pop up, then vanish a day later. There seemed to be a high demand, unless the bosses spotted the ads and took them down.

If he left a key code in a Pure's quarters, she might escape into his arms. It would take planning. The code was in her chart, easy for him to copy. The best time was coming up, when the new Pure transferred from the Precautionary Wing to the Fertilized Wing. He had to figure out how to get the key code into her room, what kind of note to leave with it, where to take her, how to keep everything a secret.

It was just a game. He was not brave enough or reckless enough to chance it. Too much might go wrong. But it did not hurt to fantasize. It was a way of being distracted, not dwelling on the past. The bosses urged future thinking. Once enough Pures had been born to fulfill the repopulation objective, there was a new society to build. So far, they had contained COVID-35 by isolating active cases, Spreaders, and Pures, with only well-tested Recovereds acting as go-betweens.

Through the hours of dozing and waking, his thoughts continued to circle. Dust motes not trapped by the building's filters circled with them, floating on air streams from the vents.

He toyed with the idea of slipping a key code into one of her pockets during the ultrasound and blood tests just prior to the egg retrieval. Someone from Obstetrics would enter the Procedure Room as he left. Constance would watch the doctor, not him. The Pure's clothing would hang on hooks near the door. That would be his chance.

He would not risk the other steps he needed to plan. All he would do was the key code part, leaving the rest to chance. If she escaped, and he spent time in the gardens dozing on the benches, he might catch sight of her. He might catch her.

When the day came, he bounced between excitement and anxiety. During the testing, his stomach roiled. *His only chance.* Was it worth it? They would fire him if they found out. They would transfer him to a factory. Or worse. Images of a prison cell flashed through his mind, superimposed on images of catching the Pure, putting a hand over her mouth to keep her from screaming. His imagination went no further. He did not know how he would get her to the secret hiding place he did not yet have.

When the door opened, the doctor from Obstetrics entered, nodding at him. The Radiologist handed him the device with the test results. He shook, but the Obstetrics guy did not notice. He turned toward the door. The key code was already written on a folded piece of paper, hidden in the fist of his glove. Dizziness overtook him. *Don't,* a voice said in his head. Without willing it, the fist opened above the Pure's pocket and the paper slipped in.

As the Radiologist stumbled to the elevator, the dizziness increased. He was the only passenger. When the door closed, the vertical motion of the descent and the horizontal spinning made him vomit on the floor. He got off at Hazmat Storage without looking back.

Numbness set in. Whatever he had set in motion, no one could undo. He would have to live with the fear that it would not be the Pure who would be caught. It would be him.

CHAPTER 10
AZURA

When she found the paper in her pocket, Azura's skin crawled. She reread it many times. They transferred her to the Fertility wing, and she was adjusting to her new quarters, not in any way different from her former one, when she reached into her pocket absent-mindedly, not for any reason. There was a folded piece of paper. She remembered the one under the coffee pot in her old room.

Get out while you can.

This paper contained a number. Could it be it for the keypad? If it was, they might detect her if she used it. There might be cameras or a special alarm if an unauthorized person unlocked the door. Her white outfit would also be a problem. Only Pures wore all-white. The Recovereds she met wore street clothes of different colors under white lab coats. Their shoes were black or brown. The Hazmat suits were silver.

She took the precaution of memorizing the number and flushing the paper away, as she had done with the one under the coffee pot. No one doing laundry would find it. No cleaner would discover it hidden in her quarters. These invisible people, who came and went when they took her to the exam room, or who received the used dishes and the laundry bag on the conveyor belt, could not be trusted.

Someone got messages to her, but who? Perhaps the patient who popped out from behind the curtain during her first exam. Or Marie, the Pure in the long white dress, faking allegiance to the bosses. Or someone who knew about her, but of whom she had no unawareness. Or someone she knew who did not reveal his or her true purpose.

Martin? Constance? The Radiologist? The Nurse? The doctor who did the embryo transfer? They had sedated her for that before he or she entered the procedure room. One of them might be a possibility, but which?

She did not know the floor plan of the building, which was said to be maze-like. There was no escaping without Noam. Another obstacle was finding the location of the children's wing. She thought of a way of finding out if it was nearby by texting Constance.

I thought I heard my daughter. Is she on this floor?

She held her breath, waiting for an answer. Constance replied with a single word.

No.

It was information, however meager. Azura guessed Noam could not be on the medical floor, either. There would be too much opportunity for children to be frightened by a stray sight or sound. She was on one of the other floors. Azura tried to remember how many stories tall The Pure House was. Six? Seven? Not counting the lobby, that left four possibilities.

In a wing on one of those floors, her child lived in quarters with two other girls, Sandy and Ju. Her child. Her Noam. She recalled the scent of her hair. From the moment of her birth, she had taken the smell of her scalp deep into her lungs. When she held her, she inhaled the aroma rising from the top of her head. If she became blind and deaf, she would recognize her daughter by her scent. If she had amnesia, her lungs would remember. Often she sat with her baby girl on her lap, with the tip of her nose on the child's soft fontanel, taking her in with the air.

The bulge of her first pregnancy had collapsed into her now flattened stomach with the birth of Noam. It reminded her of how her daughter had grown inside her, enlarging her, ballooning her out until she felt she floated over the ground like a Zeppelin, cruising toward the cave in the forest where she would land when her due date neared. Her great grandmother knelt between her legs with a clean towel spread to catch the baby as she emerged. One of the elderly Nathan sisters sat behind her with bent knees for Azura to lean against, bracing her shoulders when it was time to push.

With the last contraction, Noam tumbled into the towel. The odor that arose came from all of them — the yowling newborn, the placenta, the blood, the perspiration, the effort, the pain, the astonishment, the delight. They all — Azura, her great grandmother, and the two Nathan sisters — committed the fragrance to memory without knowing it. When the elders died, their portion passed to Azura, who recognized it whenever she sniffed her daughter's head.

That's what she missed the most and craved — the distinctive smell of Noam.

It would happen with this pregnancy, too. But they would take her second daughter from her minutes after her birth, when her smell had already been implanted in Azura's nostrils, impossible to eradicate. She would spend years searching for that scent, grieving its absence, thinking it was just for her physical child and not for the odor that would accompany her as well.

She had to find Noam and escape. Before that, she had to find out if the numbers were the key code. She faced the same dilemma she had when she wanted coffee after her first night in The Pure House. Back then, she feared lifting the coffee pot would set off an alarm. Would that happen if she tried to punch the code into the keypad next to the door?

For a long hour, she paced and worried. If she did something wrong, she was unlikely to be kicked out, now that she was a Pure in the Repopulation Program. The worst punishment would be to deprive her of her evening communication with Noam. But that would punish Noam, too. They did not want to traumatize a Pure child. Their methods had been manipulative, not brutal.

Her obsessive thoughts became more irritating than stressful.

Screw it, she said to herself.

After a deep inhalation, she held her breath while punching the numbers in. The familiar click sounded. She took a step back, holding a hand on her chest to quiet her beating heart before it alerted everyone in the building. Gingerly, she stepped forward and put the other hand on the doorknob. On her next inhalation, she turned the knob. The door opened as easily as when Martin came for her. No alarm sounded. There was still the possibility of a camera. She had to take the chance of stepping outside. Nothing. No one was there. She stood still, just outside her quarters, sniffing without being aware of what she was doing. No Noam. She counted to ten. When she reached ten, she darted back inside and relocked the door.

An hour later, she unlocked the door again. No one was in the hallway this time, either. She walked to the end of the corridor, passing two doors with keypads like hers, then a door without one. She turned the knob. A broom closet. Somewhere to hide if anyone spotted her. A few steps more and the hallway met another at a ninety-degree angle. This one was much longer. She could see several doorways. Half-way down, someone stood with his back to her. A Recovered man in a white lab coat. After retreating to her door, she walked down the hallway the other way. It was the same. Two locked doors, then an unlocked one—containing an ice machine, this time—then a sharp turn to a longer corridor. It was not a maze. It was a rectangle, similar to the layout of hotels. She returned to her quarters with that knowledge. A staircase had to be at the end of one of the long hallways. A possible way to escape.

Back in her room, she panted with fear. She put a hand on her stomach, wondering if she would miscarry from the stress. Leaving her quarters, even for a few moments, was a bold and risky step. It had been an impulsive act. From now on, she would have to plan before making a move. And she would need the help of whoever had written the notes.

But now she had to calm herself. The remote for the TV lay on the nightstand. She used it to channel surf, hoping for a soothing program. At least it was not all cartoons. Classic movies, animal shows, history, games shows, sports. There were hundreds of channels, but no news. She reached the higher numbers. The last one was the Public Service Station.

On it, an interview was conducted by a young mixed-race man with an older white man. The interviewer called the older man Boss Franklyn. Franklyn might be his first or last name. Boss appeared to be his title. He was one of the so-called bosses, sitting in a relaxed way in his chair, while the interviewer leaned forward in his, looking interested and tense.

She gaped. Perhaps the program was a mistake, stuck in the last channel slot because they did not want her to see it. How ordinary the boss looked, like someone's retired father, sitting in his easy chair before going to the garage to putter around. She half-expected him to joke about his "honey-do" list or talk about the travel plans in his "bucket-list." He had a kind face and a serene smile. He might help her, she thought, before listening to his answer to a question she had not heard.

"The obligation of the government is to protect civilians from any threat, whether from another nation, climate change, or disease. The more serious the threat, the more ruthless the government must be. Many of our actions are in response to the severity of the threats we face."

The interviewer hesitated before asking his next question.

"Some would say that the cost of protecting us from threats is a threat, too. How do you respond to those who make that point?"

Boss Franklyn flipped his palm upward, as if receiving a feather floating down from above.

"What's the alternative? Give everyone the choice to die from the virus or the heat?"

"Some would say people can't thrive without choices. They are being robbed of free will."

"Thrive or survive. It can't be both. There aren't any good choices. We're long past that. Government has to choose the least worst solution and enforce it."

She turned off the TV. An appeal to Boss Franklyn or any of the bosses would not reunite her with Noam or release her from the Repopulation Program. The kind face of the man being interviewed belied a believer in ruthlessness. A practitioner of ruthlessness. Santa Claus with a machete, living on the top floor of the building, trampling on her with every footstep.

But the interviewer had started his question with "some would say." Who were those who opposed the strategy of the bosses? The minority party or a rebel group? If she connected with them, if they were rebels, it might be her only chance. If only she could figure out how.

A rebel may have left the two notes on folded paper. They knew she was here, and that she wished to escape. It had to be someone who prepared the coffee, or someone with access to the medical floor. One note on a folded piece of paper under the coffee pot, the other in the pocket of the outfit she wore on the day of the embryo transfer. Who would have been able to plant both? The Radiologist was her best guess.

Would he help her locate her daughter? Without consciousness, she kept sniffing the air for the aroma of Noam. Now, she stood on a chair with her nose to the air vent, hoping for a whiff. There could be a trail of scent molecules that would lead her to her daughter, like the bread crumbs in old tales followed to bring children back to their home. Her nose would continue the search.

CHAPTER 11
CONSTANCE

That afternoon's call from Molly caught Constance off guard.

"Mom, I met a guy."

Constance sat up straighter in bed, adjusting the monitor to see what her daughter's image revealed. The young woman who became so distraught during their last conversation was all smiles. Her excited eyes danced across her mother's face, sharing her electrifying news, hoping it would thrill her mother.

Constance remained cautious.

"What's his name? Where did you meet?"

Molly chuckled, as if saying his name delighted her.

"Vic. Victor, but he goes by Vic. We met in the break room in the factory. I waited for my coffee to cool, when he sat down next to me. There were plenty of seats, but he chose the one at my table. He got right to the point. 'I've been wanting to talk to you,' he said."

Constance sighed to herself. Here we go again.

"What else did he tell you about himself?"

"Let's see. He's a Recovered, of course. Just got back to work after a little relapse."

Or a little time in jail, Constance thought.

"He's a proper gentleman, Mom. Took my coffee mug back to the dirty-dish depository along with his."

Proof of a gentleman. All it took was the gallant return of a mug to win over Molly.

"After my nap, we're meeting for drinks."

Constance felt her eyes droop. Sleep called to her. Her daughter's romances fell into a pattern—meet someone, forget birth control, get pregnant, miscarry or deliver a stillborn or a baby that lived a few days, threaten suicide. Molly had the stamina to go through the same scenario again, but Constance flagged.

She detected the reservation in her mother's unsmiling expression.

"I've met the love of my life, for sure. I want you to be happy for me."

She had to give her daughter something.

"If that's what Vic turns out to be, I'll be happy for you. If he cares for you and treats you well. But you can't know yet. You've only been with him for a few minutes."

"I do, Mom. I can tell."

"How?"

"I have good instincts about people."

Really?

"Be careful, okay?"

"Sure," she yawned, worn out by the stress of emotions, even joyful ones.

Add alcohol, and he would seduce her within minutes. No Recovered had the energy for long hours in a bar or for extended conversations.

Constance wished she could call Gary, her ex, Molly's father, now deceased. She caught the virus first. During the long months of her illness, he cheated on her, unable to wait for sex until she recovered. When he caught it, maybe from her or most likely from one of his girlfriends, it was a severe case. He gasped out a confession when he knew he would die. Constance felt like someone had grabbed her by the shoulders and given her a shaking for being so stupid. Gary was not who he seemed.

She stayed at his bedside every minute, at home, in the hospital, in ICU, the funeral home, delaying her return to work. When she lay in bed, with every inhalation an effort, he came and went. When he went, it was to the arms of other women. He claimed that the fact there were several proved it was just sex, meaningless, without love, unlike a genuine affair, cheating with one woman.

One part of her understood this is what men are like, they cheat, they confess, they want forgiveness; they think cheating has no meaning, and if the woman doesn't forgive, they blame her, the bitch, for lack of understanding, for not forgiving even though they humiliated themselves by crying on the floor, holding the legs of the woman to keep her from leaving. She hated him for it, while still loving him with another part of herself to this day.

Constance was only fooled once, but Molly succumbed several times, even before her parents had gone through the same thing, without complicating things with another pregnancy. COVID-35 took care of that with Constance, but not with Molly, one of the few with undamaged ovaries. Her daughter carried a baby to term. She was eligible for the Recovered Repopulation Program. It was high risk with a low success rate. The strict quarantine kept Molly from enrolling. She would not meet her next soul mate if they confined her to quarters, even if it was roomier than her cell.

"It's not like I have to enroll, Mom. I'm not a Pure. They won't force me."

Constance was not unsympathetic.

"No, they won't force you. It would be a break from factory work and the possibility of re-infection. But you wouldn't raise the baby. It would live under quarantine in the Recovered Children's Residence to give it a better chance of survival. It's a tough decision, but one you should consider."

An idea popped into Constance's head, like the light bulb over the heads of characters in comic strips. A ridiculous thought, but there it was. What if, somehow, she substituted Molly for the newest Pure, Azura? It was what Molly asked for. If Molly had sex with Vic that day, she might be pregnant, only a few days after the Pure. And since they had tested the Pure for exposure to the virus, they would not repeat the test on a Recovered who replaced her.

She might persuade the Pure to step into Molly's shoes, working in the factory, but with time off for pregnancy. It would be easier to escape with her baby and raise it herself in the forest. All she would have to do is walk away before they discovered her pregnancy. No one would look for a Recovered.

Such a stupid fantasy, a way to amuse herself before falling asleep. She allowed herself to continue. Molly would have to be disillusioned by Vic, the latest "love of her life," first. As if that would not happen. Then she would have to be persuaded that nine months of isolation as a Pure would be preferable to the weeks of bedrest given a Recovered. Better food and quarters might do the trick. Molly had always had a materialistic side. A better chance for the baby's survival would appeal to her maternal side. For all of her daughter's flaws, she did love the baby who died.

The biggest obstacle was Noam, the Pure's child. She was also the Pure's biggest incentive. If she promised Azura reunification with her daughter, the Pure would do anything. Constance had no access to the children's wing. That was a problem. There would be a lot of sneaking, getting Molly into the Fertility quarters, getting the Pure out, getting the child out, getting them all past guards and possible hidden cameras.

It was unusual for her to have trouble falling asleep. Her mind whirled with excitement and worry. Who knew what punishment she would visit on her head and her daughter's if the authorities read her mind. Even worse, if she tried to execute the idea and failed. A long prison term, no doubt. She forced herself to stop her thoughts and allow sleep to overtake her. It would seem absurd the next morning.

She woke up to a text from Molly.

Don't say I told you so. I had sex with Vic in the alley next to the bar. Got covered with filth. My hair was disgusting before I washed it later at home. When I got out of the bar's bathroom, he was gone. Vanished. We were supposed to have another drink. He would walk me to my cell. He was nowhere in sight. What's worse, I took one of the rapid pregnancy tests this morning, and, Yup, it's positive.

Constance made herself have coffee in The Pure House cafeteria before allowing herself to react. She took the unusual step of not sitting with her team, which was recommended, not ordered. The bosses understood sometimes people just wanted to be alone. It was harmless if they sat with their teams regularly.

After she drained her cup, she opened the door in her mind to the thought that had been pushing against it. The first step in her fantasy happened. Molly had sex with Vic, got herself pregnant, and then became disillusioned with him. All within minutes. Soon she would weep for help from her mother.

Please, Mom. Tell me what to do. I'll kill myself if I lose this baby.

Constance bit her lip. The next step, if she took it, would be to tell Molly what she had spent the evening considering, while Molly had sex with the love of her life. Her impulsive daughter would jump at the chance for the emotional relief an actual plan might bring, while leaving the details to her mother. Details were not Molly's strong suit.

Later in the day, Constance received a text from Molly with the wording she expected.

Mom, you must help me. Fix this. I'll kill myself if I lose another baby.

Before Constance could stop her fingers, they typed out a response.

I have an idea. We have to meet for me to tell you. After my nap on our usual park bench.

It took an hour for her to fall asleep. She had started something and acted as impulsively as her daughter. Having sex with the wrong man was not illegal. Switching a Recovered and a Pure was. Sneaking a Pure child out of The Pure House was worse.

And she had not figured out how to pull any of this off. But the ball was already rolling.

When she met her daughter and told her, Molly stared at her mother with an open mouth that soon lifted at the corners into an excited grin.

"I'm stunned! You of all people, my cautious, never-take-a-chance mother, came up with this. Oh, my God. How long have you had this idea?"

Could she trust Molly to keep a secret? From this Vic or the next love of her life?

"No! And you mustn't tell anyone. The authorities would haul us off to prison if they overheard this conversation."

Molly almost bounced in her seat.

"My lips are sealed. I swear."

Constance was not so sure. Now it was imperative to get Molly into seclusion in the Pure House, where she could watch over her and make sure she did not talk, before she did anyway. She knew her daughter, but had not thought through how impetuous she might be. How stupid! Would she last nine whole months without opening her mouth? What did Constance get them into?

Of course, she should say she changed her mind. Molly would be furious. After a while, there would be a new distraction, a fresh man, an ultrasound of the baby, and she would get over it.

Yet, losing this pregnancy might push her over the edge. She might take her life. Constance always thought it was possible. This might be a way to save the pregnancy, since it was in most danger from her being reinfected, by getting her into the sterile conditions in the Fertility wing as fast as possible.

"I have to talk to the new Pure. If the plan interests her, we can consider — I said 'consider' — the next step. If it does not interest her, we drop it. Agreed?"

Molly put her hand on her stomach. Her eyes moistened.

"Sometimes I doubt you love me, Mom. If you do this for the baby and me, I'll know you do."

Constance took her daughter's hand.

"You frustrate me, and you scare me. You are my daughter, and there's no way I could not love you. If it turns out we don't go ahead with this crazy plan, it will be because I love you, not because I don't."

"I understand," Molly said. She sniffled. "And deep down, I do know you love me. I wish you had faith in me, too."

"We'll need a lot of faith if we do this. For now, I need you to be patient. Consider how you will keep yourself sane if you are quarantined for your entire pregnancy. I need your commitment even if Vic shows up again."

Her eyes did a jerk from left to right, then she gave her mother a sober look.

"I realize what's at stake. If you talk to the Pure, and she does not agree, I won't agree, either. I'll be a grown up about it. Promise. It will be a disappointment, but I'll be okay."

It was a mature statement from an immature young woman. But it was enough for Constance to go ahead and plan the talk with the Pure.

CHAPTER 12
AZURA

Her throbbing breasts and morning nausea reminded her — this is what early pregnancy is like. It assured her, more than the rapid test, that the embryo transfer had taken. For the next nine months, no one would enter her quarters or examine her in the medical wing without a Hazmat suit.

The first time the lock clicked and someone entered as covered as they would be in a *burka*, she saw Constance smiling at her through the face shield. It did not look like her usual fake mouth stretch. The grin was not as wide, and a slight tic appeared in one corner. It was a nervous smile. Constance was uneasy, even scared.

That scared Azura, who prepared for the worst.

"Is Noam okay?"

"Yes. She's fine." The shield muffled Constance's usually sharp voice.

Azura relaxed. If her daughter was good, the worst was avoided.

"I've made an excuse to visit you. Because they have upset you, and you need calming. My team will believe me since you have reason to be."

She nodded. Separation from her daughter and a pregnancy she did not choose were good reasons.

"You've made it clear you don't want to be here. What I want to say to you is dangerous and must remain our secret. Shall I continue?"

CAROLYN GEDULD

Azura sat, not wanting to stumble if Constance was going to say something shocking. Constance sat and pulled her chair close, speaking just loud enough to be heard through the shield.

"I may have a way for you to escape. It's not a developed plan yet, but I need your assent before going further. If you don't want to risk it, I'll understand."

Azura gripped the arms of her chair.

"Escape with Noam? I won't consider leaving without her."

"I understand. That's one part yet to be developed."

Was Constance responsible for the notes? Had she already proceeded with her plan?

"Did you leave me anything?"

"What do you mean?" Her smile vanished.

She would not reveal the key code yet.

"In my first quarters, I found a note under the coffee pot."

"A note?"

"It said I should get out while I can."

The corner of Constance's mouth twitched again.

"I didn't leave it. There are rebels on the staff. No one knows who they are, but it may have been from one of them."

She paused, then reached for Azura's hand, failing to grasp it with her thick glove.

"You must let me know if you receive any other notes."

Azura nodded, not promising anything. Her suspicions remained.

"I won't tell you everything. But here's my intention—to get you and Noam reclassified as Recovereds. They would make you both leave The Pure House and assign you to a beehive for women. If you hide your pregnancy, no one will care if you leave."

"I could leave?"

"With caution. The bosses would want to place your daughter in the Recovered Child's Residence, but that wouldn't happen for a few days. There would be a brief window for the two of you to make your way back to the forest."

"If I get out of here with Noam, why can't we head for the forest right away?"

"I have my reasons. As I said, I can't tell you everything. It might compromise another person."

Azura did not know if she trusted Constance.

"I won't assent without knowing your motive."

Constance remained silent for several seconds. Her eyes darted. Azura knew she was trying to figure out what to say.

"To be frank, my motive is to help the other person. I'm sorry I can't tell you more. It's better this way. If we're caught, you'd have some deniability. You can insist you didn't know everything."

"What would happen if we're caught?"

"Nothing much to you or Noam. You're too precious to them. A pregnant Pure with a child who could become pregnant when she is old enough. Tighter security in the future, losing some privilege like TV."

"What would happen to you?"

Constance expelled a deep breath, fogging her face shield. It cleared in seconds.

"Never mind that. Look, I hate pressuring you, but I need your go-ahead now. My visits to you have to be infrequent."

Azura nodded. "I have nothing to lose, from what you say."

Now Constance's smile was authentic. Crinkles appeared next to her eyes.

"Thank you, my dear. I'll be in touch when everything is set."

The door clicked, and Constance left, saying nothing more. Azura was alone again after the quick visit. She paced across the room—twenty steps each way. Soon, she might leave with Noam and her future daughter. Constance forced her to give her assent within minutes. There was so much to worry about—trusting Constance, getting caught, making it to the forest only to starve. The price of freedom might be to go hungry while pregnant, risking the life of her baby and Noam. That was the point Boss Franklyn made. Survival costs freedom. If she and Noam were freed, they might not survive.

As the interviewer said, some would say the price of survival was too high. The cost was virtual slavery for everyone, no matter what their disease status. The difference for Pures was a matter of degree. A Pure was more tightly guarded, but a Recovered had fewer privileges.

Neither raised their own children. This might be less of a concern for most Recovereds who could not conceive or bring a baby to term.

Constance made it clear she left neither note. If it she had left the first, she would have asked about the second one. She did not know the second one existed. A rebel among the staff was a reasonable supposition, except none of the kitchen staff was likely to be in the medical wing. Azura's best guess was that the Radiologist or the obstetrician bribed a kitchen worker to leave the first note.

It occurred to her that only Martin and Constance had the key code, or at least they were the only ones she had seen use it. Constance did not leave the code. Azura had established that. And Martin left her at the door of the exam room without entering. He did not put the key code in her pocket.

She turned her thoughts in the other direction. One of the kitchen staff could have left the message under the coffee pot. That person could be in league with another who serviced the medical floor. During the time they sedated her, the medical one might have entered the exam room without her being aware of it and deposited the paper in her pocket.

Azura sighed. Unless whoever left the folded papers revealed him- or herself, she had no way of knowing. If she was beginning nine months of solitary confinement for each of a multiple number of pregnancies, she would wind up talking to the walls and hearing them talk back. Noam was less isolated, with two girls to interact with. Just two. It would affect her social development without boys, older and younger kids, and a more varied choice of girls her age. If she developed a special interest the other two did not share, like science or dance, they might tease her for differing from them. In a larger group, she might find friends who would support her talents.

At the thought of her daughter, she sniffed the air unconsciously. Her nasal passages, her lungs, and the olfactory part of her brain kept searching, like a hound nearing its prey, when she saw Noam's image during their evening talks. She should prepare her daughter for possible reunification without telling her it might happen, starting right away. Constance implied it would be soon, before her pregnancy showed.

"Hi, Mommy."

Although she only saw the top half of the child on the monitor, it seemed she had grown. She appeared taller, older, more mature, even though she hadn't had her sixth birthday yet.

"Hi, Sweetheart. What did you do today?"

"Ju wants to be called Daisy, now. Because her name means Daisy in Chinese."

"That's a nice name."

"We're friends. We don't like Sandy anymore."

"Why not?"

"She's not nice."

Noam had a well-made stuffed bear in her hands. It looked new. She glanced up at Azura, then concentrated on the bear.

"What's your bear's name?"

"Teddy."

"If we visited the forest, would you want to take Teddy?"

Noam kept silent, turning her bear this way and that.

"I share Teddy with Daisy, but not with Sandy. I like Daisy better."

Azura tried again.

"What if one day we visited the forest with Teddy?"

"I don't want to, Mommy. There's no food there. I want to stay here."

"Not even a visit?"

Azura's eyes jerked up, meeting her mother's stare.

"No! I won't go. I like it here."

The next thing she said chilled Azura.

"I'm a Pure. You can't make me. I can do whatever I want."

With that, the child reached for something off-screen. It was a toddler-scissors, with blunt ends. Her face scrunched with effort as she began cutting off the bear's ear.

"What are you doing?" It horrified Azura.

"I don't like this ear."

The next moment, Noam's face relaxed into the cute, lovable one Azura cherished. She held up the bear for her mother to see, proud of her work.

"It's better, now," she said.

As soon as the call ended, Azura took a deep sniff, as if trying to detect a difference in her daughter's scent. The conversation made little sense unless her daughter had changed. They had to be brainwashing Noam, preparing the preschooler for her role in the social order, even at this young age. She wondered about Sandy. Noam had described her as dark. She could be a black girl, made to feel second rate despite being a Pure. Who put the idea into Noam's head that Ju or Daisy was nicer? Maybe biases don't die when the government imposes a new ranking system. Within each rank, the old prejudices might still exist.

Cutting off the beautiful bear's ear made Azura shudder. Perhaps it was a normal thing for a young child to do, part of mastering her environment. But Noam did it right after challenging her mother, refusing to entertain a visit to the forest, throwing her status as a Pure in Azura's face, then making her will known by mutilating a stuffed animal. Her daughter never had a defiant streak before, not even during her "terrible twos." She had refused to do some things her mother wanted her to do, but not with the arrogance she had just displayed.

If Azura hesitated while agreeing to go ahead with Constance's plan, now she was all-in. She had to get Noam away from the town before it corrupted her personality. Some said the cost of life here was too high. Azura wanted to join those who said that, the rebels, if she found them. In her heart, she was already one of them.

As the night wore on, she softened. She made a lot out of one moment in her daily contact with a young child. She might be over-reacting. Noam had a few ill-tempered seconds, not a sign of a complete change of character. And the child had a point. The forest was no longer a fun place to visit, without food or baths or toys. They had half-starved in the woods, an experience bound to leave its mark on a child. She might remember the deaths of the three elders they had both loved.

Her adamant refusal to visit and her show of anger taken out on her bear were rational. It did not matter how Azura interpreted it. Noam might be defiant or arrogant or fighting for survival her own way. The Pure House was not good for her. Azura was her mother. She would decide what was best for both her children.

CHAPTER 13
MARTIN

When he did not escort or provide security, Martin chewed over ways to force-feed the truth to his daughter, Penny — she was a Spreader. No red cow would change that. He understood the consequences. Accepting the truth meant admitting she may have infected her mother, maybe others, and that the disease had ruined her own chances for motherhood. But he did not want her to be unhappy. By lying to herself, she was angry, not unhappy. By believing in the myth of the red cow, she was hopeful, not depressed. So what did he want?

He shook his head. He wanted both — for her to admit the truth and still be happy. It was the dream of so many parents. They wanted their children to give up drugs, stop dating the wrong people, get a proper job instead of doing art, wear modest clothing, come home every night before midnight, obey speed limits, open a savings account, and be happy. Most parents knew from their own youthful experiences that happiness does not come from pleasing the older generation, but it does not make a difference to them.

Take the new Pure, Azura. Her present life may have been what parents hoped for — a high social status, material goods, and safety for her and her children. Yet, she cried or verged on tears every time he saw her. She did not want to be a pregnant Pure. Penny did not want to live on Spreaders Island. Young people wish for freedom, not safety. It took age and a lot of loss to reverse the equation. He, for instance, preferred safety.

Memories of the risks he had taken years ago made him cringe. He hitchhiked across the county, shoplifted, had unprotected sex, drank water from streams, took whatever drugs others gave him, dabbled in radical politics and published his views in student papers. When he married and Penny was born, he flipped into a conservative lifestyle. He gave up drugs, got a job, opened a savings account. He became like his parents and enjoyed visiting them, delighting them with his infant daughter.

He wanted that delight again, for himself, not for his deceased parents. But not while Penny had a lunatic belief. She seemed to be content with it. Was he being selfish?

No, he replied to himself. The red heifer cure was unscientific, demented. She and the others would still be Spreaders, even if her group bred one without a single white or black hair, and they ate the whole thing.

He was angry at her. He was angry at the sun that smoldered behind a perpetual haze, the result of the air pollution spewed by prior generations of vehicle owners. He was angry at the extinction of songbirds and the abundance of scorpions, fire ants, and armadillos invading the Midwest from the south, now that the summer temperature had shot upwards to scorching. He was angry that only Spreaders Island evaded the hot flow of surrounding air and attracted whatever rain there was. It retained pasture land, the source of cattle that fed the population dairy products, since the bosses outlawed meat-eating. They wasted a portion of the same pasture breeding the damned red heifers.

He read all he found on the treatment for brainwashing and indoctrination into cults. The only thing that worked would be presenting the victims with rock-solid evidence that countered their beliefs, like pointing out that the leader could not be reincarnated from the time of dinosaurs because no humans existed then. Sometimes that worked, sometimes it did not.

It was worth trying. It dawned on him that if he isolated Penny with a Pure, and the Pure contracted the virus, Penny would have to believe it came from her, that she was a Spreader. The Pure would have to be tested right before the isolation, or Penny would claim the virus infected her before he locked them in together. There would be no way for the Pure to become an active case unless Penny was contagious. It seemed an airtight argument.

If there was a way to get Penny off the island, he would sneak her into the new Pure's quarters. He had the key code. Both must agree. Penny would do anything to get to the mainland. But what would convince the Pure?

She would have to endure the illness. He had to assure her it would not harm her baby. Health experts said it was safe in the first trimester. But there was no way of telling if a case would be mild or severe. The Pure had to be convinced that a Recovered status was worth it. There would be a day or two of preliminary symptoms — low fever, sore throat — if Penny infected her. He would have to get her out of The Pure House before coughing alerted everyone. He would take her to an active case beehive and leave her at the entrance. How she got there would not be a concern. If she survived, they would assign her to a Recovered unit. He would smuggle her daughter to her. Martin knew where the child was. He had the key code to her quarters. They gave it to him when he transported her. The Pure and her daughter could escape to the forest once he reunited them. He knew it was a long shot. She had several reasons to refuse and only one reason to accept. Liberation.

His shift lasted two hours. That left twenty-two, less his sleep needs, to plot and plan. He would give one of the boat owners a substantial bribe to bring Penny from the island to The Pure House. It would be at night, which was more treacherous to navigate, but safer from prying eyes. And, the idea came to him, he would also offer a bribe to the Pure. Money might grease the wheels.

He shared his idea with Penny, framing it as a fantasy.

"I've been having this daydream, a wild bit of imagination, just some silliness."

"What is it?" Penny asked. At least she was curious.

"What if I proved you are a Spreader?"

She laughed, then humored him.

"And how would you do that?"

He explained.

"That is the craziest thing you ever said."

"What do you have to lose? If they discovered you, they'd take you back to the island."

"Or haul our asses to jail."

"Just think it over. That's all I'm asking. If you're interested, I'll talk to the new Pure."

"I'm not leaving during the breeding season. I'd have to be here if a pure red heifer is born."

Unless his plan worked.

"Okay."

"What's the Pure's name?"

"Azura."

It made a difference to Penny when she heard the Pure's name. She looked at him on the monitor with solemn eyes. The Pure lost her abstraction. She became a woman with a name. A woman who might become ill, if Martin was right. But, of course, she did not think he was right. If the experiment proved he was wrong, he might stop pestering her and support her, instead.

"If Azura doesn't get infected, I'm not a Spreader, right?"

"Right," he said.

"Then you'll help me stay off the island? If I'm not a Spreader?"

She wanted to stay on the island if a red cow could change her status. Another way seemed to be acceptable to her. Martin guessed she had unvoiced doubts about the cow delusion.

"Yes. If you aren't a Spreader, I'll help you in every way I can. You could stay in The Pure House, impersonating a Pure."

She pursed her lips.

"Talk to the Pure. Take the next step. But I'm not convinced. Let's see what she says. If she won't, it's just going to be a daydream. That's all."

"Agreed."

"And be careful. You won't have your cushy job anymore if you're discovered."

He wavered before speaking to the Pure, wishing they did not monitor texts. It would have to be in person, suited up. There was no reason for him to enter her quarters, since she was not being escorted anywhere, unless it was to be examined in the medical wing. Then an opportunity would be for a minute in the elevator. That happened once a week. He could also take a chance when escorting her back after her exam. After unlocking her door, it would be possible to go in with her and spend a few minutes. Sweat ran down his back. She might scream or order him out or tell the Bitch. He would have no explanation and would wind up in a factory where he could not help his daughter or himself.

And if she let him speak? She might laugh in his face for being so absurd. Humiliate him. A muscular man prostrating himself on the floor, whimpering and begging for mercy from a slip of a young woman. *Please, please don't tell.* He winced at the image. It would be worse than any other punishment. And Penny would rub it in, calling him an old fool.

It would be more difficult to smuggle out the child. She might make a noise. No one would prepare her. He would have to tell her caregivers she needed an exam and a medical slot just opened. They would be angry about not being told in advance. It would be plausible. Kids need vaccinations and check-ups. He hoped the girl did not remember him from her original separation from her mother.

Martin's livelihood depended on appearing tough and not revealing any weakness despite being a Recovered. If he spoke to the Pure, he would not let her know how scared he was. He bit his lip, working up his courage. It took a few days.

When he told her in her room after her exam, she did not say a word. They both stood, not taking the time to sit. Martin kept looking over his shoulder, as if expecting the door to fly open, with officers storming in to arrest him. Despite himself, he wound up pleading.

"Please don't tell. It's for my daughter. I'm trying to save her. I'm asking a lot of you, hoping you'll help me. I have savings. I'll pay you ten thousand dollars. You'll have enough for a new life with your daughters."

Her face was unreadable. She asked a single question.

"Did you leave me the notes on folded paper?"

"Me? No. What notes?"

She shook her head, saying nothing.

His mind reeled. He tried to persuade her to accept his proposal, and some papers were her only concern. Did she even hear him? He went over his idea again, emphasizing the money and way it might be an escape route for her and her daughter.

"Do you understand? Will you think it over? You can tell me next week after your exam."

How dry his lips were. He kept licking them. Did he trust her? A Pure?

Later, he wished he could hit his head against the wall. She had all the advantages. Luxurious quarters. Good food. He asked her to give these up for what? To become an active case, perhaps die a terrible, airless death. For the slight chance to die another horrible death by starvation in the forest. She and her unborn baby. And her older child.

What was he thinking? Penny would be right to call him an old fool.

Unless a taste of liberation with money for a new life seemed better to her than an endless round of pregnancies. He would know in a long, hard week.

CHAPTER 14
AZURA

Azura stared out her window at The Pure House gardens. The unrelenting green of the artificial grass and bushes did not soothe her, as nature had when she lived in the forest. The natural world shimmered with color—leaves of emerald green, lime green, and olive green. Undergrowth from verdant to sage. Brown loam, naked or moss covered. Vines and bark, intact or revealing yellowish flesh.

Dust swirled above the garden greenery, blown up from the arid earth, the real earth, now packed and dry, whether under the grass carpet or stretching out from beyond The Pure House gates. Hot breezes tossed the dust against the window panes, where it stuck and clouded the view. No one would open the windows, allowing the choking dust to dilute the filtered air inside.

For three years there had been a severe drought. The ground baked and cracked. There might be a deluge, flooding the town and filling farm land with false promise, the next spring. The weather had become inconsistent. Hot, dry winters or cold, wet summers or the reverse. The virus ground on from a mild season to a severe one and back again, without abating.

The view outside reflected her choices—the deceitfulness of a plastic garden or the reality of tumbleweed and sandy scrub. Alone in her quarters, she had little to do but think. One choice was not to do anything. Enjoy her privileges, even the fake plants. A staff person would wash the windows. Or she could take advantage of what Constance and Martin offered to free herself and Noam from The Pure

House. That way led to the ugliness of the town or the dying forest beyond it.

Her mind revolved around her three offerings. Three! She had not been the center of so much attention in a long time. First Woman, her mother, organized a forest cooperative during COVID-19. Great Mother, her great grandmother, won respect as a healer. Her father, Rabbi Isaac, led a congregation that used drugs to invoke spiritual visions. They commanded attention, interviews, articles, social media presences.

What was she? A child raised in the forest, feral, unsocialized, uneducated until her mother's death when she was twelve. Then she discovered the wrong type of attention when she kidnapped her father's newborn son. She was sentenced to Juvie and began a downward spiral until she returned to the forest and put herself under the wing of her great grandmother, Great Mother.

Now, three people, perhaps more, wanted to free her. The secret liberator gave her the key code. Constance had a plan to switch her with some unnamed person. Martin had a complicated scheme to pay her to get infected for the sake of his daughter. She stood at the center of a ring, not a negative one this time. Or was it?

No one was concerned about her as a person. They had their own reasons for helping her, all for the sake of others. If the authorities caught them, there would be a media circus again for the short time it took to confine them. Her helpers would go to prison. They would lock her away in her quarters to be forgotten. Only now, she had her children to consider. Whatever happened to her also happened to them.

She, Noam, and her unborn baby were Pures. The entire town was dedicated to serving them and the other Pures. The factories pumped out luxury goods for them, designed to keep them content. IVFs took more often in women who were not stressed. A large staff ensured she would never have to lift a finger. She produced for society by becoming pregnant. After the difficulties of life in the forest, Azura needed the rest. But her life was without purpose, except as a reproduction machine.

Without peers, authentic relationships, or a meaningful life, she was lonely and restless. She did not want this for herself or her daughters. She had never been a cunning person, able to concoct ways of using others to improve her lot, but now her situation emboldened her. If Constance and Martin wanted her help, she would make them help her first.

She texted Constance, trying to be indirect so the text observers would not catch on.

I'm sick of white clothing. Can I have some with color?

The response did not tell Azura whether Constance understood.

All Pures wear white.

Later, the lock clicked, and before she turned around to see who it was, the door opened just wide enough for a package to slip in. It contained a brown outfit and matching shoes. The fit would be poor, but it did not matter. She would be able to dress like a Recovered. Constance would think she agreed to her plan to switch identities with an unnamed person.

But Azura could not trust Constance or Martin to smuggle Noam out to her. They said they would, but it did not mean they would follow through. The risk was much greater abducting a child than an adult. The only one to depend on was herself.

In the elevator with Martin on the day of her next medical exam, Azura made her next request.

"If you want my help with your daughter, you must help me with mine. Tell me where she is and give me the key code to her quarters."

Martin said nothing. But when he brought her back to her quarters, he slipped a note to her.

Third floor. Room 318. Code 4387. Memorize and destroy.

She had what she needed. Now she had to create a plan. But had Martin been truthful? He could have given her any location, any key code, just to manipulate her into accepting his offer. She had to find out before he made a request of his own. She did not intend to be infected for the sake of his daughter.

That night, she changed into Recovered clothes and left her quarters, planning to find a staircase at the end of the long hall. If she set an alarm off, she would sprint back before they caught her. That was her hope.

The hallway light was dimmed. She had taken only a few steps to the right when a hand gripped her upper arm and another covered her mouth. Her knees buckled.

"Don't scream," a male voice said.

Whoever it was shoved her further down the hall, then into the broom closet. When the door shut, it was as dark as a moonless night in the forest. Her captor held her against him, keeping his hand over her mouth. He whispered close to her ear.

"I have the key code for your room. I didn't expect you to have it, too, and to use it when I was about to. You may not believe this, but I'm a friend. They call me a rebel. I try to sabotage the system. I'll release you if you promise not to scream. If you do, they'll arrest both of us."

The thought of being arrested made her nod. He uncovered her mouth. The trembling that started when he grabbed her continued. There were rebels in the town. He might be one or just impersonating one.

Some say....

"Are you trying to escape on your own? It's not as easy as finding an exit and walking out the gate. Where would you go? If they don't assign you a room in a beehive, you'll have to survive in the streets. The gangs that rove there will do worse to you than the bosses."

She collapsed onto the floor, weeping. He overpowered her and might do anything. And if he told the truth, her escape plan would be too dangerous for Noam. She did think it was possible to walk away from The Pure House. She forgot about the gate and the gangs, although they ruled the streets five years ago, when she last lived in town. Helplessness crushed her bold thoughts of exploiting Constance and Martin. She had not even been clever enough to avoid capture two steps from her door.

"We can't see each other in the dark. You don't know what I look like, and I've only seen you from the back. We can't identify each other. I'm going to open the door. You run back to your room. Wait for me to help you. It may take a few days."

"What's your name?" Her voice shook.

"Some call me Vic. Maybe it's my real name."

The door opened. A shaft of low light entered. She hurried back to her quarters, so shaken, she wondered if she would miscarry. Through the next few hours, she checked for spotting. The sensation of her back squeezed against someone's body and a firm hand over her mouth stayed with her through the sleepless night. This Vic, whoever he was, could have done anything to her — molest her, kill her, bring her to the authorities. He chose not to. Did that mean he was her friend, as he claimed? Or was he just another opportunist, like Constance and Martin, pretending to be a rebel?

He had her key code. It would have been easy for him to follow her into her quarters and rape her, if that was what he wanted. An opportunist would have thought that an opportunity. One he did not take. She wracked her brain, trying to figure this unseen person out. He prepared to visit her just when she was leaving to find Noam. A few minutes later, he would have entered an empty room. Then what? What if he came back?

But as the hours passed, he did not come back. She remained wide-awake, alert, waiting. The sensations aroused by him were still there — the skin of his palm on her lips, the solidness of his body supporting her back, the brush of his hair against her cheek when he whispered in her ear, his hand in hers as he pulled her up from the broom closet floor. She brought her fist to her mouth and bit the joint of her curled index finger. She recognized desire, not felt in over five years except in dreams — a dangerous wish for someone who might as well be an enemy as a friend.

He called himself Vic, although that might not be his real name. She called him Vic in her mind. Vic — a masculine name, a sexy name. *Stop it!* She had to yank herself away from wallowing in the wild imaginings loneliness brings, and the risk it might lead her to attempt. He might still rape her, betray her. He had the key code to her room. She had to escape before he returned. It would not be that night. He said in a few days. She hid the Recovered outfit under her mattress and the shoes on the upper shelf in her closet. Her best option was figuring out who besides this Vic to trust. If Martin gave her Noam's location, she would know he was honest, although she was still unsure if exposing herself to the virus was worth considering.

The next night, she dressed as a Recovered again and left her room. This time, she waited for her eyes to dilate enough to see down the hall in the dim light. No one was there. Vic was not there. Despite herself, she felt both relieved and disappointed. She went to her left this time, turning right when the short corridor met the long hallway. Again, she waited, checking the passage out. It was empty. Halfway down, she saw a niche. She paused there, wedging herself next to the water fountain it contained. Still no one. She stole down to the end of the hallway, where there was, as she suspected, a staircase door.

Taking a deep breath, she opened it. No alarm sounded. Inside the stairwell, she heard someone climbing up. A Recovered woman, carrying a tray, nodded to her in passing. Azura nodded back as she descended the stairs, praying it would not seem strange for an unknown Recovered to be there. The same thing happened on the next flight. This time, a Recovered man with a box under his arm rushed past, not acknowledging her. The staircase must have been for the staff, some of whom worked at night. A new Recovered did not appear to be remarkable or worth a glance.

When she reached the third floor, Azura followed the room numbers until she reached Room 318. A sign read "Pure Children's Quarters. Do Not Enter Unless Authorized." Would the key code work? She tried it. There was a click. The door would open if she pushed the latch. She flinched back when it opened a crack from the inside.

"Can I help you? The children are asleep," a voice said.

"Oh! Sorry. I have the wrong room."

Before the person questioned her about how she knew the code, Azura fled. She got back to her quarters the same way she came. Martin's information was accurate. He had not lied. But whoever opened the door might report the Recovered who had the code. Proving Martin right may have been reckless, putting both of them in danger if the person inside the Children's Quarters figured out who she was.

CHAPTER 15
CONSTANCE

She worked everything out except how to get the child from the Pure Children's Quarters. Martin had transported the girl from the Preliminary Quarters to her permanent residence. He would know the location and the key code.

What did she have on him that would force him to reveal this information? He had a daughter on Spreaders Island. She could say she would tell the authorities the daughter planned to escape. But there was no proof. They wouldn't believe her. She could threaten to tell the authorities his daughter was involved in the crazy red heifer plot. Everyone knew that. It wouldn't persuade Martin.

She had not been using her head. The authorities would require proof. All she needed to scare Martin was a threat, such as that she had proof Penny planned to escape, even if she had none. How was he to know she did not have evidence? When she approached him, she would have to *ad lib* some of what she would say depending on his response.

If he got huffy, she would tell him she was told of the escape plan by a friend of Molly, a guy named Vic, who befriended both young women. If he clammed up, she would raise the threat, saying she would go to the authorities that day unless he cooperated. If he got scared, she would promise to protect him and his daughter.

She sent him a text.

Have to see U ASAP. About team morale. Meet me in the exec dining room at 4 p.m.

If the observers viewed the text and wanted more information, she would tell them about the hostile relationship between Martin and the Radiologist. It was a problem they required her to address. That must have been old news to them. They did not contact her.

After her nap, she arrived at the designated meeting place. Martin was already in the room, sitting erect in a chair at the table with his beef-up shoulder muscles tensed, hunched to his neck. He waited, expecting to be dressed down for his attitude toward the Radiologist.

"You might presume from my text that we're here to talk about the team. This meeting is about another matter," Constance said.

He blinked.

"Martin, you're helping your daughter escape from Spreaders Island."

She did not intend it to come out that way, as if he were involved in the escape. It was a slip of the tongue. There was no way to take it back.

"Who told you?" He asked.

His eyes darted. Her brow knitted.

"Who told me what?"

"That I'm helping Penny escape."

They stared at each other. For several seconds, Constance fell into a hypnotic daze, brought on by extreme confusion. When her mind cleared, she realized she had stumbled onto some secret of Martin's. Her slip of the tongue gave her the upper hand. They both conspired. But, for the moment, only she understood that.

"I can't reveal my sources."

Martin opened his mouth and closed it again several times, like a guppy out of a fishbowl.

"But… there can't be sources. No one knows."

Constance stared straight at him, riveting him with her eyes. She stayed one step ahead of him.

"Your daughter knows."

"Penny told? Who?"

"Never mind that. What's important is you know I know."

He sagged, a big, muscular man with the energy of a slug.

"Are you going to the authorities?"

Constance made everything up as she went along.

"It depends."

Martin sniffled. Was he going to cry? At that moment, she felt sorry for him. He helped his daughter, and she helped hers. That is what parents did at the time of COVID-35. Whatever status their children wound up having, it was the secret duty of their mothers and fathers to get them to the next level. Spreaders to Recovereds, and Recovereds to Pures. It was likely that each rank contained more of a mixture than the bosses suspected. Some children raised a rank, but some fell below. People paid enormous sums to buy their Spreader children a Recovered rank, where they would continue to infect other Recovereds. But the jump from Recovered to Pure required more than money. Connections gave a parent that advantage.

"What do you want?"

Martin's voice was subdued with defeat. His face drooped, as if overpowered by gravity.

"The key code for the Pure Children's Quarters."

His head jerked up. His sagging cheeks drew up again. He had something she wanted, something it was dangerous to share. There was a pause while his thoughts revolved. If he told the authorities what she had asked for, there could be a problem for the Bitch. The conversation was not being recorded. If he thought of it, he would have turned on his device before she entered the room. His device was in his trouser pocket. Hoping she would not notice, he fiddled with it. His finger hit Record.

"You want what?"

He forced her to repeat her request.

"The key code to the Pure Children's Quarters."

She had fallen into his trap. He took his device from his pocket and lay it on the table between them. It had recorded. He clicked on Play. Constance's voice was clear.

"The key code to the Pure Children's Quarters."

"I have you recorded, but you don't have one of me saying I'm helping Penny escape." His triumphant lips curved upwards.

Constance sat back in her chair, forcing herself to exhale. She was the clever one. That was why she made the head of the team. Martin did not know yet that Penny did not tell anyone about the escape.

"I have a witness, Martin. This boy Penny knows, Vic. She told him. My daughter is his girlfriend. He'll testify against you if I ask him to."

"Why would Penny tell him?"

"Who knows? She might want him for herself. Ask her. The point is, I can come up with a reason for asking for the key code, if you'll tell the authorities. You can't for helping Penny escape."

She bluffed while watching Martin's eyes shift from right to left, a sign he was deciding between his two options. Finally, he sighed, turning to gaze out the window at the dust.

"I have an idea," she said. "You keep the recording as collateral. It will assure you I won't go to the authorities. Give me the code. It will be a safe thing for you to do."

They had entered a negotiation. Constance was aware of it. Martin seemed more confused.

"If you report my plan to help Penny, we'll both go to prison. I can't trust you to keep quiet without collateral. You're right. I'll protect myself by keeping the recording."

"And the code?"

He gave it to her.

"I can find the location myself, but it will be simpler if you give it to me."

He gave her that, too.

She had what she wanted. When Martin talked to Penny, he would realize he had been outsmarted. The next step for Constance was to try the code. She would not put it past Martin to give her an incorrect one. The worst outcome would be if she switched Molly and the Pure, then discovered the code did not work. The Pure would make a fuss, alerting the authorities. They would all wind up in trouble.

That night, she set her alarm for just past midnight, giving herself the few hours of sleep she would need to function. Her excuse for leaving her cell would be to return to the executive dining room. She left her jacket there at the close of the meeting with Martin. She headed in that direction, then veered to the staircase. No one cared about Recovereds using it. She reached the second floor, with no one stopping her.

When she found the door, she tried the code. It clicked. Martin had given her what she asked for. Before she turned to go, the door opened a crack. Someone inside spoke in a harsh whisper.

"You again? That's the second time. If you come back, I'll report you."

Constance backed away, shocked, and raced to her cell.

The second time. What did that mean? Did Martin give the code to another person? She took the chance of texting him.

About that file you gave me today. Have you shared it with the Radiologist or anyone else?

He must have been asleep. There was no response until early morning.

I'll look at the Share History on my device and get back to you. Did you look for your jacket? You left it in our meeting room. I took it and am keeping it for you. Tell me where you'll be this morning, and I'll bring it.

He was arranging another meeting. That meant he wanted her help with his plan before he would tell her who else had the code. She texted him, suggesting a quiet spot where they could meet. She did not want involvement in whatever he was up to, but she was being forced.

He arrived at the spot with her jacket.

"I need you to convince the Pure to allow me to bring Penny to her quarters. Tell her I'll pay her."

"What? You want your daughter to infect a pregnant Pure for money?"

"That's the point. I want Penny to acknowledge she's a Spreader."

"That's crazy, Martin. Why would the Pure agree to become an active case, no matter how much she could earn?"

His smug eyes look straight at her.

"Figure it out. You're good at convincing people."

"Not to commit suicide. She might die, Martin."

"It's not my problem."

"You think it will convince your daughter if the Pure dies. Then what?"

Martin said nothing. She realized he had not thought everything through. He might sneak Penny into the Pure's quarters. In a few days, the Pure would cough and have a fever. She would be an active case. The Radiologist would report her after the next medical exam. They would fumigate her quarters. If Penny did not leave in time, they would find her there. But there seemed to be no plan to get her out. There would be an investigation even if Penny escaped to find out who infected the Pure. They would all be in danger.

Constance's plan was complex. Besides switching the Pure and Molly, she had to kidnap the child and convince the Radiologist not to report the unknown pregnant woman who had replaced the Pure. But compared to Martin's, it was simple. What she had to do now was string him along. She would give up discovering who he had given the code to for the time being. It did not matter. At least she figured out she was not the only one.

"I'll give some thought to how I might convince her, Martin, but don't be surprised if she refuses to go along."

He nodded, handing her the jacket. He seemed satisfied.

"I'll tell you anything you want when the Pure agrees to the arrangement."

It was so unlike Martin to be irrational, putting himself, Penny, and the Pure at risk. Except for his senseless quarreling with the Radiologist, he had always seemed coolheaded. There must be something she did not know. Maybe the red heifer thing. Many on the island believed they could breed a cow without white or black hairs. That was possible, from the little she recalled of high school genetics.

But the Spreaders believed in ancient curses and miracle cures. She had not paid attention to the details. They had a concept of purity that competed with one of contamination. The virus contaminated. The heifer purified. Or the heifer purified the virus. Something like that.

For once, she wished she were still married so she would have someone to confide in. Gary had filled that role until he had not. Before his betrayal and death, they whispered to each other in their couple's cell in the dead of night. They told each other their suspicions and their dreams. The virus ruined it, just like it ruined so many relationships.

It purified distrust. No one trusted anyone anymore.

CHAPTER 16
AZURA

There was nothing to do but daydream. Images drifted into her mind, seeping through cracks in her thinking, like the dust that settled everywhere. Despite the filtration system, she traced her initials on the tops of furniture. When sunlight poured through the windows, dust mites floated their lazy way through the air, swirled by drafts around the room like snowflakes. A blizzard of dust, coating her hair, drying her eyes, making her sneeze.

In the Pure's quarters, scrubbers filtered the air until it was as pure as air could be in the town, less polluted than the air in the Recovered's residences or in the factories. But it had become worse. Outside, after a walk in the garden, clothing had to be brushed. They hosed the fake grass with some of the rationed water. Patrons in the bars used paper napkins to blot up sand residue from the tops of their beer foam. Barbers blew grit out of hair and beards with hair dryers.

Azura forced herself to stop remembering the man she had not seen, Vic, but the thoughts of him were like dust, present even when invisible or shrouded in darkness. Everything he said came back to her in constant repetition, accompanied by what she might have said in response if she had not been so terrified.

"Don't scream."

"Take your hand off my mouth."

"I'm a friend."

"A nice way you have of showing it."

"Did you think you could just walk away?"

"Did you think I'm stupid?"

"I'll be back in a couple of days."

"I may be gone by then."

She would not allow herself to imagine saying, "I'll wait for you." She tried pictured him as unattractive—short, fat, greasy, too old or too young. It did not work. The romantic image in her head was of a tall, lean, handsome man. Rescue fantasies arose to annoy her. He would enter her room, smile, lift her into his arms without a word, carry her off.

She needed to occupy herself until the time came to escape. Which of her forest skills could occupy a princess locked in a tower? The elders had taught her trapping, tanning, starting a wood fire without matches. None of these were useful here. She thought of Marie, the Pure in the white dress in the garden, imagining her doing needlepoint or embroidery, perhaps tinkering on a piano, like a Victorian woman of leisure. Nothing meaningful. Nine months of whiling away the time before childbirth. Then starting the cycle again.

She had not gone to college or made much of her life, but she had done more than wait for rescue. The time she spent in Juvie and Rehab was put to good use. She got her GED, finished the twelve-steps, and took stress-management classes. She stayed sober. Her life straightened out before she got pregnant. When she returned to the forest to live with her great grandmother, it was the best decision she ever made. Now it was up to her to make other good decisions that would not have disappointed her great grandmother.

Instead of waiting for Vic, she would pretend to turn down Martin's offer and to accept Constance's with its promise of an easy escape. Or maybe she would accept Martin and turn down Constance. Whoever left the notes, assuming it was not Vic, might have a proposal for her, too. She would pretend to accept whatever the note writer offered. After sorting through all the offers, she would decide what to do.

Courage defined her thinking some of the time. At other times, she panted with anxiety. Escape might be a foolish notion. Escape to what? Where? She would put Noam, who was safe in the Pure Children's Quarters, in danger—from a virus that targeted children, from gangs, or from heat stroke. Boss Franklyn had a point, didn't he? It was worth giving up some freedom to survive.

Soon after, she would reverse. *Some say....* Mere survival without freedom had too high a cost. There were decades ahead of Noam and her unborn daughter. Who knew whether freedom might return one day. Survival for the time being. Freedom in the long run. She should endure three or four pregnancies before trying to escape, depending on future conditions.

But what if conditions worsened? So far, the climate had not improved. In the time she had been in The Pure House, the dust increased. The virus was a fire that smoldered without being extinguished. The bosses had a tight grip on society. She recalled Vic saying, "Wait for me to help you." What power did a rebel have? Help her how? She should take the best chance to escape and save herself and her daughters.

Brave and fearful thoughts circulated, like a plane low on gas without a landing strip. They kept her from taking any action. Or was she waiting for Vic despite herself? He said a few days. Constance and Martin would pressure her before then. She needed to forget her broom closet savior.

The time came for her bedtime talk with Noam.

"Hi, sweetheart."

"Hi, Mommy. Guess what? Sandy's my special friend now. We don't like Daisy anymore."

"Why not?"

This was familiar.

"Sandy's nicer."

"What else happened today?"

"Uncle Frank visited. He brought me this special doll, just for me."

Uncle Frank had to be Boss Franklyn. Noam held up a large doll, close to her size.

"Wow! That's a big girl doll. Why did he give you a special doll?"

Noam hugged the doll.

"Because I love Uncle Frank. He says he will let me stay here always and always."

"Did Sandy and Daisy get special dolls?"

"No. Because they cry to be with their mommies."

Azura sighed. She wanted her child to miss her as much as the other two did, but she did not want her to cry or get depressed. And she did not want her loving Boss Franklyn. Her daughter was disappearing into a Pure House mirror, where everything seemed the opposite of what should be. Whenever she spoke to the child, her mind cleared. She had to get Noam out of this awful place.

The next morning, the lock clicked, and Constance entered wearing a Hazmat suit.

"I can only stay for a minute. Just want you to know I arranged everything."

Through the face shield, Constance pursed her lips.

"Look. I've found out that mine is not the only offer you have. What I can tell you is that my offer is the simplest and the safest. The person you'd switch with, I'll tell you now, is my daughter, Molly. You're both pregnant, so switching will resolve that complication. The risk of discovery would be higher if you're switched with someone who isn't pregnant. And I have the key code to Noam's quarters."

"What about getting me assigned to a cell and factory job in town? And who would take care of Noam while I work. I'm not putting her in a Recovered day care where she might be infected."

Azura waited to see how Constance developed her plan.

"I'd give you the code to Molly's cell. You'd only stay there until I brought Noam. Then you'd leave for the forest in the night, when no one's around. You'd never work, and your daughter would stay with you."

Constance paused, having just come up with another possibility.

"Unless you'd rather stay in town and work. You wouldn't have to get pregnant again if you lost your Pure statues. But that would be a risk for Noam."

"How would I account for her? Molly doesn't have a child."

"I'll get documentation, forged, of course, establishing Noam's father as having custody of her and transferring custody to you. You could say the virus reinfected him, and he couldn't take care of her any longer. The bosses don't care enough about Recovereds to check."

Constance was smooth, but Azura had the sense she made a lot up on the spot. Would it be so easy to forge a document?

"I'm not agreeing unless you bring me my daughter at the same time as we make the switch. I won't leave here without her."

She would not trust Constance to show up with Noam after the switch. What would stop her from abandoning her as soon as Azura was out the door?

Constance nodded.

"If you agree, you'd have to be ready without advanced warning. I'd just show up with Molly and Noam. Understand?"

"Yes. Okay."

Had she just agreed? If Constance brought Noam and did not trick her, it would satisfy her.

"Have a bag packed. Then hide it."

Constance left. An hour later, the lock clicked again. Her speed shocked Azura. It did not seem like enough time to round up both daughters.

But it was not Constance. Instead, a man appeared, not wearing a mask nor the required Hazmat suit. Azura stepped back.

"It's me. Vic. Your friend from the broom closet."

He was not what she imagined, neither unattractive nor handsome. What she noticed at first glance was his rust-colored ponytail, his red-head's complexion, and his lankiness.

"Thanks for not ratting me out. It's difficult for me to sneak into and out of this bastion of purity."

His eyes crinkled at his witticism, putting her off by joking about the risk he took and put her through.

"What do you want?"

"I'm a rebel. I want to upset the system. If you let me help you escape, we'll both get what we wish for."

She stared, taking in his appearance, so different from what she imagined. She had an impulse to refuse. But that was to keep herself from accepting too readily. She did not want him to know how much he had woven into her daydreams. She delayed.

"Did you leave me the two notes?"

He cocked his head.

"No. I didn't. Tell me about them."

Instead of remaining silent, she confided.

"There was one under the coffee pot soon after I arrived. I found the other in my pocket after the IVF procedure."

He shook his head. She went further.

"The first one said 'Get out while you can'. The second contained the key code to this door."

She tilted her head toward the door to her quarters. His eyes moved in thought.

"The first one might have come from a rebel, but it wasn't me. I didn't get the code until the day I hustled you into the broom closet."

"Two days ago. I've had the code for a week."

She had slipped into cooperating with him, telling him more than she intended. It was too much. She pulled back, reverting to an attitude of suspicion.

"Someone besides me wants to help you escape. Be very careful."

"Why?"

"Many have their own agendas. You don't want to wind up a part of someone else's scheme."

"I can take care of myself."

She was not being honest. Without the key code or "someone else's agenda," there was no escaping. She should throw him a bone.

"But I would appreciate your advice. And you should know, I have a daughter in the Pure Children's Quarters. Plus, I'm pregnant. Not that I wanted to be. It's by *in vitro* fertilization. I don't know who the father is."

That was more than a bone. She was being too open.

"I can get you out. Your daughter is a problem. The Children's Quarters are well-guarded."

His eyes crinkled again.

"It's no surprise you're pregnant. All the Pures are."

She changed the subject.

"Others say they can bring Noam to me."

"So there are others. Don't take their word for it. Insist they bring her to you before escaping."

"I have."

"Getting you both out requires more planning. I intended to spring you tonight. I'll need another couple of days. Will your daughter protest?"

"It's probable. She likes it here."

"That's a problem no matter who wants to bring her."

He did not give her empty promises. She could imagine Noam screaming if anyone tried to rescue her. There was no way to prepare her. She would have to be sedated. This was another consideration Azura had to think through before deciding whether to escape. She would not consent to sedation from just anyone. It had to be a medical person.

CHAPTER 17
THE RADIOLOGIST

There was extra work cleaning the dust out of the medical equipment. He had to take apart the imaging machines. It amazed him the way dust crept through the joints and tiniest openings. Special care had to be taken cleaning the lenses. Each cost tens of thousands. It irritated the Radiologist to have to use his precious energy this way because the bosses had not updated the air purifiers. They needed updating every six months. The filters became too clogged to be washed clean after that.

The newest Pure would have her exam that day. Obstetrics wanted assurance that the zygote remained implanted and that cell division occurred at the normal rate. The future baby would be as small as one of the dust specks he wiped off the lens. The Micro-Ultrasound would be used for the test. Although it was pleasurable overkill, he would make an excuse to use the hand-held vaginal ultrasound as well.

He wondered if the Pure found the note he left in her pocket, and if she figured out it was the key code. He had been waiting on a park bench for her to use it, but had not spotted her in the garden yet. Some Pures were too thick to take hints. She might have thrown the note away without understanding what it signified. Or, he thought with a shudder, she could have given it to Constance.

He prepared to take another risk. This time he would leave a note in her pocket that read 147A, the number of his cell in The Pure House. He dreamed she would use the key code, then find her way to him. It was better than choking in the garden or his ridiculous plan to bring her to a secret hiding place. What hiding place? He had no idea how to secure one.

Simple curiosity would lead her to him, he hoped, imagining her shy knocking on his cell entrance, her trembling in the hallway, her stumbling in once he gave permission.

"You must do whatever I tell you," he would say.

First, he would order her to undress. Then lie on the bed. From there, he had several scenarios. She might beg, either for him to do nothing or for him to do something. Her begging would increase his excitement.

He tried to fantasize how he would get her to remain in his cell, with no one finding out. That was as likely as hiding her in a secret place. If she went missing, a general alarm would go out, and they would assign that asshole Martin to find her. They would search the building, including the cells. His cell, too. It was better to skip that part of his dream. Once would have to be enough.

The time came for her exam. On the dot, Martin delivered her, gave him a look, and left saying nothing. They would wait for Constance. The Pure surprised him by stepping close.

"I must talk to you in private. After the exam. Tell me where and when, and I'll meet you."

She kept glancing over her shoulder, fearful of being overheard. He turned to the Micro-Ultrasound, fiddling with the dials to hide his astonishment. The folded note was in the pocket of his lab coat, waiting for transfer to her's. He reached in and thrust it at her.

"What's this?"

Instead of being smart enough to hide it and read it later, she stood looking at it as Constance arrived.

"Is everything okay? What's that in your hand?"

With a racing heart, the Radiologist raised his voice to a shout.

"We must get on with the imaging right away. I'm behind schedule because of extra cleaning, and I still have to report to Obstetrics about the results. Now, please, Miss, lie down on the table."

Constance backed to a chair. He did not see what the Pure did with the note. Pretending to be in a huff, he adjusted the imaging machine again. If Constance dared to intervene, he would order her out.

Back in his cell after his shift, he lay on his bed staring at the ceiling, only a couple of feet above him. His fearful heart raced. He thought he wanted her with him, but now that it might happen, if she figured out the note, his mouth was dry. It was a major infraction to allow a Pure in his quarters. Maybe he only wanted the dream, not the reality.

A thump startled him. He thought it was her. But it was only some poor bird blinded by the dust, hitting his porthole window. He held out his hands, noticing the tremor. *Calm down,* he told himself. The chances of her showing up were slim. The note only had three numbers and one letter. It meant nothing. But the authorities would understand it, if she turned it over to them.

Yet, she was the one who asked for a meeting. He never said "yes," he never said "no." If anyone recorded their conversation, they would not blame him. A plan was needed in case she showed up. Don't open the door. Tell her to leave. Threaten to call Security. No, that would be disastrous. She might show Security the note.

He lay in a light doze when the knock came. In an instant, his eyelids bolted open. He sat up. What if someone in the hallway saw her? He had to get her inside right away, he realized. He opened the door, and there she stood. She crawled right in when he made enough room for her by scooting to the end of the bed. She closed the door.

"How did you know the number in the note was for my cell?"

"I lived in a beehive residence before going to the forest. They number all the cells, followed by an 'A' for a lower one and a 'B' for an upper. I remembered."

"And you figured out the first note was the key code?"

"You left that?"

Her eyebrows raised. He nodded.

"What about the first one?"

"What first one?"

"You only gave me two?"

"There was a third?"

Both became confused. She shook her head.

"Never mind. Here's why I'm here," she said, moving closer. "I'm getting my daughter out of here. But I need a safe way to sedate her for an hour during the escape, so she stays quiet. You can get me the right medication for a five-year-old."

He leaned away.

"Me? I'm a Radiologist. I'm not in Pediatrics."

"I need it tomorrow."

"There's no way!"

"I've saved the notes. Find a way, or I'll show Constance. I can get you in a lot of trouble."

In the distance, a siren blared. Were they coming for him already?

"Don't... don't... I'll die if I go to prison. My heart is weak."

"Tomorrow. Bring it to my quarters. Do you need my room number?"

"Yes. No. I've got it. But... what you're asking is...."

"This is my maternal instinct talking to you. I will do anything, *anything*, to free my daughter. Understand? I don't care about your heart. I care about Noam."

Her eyes were narrowed and menacing. He wondered if he would have a heart attack right then.

"I'll try."

"Do it."

When she left, he lay back on his bed, attempting in vain to relax. He put two fingers on his wrist. His pulse was fast. *Calm down. Calm down.* But he did not calm down. He was close to panic. Then it came to him. He could bring the Pure any medication. She would not know the difference between the right one from a dangerous one. He could get a narcotic, like Xanax or Valium, a single low-dose pill, and tell her to cut it in half or quarters. The child would sleep for who knows how long? An hour? A day? He was no expert. As long as he did not overdose her, the Pure should be satisfied.

He would go to the medication room at the beginning of his shift, saying a Pure he planned to test was too anxious for him to get a good read. If the dispensary nurse asked him.

"Valium. 10 mg," he would say in a firm voice. She would record it for the first Pure he tested that day. Then he would bring Azura the pill before going to the imaging room. 2.5 mg should not hurt the child. He hoped.

If only his weak heart had let him stand up to the Pure. He should have ordered her to undress and lie on the bed.

"You want a pill to sedate your daughter? Then do whatever I tell you to do. Right now."

That is what he should have said. He wanted to kick himself. *Fool. You are giving her what she wants with nothing in return for yourself. Fool. Idiot.* But she had the hand-written notes, the paper evidence, in his writing. He did not want her anymore. He just wanted a way out of a situation that could go on and on. She might ask him for more medication, for her daughter, for herself, often. Once would have been enough for him. It might not be for her.

The day's unpleasantness had not ended. Constance sidled up to him during his next shift, saying she wanted to speak to him.

"This is for your ears only. I'm switching the Pure, Azura, with another pregnant woman. Don't ask me anything. The less you know, the better. I'll need you to keep recording the results of your tests in Azura's chart."

"But it won't be Azura. And it won't be consistent with Azura's history. Obstetrics will spot it in a minute."

"Make it consistent."

"Why should I involve myself in whatever this is?"

He had enough on his plate already, with Azura's demand.

"Because I am the team leader."

"So?"

Constance stood taller, looking down at the Radiologist, as menacing as the Pure had been earlier.

"I've seen how you take advantage of the Pures with your handheld device and your leering looks at their privates. Did you think I never noticed?"

The Radiologist swallowed hard. He feared this conversation was recorded, too. That Constance recorded it herself. He would not incriminate himself. Instead, he denied.

"You're mad. I've always acted professionally. No Pure has ever complained."

"I could arrange a complaint."

Later, he realized that twice that day he had allowed women to take advantage of him. He should have threatened to tell the authorities about Constance's intention of switching Pures. Why would she want to do that, anyway? One was like another.

CHAPTER 18
AZURA

The lock clicked. In came Constance in her Hazmat suit, lugging the sedated girl on her shoulder. Azura leaped up, running to take her child in her own arms. While she rocked and petted her, another woman entered.

"This is my daughter, Molly. She's switching with you. Here's a paper with the building and cell number you'll need. Where's your bag? I'll put them in. Grab it and let's go."

Molly gaped at the luxurious quarters.

"Wow! I get to live here?"

She dropped her own bag on the floor, transfixed.

"Hurry!" Constance said to Azura, who was inspecting Noam the way mothers do if their child is injured. She moved each limb and checked the girl's face, kissing each part of her with ferocity. Meanwhile, she took a deep sniff of her head, burying her face in Noam's hair. The authorities had separated them when they came to The Pure House. The child may have changed, but her scent was the same.

"I'm not leaving until she is alert enough to walk. I wanted her sedated, not sound asleep. When I see she's okay, I'll go."

"She's fine," Constance said. Her impatient, gloved hands gestured toward the door.

"Geez, Mom. You didn't tell me it'd be this glamorous. It's like where movie stars live."

"We have little time."

Molly crossed her arms.

"I'm not staying unless you promise to tell Vic where I am and give him the key code to my new quarters."

Azura looked up. "Vic?"

"He's my boyfriend."

"Does he have red hair?"

"He's not your boyfriend, Molly. You only had one... encounter."

Azura gave Noam a gentle shake.

"Wake up, darling."

"I want to go back to my room." Her voice was sluggish.

"You're staying with Mommy now."

"No. I hate you, Mommy." Her eyes closed again.

"I can find Vic, if you tell me where he is," Constance said.

"Try the bars near my factory."

Constance sighed.

"What did you do to my child? She hates me." Azura was crying.

"No, she doesn't," Constance said. "It's the sedative talking."

Azura picked her daughter up, preparing to follow Constance, when the lock click again. The three women stood stock still, thinking they had been caught. But instead of officers coming to arrest them, Martin came in, dressed in a Hazmat suit, with another young woman.

"What are you doing here?" He asked Constance.

"I could ask you the same question. And who's this?" She pointed at the young woman.

"It's... I might as well tell you. It's my daughter, Penny. Who's that?"

"My daughter, Molly."

They all stared at each other.

"Wait," Constance said. "Isn't Penny a Spreader? You brought an unmasked Spreader in contact with two pregnant women and a child? Are you crazy?"

Constance and Martin began yelling at each other through their face shields, while Penny and Molly gaped at their surroundings. Azura picked up her bag and rushed out the still open door, carrying the sleeping child with one arm. She hurried to the broom closet, placed Noam on the floor, then changed into Recovered clothing. After putting a sweater on the child to conceal her white dress, she lifted her again and made her way to the staircase. She hoped none of the Recovered staff she passed would stop her to ask about the child. None did. At the bottom floor, she followed another Recovered through a short twist of hallways until they were outside in the swirling dust.

It was late afternoon, and staff milled around at the back of the building. Azura walked with her head high, as if she was on an errand, until she found an isolated place behind some fake bushes and lay the girl down. She sat beside her. Martin or Constance might look for them. They had exposed her and Noam to a Spreader, but just for a couple of minutes. And Noam was still asleep. Azura did not have the strength to carry her further. She would have to wait for the child to be awake enough to walk to the building assigned to Molly.

It was boiling hot. The sun was an orange smudge hanging low in the sky. The air tasted like smoke. Behind her, The Pure House shimmered. She used the paper Constance dropped in her bag to fan the child. It was not until nightfall that the temperature dropped and Noam stirred.

"Where are we, Mommy?"

"Outside."

"I'm tired. I want to go to bed now."

"We'll walk there."

After a few steps, Noam sagged. Azura was forced to carry her again. Molly's room number in her Recovered building was 2049B. The hardest part was getting the child up the ladder and into the half-door unseen. Once she was on the bed, her sleep grew deeper. With reluctance, Azura left her to get food from the communal dining hall. The choice was limited compared to the array they were both used to. She knew it might be even more limited if they left town. None of the residents, exhausted from their shifts, paid attention to her.

Without lingering, she boxed up the items on her tray, and made her way back to Molly's room, passing others in the elevator, the hallways, and along the corridors containing bunked cells. When she unlocked the door to Molly's cell, the child was still asleep. A few minutes later, there was a soft knock. Azura froze. Was it an officer? She crawled over Noam and opened the door a crack. A familiar face appeared, belonging to a person clinging to the ladder.

"Come down. No one here will care. Anyone who sees us will think we have a thing for each other."

"Vic?"

"I saw you in the dining hall and followed you. I couldn't believe my eyes. How did you get here?"

She left the door open a couple of inches to hear the child if she awakened, and then she climbed down.

"So, you live in your girlfriend's beehive residence. How convenient."

"I don't live here. I circulate through the buildings, attending meetings with others who share my convictions. And I don't have a girlfriend."

"That's not what Molly said."

"Molly? Who's that?"

"Someone who's pregnant, and who says her boyfriend's name is Vic. Know any other Vics, Vic?"

His puzzled eyes looked into hers.

"Are you mad at me?"

"I might as well tell you. I've switched identities with a woman named Molly, and she wants you to know where she is and to give you my old key code. Her mother will search for you in the bars. I guess that's where you and Molly met."

Vic shook his head.

"Look. As I told you, I circulate. When I need a cover, I may ask someone to meet me somewhere, like at a bar. Just one time. If we get drunk, it might go further than I intended. Molly may have been one of those. I try not to ask for names. It's less likely the woman will get in trouble if they round me up."

"I guess I'm your fake date tonight."

"Yeah. Like I would choose an escapee from The Pure House. Some cover that would be."

He broke into a smile.

"Are we having a lover's quarrel already?"

"We aren't lovers."

114

"Fair enough. But pretend we are. Soon, they'll be ripping the town apart looking for you. We can buy some time by claiming to be a couple. It's a win-win. A great cover for both of us."

"I suppose."

"By the way, where's your daughter? Did you leave her behind?"

Azura motioned to Molly's cell with a tilt of her head. Vic's gaze followed her direction.

"I guess we'll have to claim to be a family."

"My daughter's sedated. When she's alert, she may fuss. She didn't want to come."

"Then we'll have to leave before dawn."

"I can take care of myself." She averted her eyes.

"I doubt it. You'll need my help if you want to escape with her. The alert will be for both of you. You wait here. I'll make arrangements. Be back in a couple of hours."

He grinned again.

"Shall we kiss to make it look like our quarrel is over?"

"You wish!"

She climbed back into Molly's cell and lay down next to Noam. She had two hours to consider her situation. If she was honest, she was glad Vic showed up to help her. She needed a guide to bring her and Noam to safety. Besides, Vic may have been cocky, but in a way that appealed to her. Not that she would let him know it. Not when he might be the father of Molly's baby.

Penny was another worry. She did not want herself or Noam to become an active case. Who knew how much time they needed for an exposure to lead to an infection? She could only hope it was more than a couple of minutes and that the filtration system in The Pure House was efficient. Now they were among Recovereds. Any of them might be reinfected and spread the virus. Even Vic. It was a good thing she did not kiss him. She was a Pure and had none of the immunities a Recovered might have, if they had any. In her years in the forest, she and Noam never had so much as a cold. Not being exposed to common viruses might be a disadvantage. This was another reason to be glad Vic was taking them away from the beehives before dawn.

After dark, there was another soft knock. It was Vic, masked this time. He lifted the sleeping child, carrying her and Azura's bag to the elevator. She followed and stood at his side during the ride down to the lobby. Once again, none of the Recovereds paid attention to them. They were just another family, perhaps visiting grandparents who had the good fortune to survive the virus.

Once they were out in the choking night air, filled with dust they could no longer see, it was safe to talk.

"Where are we going?"

"To the lake. Someone is lending me a skiff hidden there. I thought of borrowing a vehicle, but they will monitor the roads while you're still missing."

"How far?"

"It's a way. Do you think you can walk a few miles?"

"I was used to that in the forest."

"I've got a flashlight and extra batteries. But if patrol cars are on the road to the lake, we'll have to walk in the dark. They will think you're headed to the forest and may not be looking for you here."

Any time a vehicle approached, they hid behind whatever little foliage grew on the side of the road. Very few travelled to or from the lake at night. It reminded Azura of her walk to town from the forest at night, hiding to avoid detection. So much had happened since then. She and Noam had been prisoners in The Pure House, she had been impregnated by *in vitro* fertilization, and Vic had come to her rescue. Unless he had come to take advantage of her. He might sell her back to the bosses. She would not allow herself to trust him — yet.

Noam coughed in her sleep. Azura wondered if children developed asthma from the polluted air. Her nose tickled, too. Even Vic cleared his throat every few minutes. Many wore masks for the dust, not just the virus. Soon the forest would be a pile of dust, sand, and ash, and the entire landscape would be desert.

As they neared the lake, the air seemed cleaner.

"The water level is very low. We'll have to climb down the bank to reach the skiff," Vic said.

He turned the beam of the flashlight to the water, shimmering like a black tarpaulin against the embankment. After switching Noam to his shoulder, he held out his hand for Azura. They sidled down to the water's edge, then stepped into the skiff. It had a motor, but Vic used the oars to keep from making noise.

Noam stirred.

"I'm hungry, Mommy."

Azura opened her bag and fished out an apple from the communal dining hall in Molly's beehive residence. She noticed Vic stopped rowing. He had his finger to his lips.

"Shhh!"

Noam's crunching bite of the apple sounded loud enough to be heard across the lake. The two adults sat without moving. There was a sound of water splashing. Vic turned on the flashlight and moved the beam across the water until it smashed into an object—another skiff. A man in a Hazmat suit was rowing, and a young woman without one sat looking back at them. The beam cast a reflection in her pupils. Azura recognized the two passengers.

"Martin and Penny," she said under her breath.

CHAPTER 19
SPREADER'S ISLAND

The skiffs stopped alongside each other.

"Dad. Isn't that...?" Asked Penny.

"It's the Pure and her child. Everyone's looking for them. And who are you?" Martin asked Vic.

"I don't like this yucky food, and I don't like the dark. Go back. Mommy, go back."

Vic did not answer Martin.

"Why are you here?" Azura asked.

"I'm taking my daughter back to Spreader's Island. Constance convinced me it's for the best. I didn't expect to find you going in the same direction with your...friend."

"Dad calls Constance 'The Bitch'." Penny smirked.

"Are you taking us to Spreader's Island? Isn't that dangerous?" Azura asked Vic.

"I'm taking you to the far side. There aren't any settlements there."

"I'm taking Penny to that side, too, so she doesn't get the other Spreaders in trouble, if we're followed. She'll make her way back to her quarters," Martin said.

While the adults cross-talked, Noam became more restless. Soon she was wailing.

"Your child will give us away to the authorities. If any are on the lake."

"He's right," Vic said.

"I don't want her on Spreader's Island. She could get COVID."

"No way," Penny said. "Everyone on the island is healthy."

118

"No one has symptoms. There's a difference," Martin said. "Let me take her back. I can sneak her into the Pure Children's Quarters. No one will realize she was gone. It'll take some heat off you."

"What should I do?" Azura asked Vic. Why did she hope for a decision from him?

"I'd send her back. They've already programmed her mind. At least you know she'll survive."

Azura held Noam's face up to hers.

"Do you want to go back or do you want to stay with Mommy?"

"Go back."

"Don't you love Mommy?"

"No. I love Uncle Frank."

"I can take Penny the rest of the way," Vic said.

While the two men held the skiffs together, Azura put her child in Martin's, and Penny stepped into Vic's. Before they rowed away from each other, Azura buried her face in her arms and wept.

"You're my hero now," Penny said to Vic. He grinned at her with a flirtatious glint in his eye.

Martin threw a bag into Vic's skiff.

"It's your belongings, Azura. The ones you brought with you to town. I figured Penny would find them useful, but now that we've come into contact, I'll give them to you."

Azura did not look up. She could not bear to see Martin row away with her daughter.

Martin threw the bag next to her. The two skiffs parted ways. While Azura kept her head in her arms, Penny used the flashlight to guide Vic to a place to dock. The three got out, and Vic dragged the skiff onto the shore.

"We should stay right here until daylight," Vic said. "Azura, you can sleep in the skiff."

But she could not sleep. While she lay awake, wondering if she had done the right thing by escaping, she heard Vic and Penny murmuring to each other. Vic might catch the virus from a Spreader. Azura was pregnant and did not want to become an active case. Did he separate her from Penny to protect her from COVID or to be alone with the other woman?

I don't care. Let Penny have him. Yet, hurt piled on hurt, like the dust that settled on dust in the town, as she suffered from the loss of both Noam and Vic's attention. It was not jealousy, she told herself. Vic was inconsiderate. He should have spent the night talking to her, after all she had been through, instead of a Spreader who had given up nothing.

In the first light of day, Azura sat up, seeing the other two asleep nearby on the ground. She opened the bag Martin brought. Her most precious possession, the book, "Roots of the Woods," was still inside. It sustained three generations of women — her great grandmother, her mother, and herself — in the forest for decades with recipes, cures, and advice for living with what nature provided. She suspected it would be helpful on the island.

As the sun rose, she saw her surroundings were not desert-like or dusty. Spreader's Island was a lush hill jutting out of the lake, with a green canopy of tree tops thickening as the level of the land rose. Before her lay a large, flat field of tall grass, stopping just before the rise to the top of the hill began. The air was clear. It was the most pleasant sight she had seen since leaving the forest.

There were two bags — the one she brought and the one Martin brought. The first contained the food she took for Noam from Molly's communal dining hall — a bun, another apple, two hard-boiled eggs, and a cookie. She divided all of it into three parts by using the knife from the second bag, There would be no coffee, but they would have breakfast.

Soon after, Vic and Penny awoke.

"I've never been to this side of the island," Penny said.

Azura kept a few feet away from Penny, but Vic sat close to her while they ate.

"What's the plan?" Azura asked.

"Penny and I discussed it last night while you slept in the skiff. Since she has never been here before, I'll accompany her to the top of the hill. From there, she should be able to see her settlement. Then I'll come back here, and we can discuss a plan for you."

"I don't much care, now that Noam isn't with me."

"You have another child to consider. The one growing in you," Vic said.

She knew he was right. While Vic and Penny climbed the hill, Azura did what her great grandmother would have advised. She opened "Roots of the Woods" to a random page. Writing in a bold font in the middle of the text caught her eye.

Your companion will arrive soon.
He will drink and be purified again.

The obscure words made no sense. Vic was her companion. And he had nothing to do with her being a Pure. She closed the book. Her eyelids drooped. She would catch up on sleep while waiting for him.

But a frightening thought bolted her awake. What if he doesn't return? What if he stays with Penny and joins her community? How would she manage? She calmed herself, knowing that the book would help in the future, even if it made no sense in the present. Then she dozed off.

The sun headed toward the west when she awoke, with Vic, masked again, standing next to the skiff, looking down at her. She hid her relief. He extended a hand to help her up and out.

"How was your little walk with Penny?"

Her tone was sarcastic, as if she cared. She did not. She would not allow herself to. Her focus had to be on her second child, not on some man who happened into her life, who had forced her into a broom closet, who was Molly's boyfriend and maybe the father of her unborn child, who spent the night and the morning with Penny, and who told her to give Noam back to Martin. Yes, he was helpful, if she overlooked all of his offensive traits and behaviors.

"It was a more strenuous climb than it looked. Downhill was easier than uphill."

"So, do you have a thing for Penny, now?"

"She's a Spreader."

"Meaning?"

"Meaning 'Stay far, far away.'"

"You didn't seem to be that far away last night."

"I'm careful not to get sick again. It's not on my bucket list. I learned first-hand that Spreaders don't believe they're Spreaders. They think they're Pures."

"But I'm a Pure."

"Penny calls you a Temporary Pure. You just haven't been exposed yet. She thinks she'll stay healthy even if she's exposed. You might call her a Permanent Pure, if you believed her."

What Azura believed was that Vic was attracted to Penny, but scared of her.

"She said she'd return with provisions for us. Meanwhile, we need to round up some food. There's a fishing rod in the skiff. How about you catch our next meal while I start a fire to cook it on?"

Now that there was something for her to do, the worry lines on her forehead smoothed. She had not done a single useful thing in The Pure House, except receive the *in vitro* fertilization egg transfer. She baited the hook with a piece of the bun she had not finished. She had learned to fish while living in the forest. At least morning sickness had the advantage of reducing her appetite, so there were some leftovers. She gave Vic the matches from her bag before he disappeared into the field to search for kindling.

If she did not miss Noam, Azura would have felt the exhilaration of someone breathing good air after smothering in the town's dusty atmosphere. The top of the hill was clear, although the sun was still hazy. A refreshing breeze blew the fine particles away. The temperature was warm, not stifling. They quarantined Spreaders in the best place in the area, the only place not affected by the changing climate and rising heat.

Later, sitting with Vic, eating the fresh fish and the remains of breakfast as if picnicking in a park, she felt friendlier toward him. Sending her daughter back was good advice. It did not have to be forever. Down the road, she could be reunited with Noam after the new baby was born. By that time, she would have figured out where to go and, with the book's help, how to survive. When Noam was older, she would realize being a Pure confined to The Pure House was not so wonderful and that Uncle Frank was not so wonderful. It was useless to kidnap her daughter before she convinced her of the truth, when no one could win her over with the gift of a doll.

This was not the time. Vic might leave her at any point for any reason. He said he had a mission. *Some say....* She was not his responsibility. He wanted to rebel against the system, and helping her escape was one way he had of doing it. Now it was done. It might satisfy him, but she had a frightening future ahead of her with no money, no job, no home, no other friends, no immunity to COVID, and pregnant. Where would she go to have her baby? How would she care for a newborn? The worry lines reappeared.

"I don't know what to do next," she said

He gazed at the field.

"You might stay here for a while. I have the skiff to get to the mainland and back. Penny and I will get you what you need."

Penny and I? Did he mean separately or as a couple? But what choice did she have other than to accept?

"I'd need a hut of some sort—like the one I lived in most of the time in the forest. And more bait for fishing. If I had a shovel, I could dig up worms. And a pot and a jug for fetching water. And..."

"Whoa! I'll have to write this down. You seem to know what you need."

"That's from my five years in the forest."

"Before I leave, I'll put together something to keep out the rain and protect you from critters. It won't be fancy. I saw a plank on the hill that will be useful."

When Vic came back with the plank, Penny was with him. Did they plan to meet, or was it a coincidence? She carried a basket and a shovel, and he carried the plank.

"I saw an outcropping a half-mile down the shore with a small cave, not tall enough to stand in, we can place this against," he said.

Azura watched from a distance while the other two worked to prepare the cave and stock it with the tools, candles, food, water jug, and blanket Penny carried in the basket. The bag Azura brought contained extra clothing, "Roots of the Woods," matches, and the knife. Vic started a fire and went back to the hill with the basket for firewood. Then he dug into his pocket for a pencil stub and a tiny notebook, writing items Azura mentioned bringing back from the mainland.

"What's a rebel without a secret notebook?" He joked.

Just before they were ready to part, Penny thought she noticed something in the field. They walked a few yards in the direction she showed. It was a large animal, standing still and staring in their direction.

"There are no large beasts on this island, except..." Penny did not finish her sentence.

They walked nearer, stopping every few feet. The animal did not move. Penny gasped.

"It's the red heifer!"

CHAPTER 20
THE RED HEIFER

Penny moved closer. The animal raised its head but did not run.

"Looks like a cow," Vic said.

"It's not just any cow. It's a heifer. That's a cow that's still a virgin. It's like a teenage cow. We breed them in the settlement. What's important is its red color. The ones that are mixed color are also allowed to breed for the milk, which we sell to the mainland."

Penny spoke in a lowered voice, trying not to spook the animal. Vic, emulating her, lowered his, too.

"Why is it important? Hamburgers are brown from any color cattle."

"If we can breed one with only red hair and not a single white or black one, we can cure COVID. Then we can rejoin society on the mainland. No one will think we're Spreaders anymore. Not that we are."

"You mean like the pure red heifer in the Bible?" Azura asked.

"Yes. It's foretold. Like a prophecy or something."

"It looks pretty red to me," Vic said. "Like my hair. Maybe I'm pure."

The two women ignored him.

"You can't tell from this distance. A single white hair could be hidden anywhere on it."

"How'd it get here?" Vic asked.

"It must have escaped. Wait here. I'll get others. Keep an eye on it."

Penny raced back to the hill. The heifer took a few steps away and began grazing.

"She's crazy, Vic. Cows can't cure disease. Even all-red ones," Azura said.

"Let's wait and see."

"I don't want to be around a bunch of Spreaders. Not in my condition."

"Stay in the cave. I'll get you when they're gone."

Azura left for the outcropping while Vic remained in the meadow, watching the heifer for Penny and her friends. Several hours later, a group of six appeared with Penny, bringing ropes, fencing, posts, and a herding dog.

"Where's Azura?" Penny asked.

"Isolating herself in the cave."

Penny introduced her friends — two women and four men. Brenner was their apparent leader's name. He was a muscular man who looked like a younger Martin from a distance, Azura noted. The Spreaders were all astonished by the heifer.

"I don't see any white or black from here."

"Me, either."

"It might be different up close."

"This may be the nearest we've come to breeding an all-red."

For the rest of the afternoon, they chased the uncooperative animal around the field. None had been raised on a ranch, and their skill with the rope was amateurish. Only the dog knew what to do, making ever tighter circles around the animal for its human companions. Azura watched from just outside her cave, ready to dart in if they neared. It took her mind off Noam and the future. In time, Brenner got a rope around the animal's neck, more by luck than expertise. While Vic held the rope, the others examined the heifer, parting the hairs on all sides with concentrated care. The heifer pawed the ground and snorted, almost jerking the rope out of Vic's hands several times.

"She's pure."

They whispered in awe, not to avoid scaring the animal, but in heart-stopping wonder in the presence of a miracle.

"We've been breeding for years to get to this one. We started with eighty percent red from a few cattle already on the island. Every season, we'd mate the two reddest," Penny said to Vic.

They got to work constructing a pen from the fencing and posts.

"We'll keep moving the pen as she eats up the grass."

"I'll get her water."

Their excitement rose. Eyes glittered with the thought their quarantine time might be over soon.

"What now?" Vic asked. "Do we drink her milk or have a barbecue?"

"Heifers don't produce milk. It's not that simple."

"We should go back and tell the others."

"Hold on a minute," Brenner said. "Only the seven of us, plus Vic and the Temporary Pure, know about the heifer, right?"

The others nodded.

"I'm thinking. If she's a cure, she'll be worth a fortune."

Everyone was silent, waiting to see where this was going. Vic took a step forward.

"I don't see how a cow can cure anything except hunger. But if you're right, give her to the world. Without cost. She'd save humans from extinction. That's priceless."

"You bet. Priceless. The bosses would pay millions. The nine of us would be very rich and have a say in how things should go. If we share with everyone on the island, we'd wind up with a few thousand each and no power."

"The first thing would be to get all the so-called Spreaders back to the mainland. When we started the breeding, we said that was our goal," Penny said.

"Why should we share with Vic and the Temporary Pure? They're not part of the breeding program," one of the others said.

"To keep them quiet," Brenner said.

While the group argued, Vic returned to the outcropping to bring Azura up to speed.

"They're already squabbling about who should profit from the red heifer cure. This will get worse before it gets better."

They sat a few feet apart, watching the group gesticulate as their discussion became more heated. When one woman left the group, walking in the hill's direction, two of the other Spreaders grabbed her and brought her back.

"I bet she wanted to tell the others in the settlement," Azura said.

Brenner said a few words to the woman, then turned to two others who crossed their arms over their chests.

"They're holding out, waiting to be convinced," Vic said. "Now they've moved their hands to their hips. They're still not sure, but have opened their minds."

Brenner put his arm around Penny's shoulders, speaking just to her.

"He's putting the moves on your girlfriend, Vic."

"She's not my girlfriend."

After more time elapsed, in which Brenner appeared to be getting an agreement from the group, hands raised in what looked like a vote. It was five to two. The discussion continued until all hands raised. A few minutes later, they looked over at Vic and Azura, conferring again.

"Let's hope they're not thinking of killing us," Vic said.

"Why would they do that?" Azura's heart raced.

"Maybe they wouldn't want to share their riches with us."

Penny left the group and approached, stopping a few feet away.

"They want you to tell them how come you're familiar with the part of the Bible about the red heifer."

"My father was a rabbi. I heard him give sermons about it."

"You're Jewish?"

"What of it?"

"According to the Bible, the high priest has to prepare the cure."

"From what I remember, that's true."

"Wait here," Penny said before returning to the group.

This time, the discussion was brief. Brenner and Penny came back together.

"Where's the high priest of the Jews?" Brenner asked.

"Are you kidding?" She gaped at him.

"No. We need the high priest. Where is he?"

Azura looked at Vic, hoping he was better informed. He said nothing.

"Jews no longer have priests. They have rabbis. That's how it's been for centuries."

"Okay. Where's the top rabbi?"

"You mean over all the Jews?"

"Yeah. The top one."

"You're mixing us up with Catholics. They have the Pope. Jews don't have a pope or a top rabbi."

Brenner walked back to the others.

"Tell him what he wants to know, Azura. As long as he needs you, you're safe," Penny said.

"What do you mean?"

"All I can say is the stakes are high. Anyone with a cure for COVID can rule the world."

"Does Brenner want to rule the world?" Vic asked.

Penny shrugged.

"There'd be a hell of a fight with the bosses if he does," Vic said.

"That's why this is top-secret."

Brenner returned.

"We've decided. If there's no high priest or top rabbi, we'll try with any rabbi. It's a gamble. The cure might not work without a high priest."

"I guess you're out of luck," Azura said.

"Where can we find a rabbi?"

"You mean, any rabbi?"

"Yeah."

If her father had survived, she could have named him. If her great grandmother was alive, she would have known many of the rabbis in this part of the state. The only one Azura remembered was the one she had known as a child. Rabbi Samuelson.

"My mother was friends with Rabbi Sam. He lived with us in the forest during COVID-19 for a while. Then he returned to the synagogue in town. I don't know if he's still there."

"Where is the synagogue?"

"On Third Street on the eastern end of town."

Brenner stared at her, as if trying to tell if she was truthful. His suspicious eyes narrowed. She might be lying about the disappearance of high priests or the top rabbi. He would not let her cheat him out of the millions the heifer would bring.

"You two," he said, indicating Vic and Penny with a tilt of his head. "Take the skiff you came in and bring the rabbi here."

"What about Azura?" Vic asked.

"She stays here. She's the assurance you'll come back. And not empty-handed."

"Brenner! That's not like you," Penny said.

"It is now that we have the red heifer. Call it the taste of freedom. The Temporary Pures have had all the advantages. Now it's someone else's turn. Ours."

"Don't you understand, man? We all should have the same advantages. No one's better than anyone else," Vic said.

"Tell it to Karl Marx. Right now, fuck off to the mainland and bring me the fucking rabbi."

Azura wished she had slipped Vic the knife. But Brenner was stronger. He might overwhelm Vic, grabbing the knife from him and driving it into his heart. Vic wasn't ruthless enough to defend himself by killing Brenner. They all knew it.

"C'mon," Vic said to Penny. They walked to the shore, then along it to the place where they left the skiff.

"You," Brenner said to Azura. "Wait here."

He went back to the remaining group and the heifer. Azura watched Vic row the skiff until it was out of sight. The two left her with the group of crazies, while they would have plenty of time to cement their relationship on the mainland. For the second time, she wondered if they would bother to return. If they could not find Rabbi Sam, if he was dead or an active case, if he had left town, if he did not want to come, what would they do? Meanwhile, she was at risk of becoming infected by the Spreaders. If she did, she might miscarry. Would that be bad or good?

Every day, she was becoming more attached to the baby growing inside. It reminded her of when she became pregnant with Noam, with no job or resources, and COVID nipping at her heels. There had been an offer to buy her baby she almost accepted. She also considered and rejected an abortion. It worked out, but this time she might not be so lucky.

The most frightening thing was the virus. On Spreader's Island, no one wore a mask or a Hazmat suit. The inhabitants did not believe they needed them. But Vic only wore a mask when near her. And he did not keep his distance from Penny. He claimed to be a Recovered, meaning he had been an active case in the past. Another puzzling factor was that he never called the red heifer cure "crazy." Was he a Spreader posing as a Recovered? But if he was, why was it a secret from the other Spreaders? Perhaps the authorities never caught him and quarantined him on the island. It would explain all his sneaking around from one place to another. Unless he was a rebel posing as a Spreader.

When he returned—if he returned—they would have a serious talk. She would insist he answer her questions and tell her his real name, if it was not Vic.

She looked across the lake. About half-way, the view became hazy. The sky, the water, and the air in between were all the same dull blue gray. As she watched, a spot on the lake darkened, slowly becoming distinct. It was the skiff. As it neared, she could see Vic at the oars, Penny in the back, and another figure hunched in the middle.

CHAPTER 21
THE RABBI

Vic and Penny approached Brenner's group, leading the third person from the skiff by a rope with one end tied around his wrists. Azura squinted until she could see that the third person was an elderly, gray-haired Rabbi Sam. He walked through the field at a slow pace. An old green cardigan hung on his round frame. Vic and Penny stopped frequently to allow him to catch up. When they passed a log, the Rabbi sat down. They did not pull him up.

Azura ran to him.

"What are you doing? You can't treat him like that. Untie him."

"He refused to come. We had to force him," Vic said.

"Now that he's here, you can untie him before you injure his wrists or make him fall."

Vic did as she asked. The Rabbi rubbed his wrists. Azura knelt before him, her worried eyes scanning his face.

"Rabbi. I'm Azura, Eve's daughter. Are you okay? Do you need water?"

"Water would be good."

She raced back to her lean-to and returned with a jug. He drank.

"Eve's daughter? Why are you with these ruffians?" His voice was thinner than she remembered. An older man's voice.

"It's a long story. I don't want to be here, either, but there's no other place for me right now."

"I see. You're a Spreader."

"No. They say I'm a Pure. I've been living in the forest and never got exposed. My mother told me you were friends."

"Yes. I lived in her forest community fifteen years ago. You were very young."

She turned to Vic.

"Did you tell him why you forced him to come?"

"Not exactly. I just said we needed him on the island."

Vic pressed his lips together. He seemed unhappy with his role. Penny waved to Brenner. He and the others joined them. She introduced them to their hostage. Vic handed the Rabbi his mask, knowing he would want one. Brenner pointed to the penned heifer.

"It's a red one. We bred it."

Rabbi Sam stared at the beast.

"A cow," he said.

Brenner pointed again.

"Not just a cow. A genuine red heifer."

When the Rabbi said nothing and failed to look amazed, Brenner began bouncing on his toes.

"There are no white or black hairs among the red ones. It could cure COVID."

The Rabbi turned his by now amazed eyes onto Brenner.

"You don't mean... You're not referring to the red heifer in the Bible, are you?"

"Yes! That one. The heifer that's all red. The pure heifer."

"If you shipped it to Jerusalem, a war might start, but it can't cure viruses."

"What do you mean, start a war? Because it's priceless and everyone would want it?" Penny asked.

"No, no no. Rumors have circulated for years about groups hoping to breed an all-red heifer because they think they could rebuild the temple in Jerusalem that was destroyed by the Romans in the year 70."

"How?" Brenner asked.

"Do you want to tell them, Azura?"

"I don't remember the details."

"The high priest sprinkled the red heifer's ashes, mixed with water, on the area to purify it before building the new temple. One of the many problems is the Temple Mount, which is holy to the Muslims, occupies that site. If they tore it down to make room for the

Jewish temple, a war would be inevitable. So no one's going to do that. Now, what do you want from me?"

"The high priest of the Jews has to kill the heifer."

"You mean the high priest of the Israelites, who lived over six thousand years ago. They were the ancestors of modern Jews. We don't have a high priest anymore."

"Azura told us. We have made compromises, like a rabbi instead of a high priest."

Rabbi Sam gave an exasperated huff.

"I am a rabbi. What do you want me to do?"

"Kill the heifer, burn it, and make the concoction that will cure COVID."

"I won't kill the cow. I won't kill any animal."

Brenner stepped toward him.

"We won't let you go until you do."

"Keep your distance, sir. Don't expose me."

He used a commanding tone. Brenner stepped back.

"Let me try," Penny said. "Rabbi, we respect you, and we respect your people. If the Biblical prophecy is right, it might save all of us. Nothing is lost if we're wrong. We're just begging you to help us in case we're right."

"Listen to me. The ritual of the red heifer in the Bible redeemed the Israelites from moral transgressions and from contaminants, like worshipping the golden calf or touching a human corpse, not from physical illnesses."

"That's not what's in the Bible."

"Everyone understood it to mean that at the time."

"This is a different time. It might have a different meaning now. Maybe it would cure the virus. If you help us, you could save humanity."

"This is ridiculous. I'm not killing an animal. Besides, you need a *Shochet* for Kosher slaughtering. That someone with special training that I don't have."

Brenner took over.

"We'll get a gun. All you'd have to do is pull the trigger."

"No! Besides, it wouldn't be Kosher. A knife has to be used."

Brenner turned to the group.

"Do any of you have a knife?"

Azura stayed quiet, not revealing that she had one. Someone stepped forward with a Swiss army knife.

"You can't use that. It would torture the animal. They do not tolerate cruelty in ritual slaughter."

"He's right," Azura said.

"Okay. Okay. We'll compromise. We'll use a gun. It'll be quick and the heifer won't suffer. If the Rabbi won't do it, he can be present," Brenner said. "Someone go back to the settlement and get the gun."

A group member took off. Everyone watched him, then looked at the heifer. It was grazing. After the initial excitement, dejection followed as they made compromises. But no one offered to slay the animal with a knife.

"I'm going to take the Rabbi to rest in my lean-to."

He stood to follow her. Then he spoke to the group.

"You have another problem. After they slaughtered the animal, they burned it. That's easy. But the ashes must be mixed with spring water. Not lake water or tap water. And pure children, raised in isolation, carry the water from the spring."

He left with Azura. For a long moment, the group remained silent as they digested this fresh problem until Penny had a realization.

"Pure children? We have them. They're in The Pure House. Azura's daughter is one of them."

"Noam," Vic said. "We brought her half-way here, then your father took her back."

"That was a mistake. We thought her fussing would attract the authorities," Penny said.

"We need a plan to get some of those children," Brenner said.

"Azura has the key code to the Pure Children's Quarters. She'd want to be reunited with her daughter," Vic said. "I can sneak her back into The Pure House."

"You'd help us?" Penny asked.

"Either there'd be a cure for COVID or the missing children would cause trouble for the Bosses. Whichever is fine with me. I'll talk to Azura."

135

The group watched him head for the lean-to. Azura was sitting outside. The Rabbi was in the cave, resting on the sleeting mat. When Vic approached, Azura stood. Penny and the group watched him explain. Even from a distance, they could tell Azura was excited when she heard the plan to bring Noam to the island. She disappeared into the cave and came out again a few minutes later, shrugging. She must have consulted Rabbi Sam. Whatever the Rabbi advised did not crush her enthusiasm for the reunification.

When Vic came back to the group, he asked if they had money.

"Why?" Brenner asked.

"We'll need to bribe the caretakers. It will have to be a lot. They'll have explaining to do the next day when it's discovered that three children are missing. And I'll have to take the gun, just in case."

"How will you keep the children quiet?"

"By taking all three girls, the number in Noam's pod. They'll be told they're going on a secret outing to a fun place. They'll play a game in which they only allow whispering."

Next came a discussion about the money, how much to take, where it was stored, who should get it, how to account for it to most of the Spreaders, who did not know about the heifer. Meanwhile, the group saw the member who left to get the gun coming toward them, across the field.

"It's a 22 mag solid point. Should work."

The hard part of the project arrived — killing the animal.

"Who's going to volunteer?" Asked Vic.

Everyone was silent, looking down or away.

"You, Vic? You said you had skin in this game."

"I'll kidnap children, but I won't shoot the cow."

"Penny?"

"I'm an animal lover and a vegetarian. Get someone else."

All the group members had excuses.

"Geez, you guys are all pussying out on me. I'll do it myself when the Rabbi wakes up."

They spent the next hour watching Brenner load and unload the gun, taking mock aim at the heifer, who stared at the humans with large, doleful eyes.

"The heifer knows," Penny said.

"No way. The thing's too dumb," Brenner said.

"It's special. It's pure. If it can cure COVID, it can tell what you're going to do."

"Don't mess with me, Penny."

"Let's get an expert from the mainland. The kind the Rabbi mentioned—a *Shochet*, or whatever. Or a regular butcher. A farmer. Someone who knows how."

"There can't be much to it. Put the gun to its head and pull the trigger."

"What part of the head?"

"Hell, girl. If it's shot in the head, it dies."

They continued to argue until the Rabbi reappeared in front of the lean-to. Vic went to get him, but he refused to come closer. He would observe the sorry spectacle from where he was with Azura.

For the next hour, Brenner approached the cow with the gun raised. The animal backed up every time he neared, mooing. He tried coming from the side, but it turned its heavy head, not taking its eyes off him, stepping away, avoiding him. When its back was against the fence, it broke through and ran to another spot in the field. Brenner cursed, pursuing it.

"Everyone. Surround the thing. Where's the dog?"

It was asleep in the shade of a tree and refused to join in.

Brenner was so exasperated, he took a pot shot at the heifer, missing, cursing it for not allowing him to kill it. The animal took off at the sound of gunfire, running back and forth across the field, staying as far as possible from its human pursuers.

"I told you. The heifer knows," Penny said. "I'm through."

She joined the Rabbi and Azura, too exhausted to continue. Soon, the others dropped out. Then, someone pointed to the lake. A skiff with two figures aboard was coming toward the island. One occupant wore a Hazmat suit. The other was a young woman. The boat docked, and the two jumped out, walking toward the group. Azura joined and recognized them.

"Constance and Molly! From The Pure house. What are you doing here?"

"Long story," Constance said, raising her face shield.

"My boyfriend, Vic, is here," Molly said, racing to him, throwing her arms around him.

"Whoa!" He said.

"What are you doing with that gun?" Constance asked.

"We're trying to slaughter that heifer. It's our first time."

"Give it to me." Constance grabbed the weapon. Without pause, she walked to the animal, which did not move, and in one skillful motion, raised the gun and shot it cleanly. The heifer crumpled to the ground.

"Where did you learn to do that?" Brenner asked.

"I was raised on a cattle ranch."

She handed the gun back to Brenner.

"Go make us dinner," she said.

CHAPTER 22
THE RED HEIFER

"How do you burn a dead cow?" Vic asked.

"You can't just throw a match on it," Penny said.

Azura asked Constance why she had brought Molly to the island.

"As the Radiologist predicted, Obstetrics figured out right away that Molly wasn't you. My guess is that you two are different on the inside. They called me in for questioning. Before that could happen, I escaped with my daughter. Martin told me that the far side of Spreader's Island was a good place to hide and that you were already there. He lent me his skiff. It surprised me. Martin never seemed to like me that much."

Penny snickered. She had already told Vic and Azura that her father called Constance "The Bitch." He must have helped her escape so she would not implicate him.

"What about the Radiologist?" Azura asked.

Constance shrugged. "If he was smart, he fled, too."

She took off the Hazmat suit.

"It's too hot for this. But I'll wear a mask. Here's one for you, Molly. Sorry, I only have these two."

She took the two from a bag she brought. She tried to hand one to Molly, who was holding tight to Vic and didn't pay attention to what her mother had for her.

"Who are you?" Vic asked her.

She untwined herself so he could see her face.

"It's me, Molly. Remember?"

"Do I know you?"

"You asked me for a date in the break room of the factory. We went to a bar and hit it off. Anyway, I'm pregnant from our time that night."

Vic stared at her with a puzzled expression.

"I... think I remember you from the factory. Sometimes I drink too much and the next day, I don't recall a thing."

"You were into me in the bar. I was into you, too. You're the father of my baby."

"You'll have to prove that. I've had girls tell me that before, and it turned out not to be true."

"But you said you'd be my boyfriend."

Molly was tearing up, clinging to him again. While they talked, Brenner and the Spreaders regarded the dead heifer.

"What do we do now?" He asked the Rabbi.

"The high priest burns all of it to ash. The corpse contaminates him, and he must stay away from the community until nightfall."

"That won't be difficult. We are already away from our settlement."

The group discussed the best way to burn the remains. If they had a shovel, they would dig a pit. They decided the next best thing would be to surround the heifer with kindling and burn it in a bonfire.

"But if we don't remove the prairie grass near it, we'll set the entire field on fire."

Someone tried to pull up a small bunch.

"The roots must be long. I can't budge it without gloves."

They could not cut the grass without a mower or scythe. Brenner cursed, kicking at the problematic growth. They thought about moving the carcass to the shore and hoisting it on the rockery, where they could burn it without the fire spreading.

"They will see the smoke from the mainland. It might attract the authorities."

"We'll have to drag it to the inland side of an outcropping."

"Not the one with my lean-to," Azura said.

The next nearest one was a quarter mile away, a long distance to drag a weight of several hundred pounds. They tied a rope around its legs, and all seven Spreaders tried to pull it, moving it a few inches. Everyone sat where they were and rested. Some took out

CAROLYN GEDULD

handkerchiefs and wiped their faces. Others fanned themselves with their hands.

"Let's cool off in the lake."

All but Azura, Rabbi Sam, and Constance ran to the shore and waded in.

"I have an idea," Brenner called to the others. "There are buckets in the skiffs. We'll use them to wet down the grass with lake water, then set fire to the heifer."

Everyone piled out of the lake and made a chain to pass buckets to the field surrounding the carcass. An hour later, the grass in the area was wet. They stamped it down until most of it lay flat. Whenever there was a break, they dipped themselves in the lake again to cool off. The next chore was assembling the kindling. They had to go to the edge of the hill to find trees that dropped branches and twigs. Dead grass was gathered and strewn over the animal.

"Are we ready?"

"I think so," Brenner said.

He borrowed matches from Azura and circled the carcass, lighting what he could. Some of the kindling fizzled out without catching, but after much effort, small flames climbed the scaffolding. They all cheered.

"They would have burned it until there was nothing but ash. Even the bones were reduced to ash," Rabbi Sam said.

"There may have to be another compromise," Conner said. "The fire isn't hot enough. I've heard it has to be three thousand degrees to burn up bones."

"Where will we store the ash?" Penny asked.

"All we have are the buckets," Brenner said.

A delicious aroma spread through the area. They had consumed the little they brought to eat from the settlement. The dog barked, scampering around the burning carcass.

"Let's pull off a chunk for dinner."

"With what?"

"I have a kitchen knife," Azura said.

"You can't eat a sacred heifer," the Rabbi said.

"Why not?"

"It spoils the ritual. A genuine red heifer belongs to God."

"We said there'd be compromises."

Azura gave Vic the knife. He walked around the bonfire until he found a spot that smoldered without flames. Everyone, even the Rabbi, shared the roast he hacked off.

By then, it was getting dark. An argument erupted about who should tend the fire all night. They drew lots to determine who would sleep and who would add fuel. Everyone lay down in the field, except the two on duty. Complaints arose about the hardness of the ground, the itchiness of the coarse grass, the mosquitos. The Rabbi and Azura returned to the lean-to. No one slept well.

The next morning, they were hungry again. Despite burning all night, there was still more cow left. Vic cut off another hunk. Then they made a chain to wet down the grass again. The day continued as the last had, with dips in the lake, foraging for kindling, and finding chunks the flames had not yet consumed to eat. When they stopped adding fuel, the fire ebbed until there was nothing left but cooled, charred bones.

"If we stamp on the bones, they'll crumble, and they'll mix with the ash."

Four Spreaders stamped on the remains as if they were grapes while the others watched. The ribs and smaller bones broke, but the large ones and the skull remained stubbornly intact. They separated these from the rest and were left with a large pile of ash and bone fragments.

"There's way more than can fit in the two buckets."

"Bring a skiff. We can put it all in."

They dragged Martin's skiff to the site and deposited the material in it with the aid of the buckets, fitting the tarp that had lined the bottom of the skiff over the top. The burning of the slaughtered red heifer had been accomplished. The happiest of the group was the dog, who was under a distant tree, gnawing at a large bone.

"Now you have to find a spring," the Rabbi said. He seemed interested in the project, despite declaring it ridiculous.

The Spreaders had passed a creek while coming over the hill.

"It has to come from a spring, right?" Brenner asked.

"Maybe," Vic said.

"Okay. We have the spring water, then. What we need now are the children."

"What children?" Constance asked.

"The ones from The Pure House. Pure children."

"You have to be joking. I took a major risk bringing Noam to Azura so they could escape together, and you sent her back."

"I did," Azura said. "It seemed the right thing to do. Now she's needed on the island."

"Don't involve me again," Constance said.

"Vic and I will handle it."

"Vic's my boyfriend. I'll rescue the children with him," Molly said.

"I'm not your boyfriend."

"Oh, my," the Rabbi said, shaking his head.

"Look, Molly. I'm not trying to steal anyone's boyfriend. I have to go to keep my daughter quiet during the rescue. You don't want three crying girls on your hands, alerting the authorities."

"I'll need the money," Vic said.

"I've sent someone. He'll be here soon," Brenner said.

They saw a figure coming across the field carrying a shovel and a bag. It was the Spreader who had been sent to fetch the bribe for the caretakers in the Pure Children's Quarters.

"Good. You brought a shovel. After we dig a pit and line it with the tarp, we can mix the concoction in it. We'll take turns digging," Conner said.

"I brought gloves so we won't get blisters."

They chose a place near the shore for the hole where the ground would be easier to penetrate. It took several hours of digging. They lined the pit with the tarp, dragged over the skiff, and dumped in the contents. Some ashes blew onto the Spreaders.

"One good wind will scatter the remains all over the island," the Rabbi said. He chuckled.

Azura allowed her blanket to be used to cover the pit. When it was dark, she and Vic boarded the skiff and set out for the mainland. After hiding the skiff, they made their way to The Pure House. Vic knew a back way in only used by staff. They climbed the stairs to the second floor. Azura put on Constance's Hazmat suit before using the code she had memorized to unlock the Pure Children's door.

From there on, everything happened as planned. The caretaker took the bribe, and three sleepy girls played the whisper game while being led back to the skiff. Noam sat on her mother's lap, while the other two dozed on the bottom of the vessel. On the island, Vic carried each of the sleeping girls to the lean-to.

Everyone woke up the next morning hearing the girls cry for their breakfast, their toys, their caretakers, their cartoons on TV.

"What will we feed them?" Azura asked.

"Break out the fishing rods," Vic said.

An hour later, several fish were scaled, cooked, and ready.

"Not fish for breakfast. That's not breakfast food. We want chocolate crunch cereal." Noam said.

"Everyone. This is my daughter Noam and her friends, Sandy and Daisy."

"Where's our dolls? They eat breakfast with us."

"We have little dishes for them. We're the mommies, and they're the children."

"There are no play dishes here. No spoons, no forks. We eat with our hands," Azura said.

"That's yucky. Our hands will be sticky."

"After you eat, you'll play a special game."

"What?"

"Carry the water to the big hole."

"From the lake?"

"No. See the hill? You carry the water from up there to the hole near the lake."

"That's work."

"Yes. A little."

"We don't work. We're Pures."

The Spreaders laughed. The haughtiness of the children was endearing, for a moment.

"It's special work. Only Pure children do it," Penny said.

"We're special."

"That's right. After you eat your fish, I'll show you where the special water is. Special water for special children."

Penny had a way with them. They ate, then followed her to the hill. She carried the two buckets and Azura's water jug, now empty. Everyone else waited near the pit in silence. When they returned, there was an inch of water in one bucket, and none in the other.

"I dropped it," Daisy said.

Only the water jug was full.

"I had to carry the jug. It was too heavy for the girls," Penny said.

"Only pure children can carry the water," Rabbi Sam said.

"What did you want me to do?" Penny asked, annoyed.

They dropped the little they had into the pit. It made no visible difference.

In the background, Vic coughed.

CHAPTER 23
VIC

When Vic started a fever, he took a home COVID test. All the Recovereds carried them. It was a piece of paper he spat on, waiting for it to turn red for positive or green for negative. When he saw he was positive, an active case, he told the others. Azura, Molly, Constance, Rabbi Sam, and the three girls planned to separate themselves from him, sheltering in the outcropping with the lean-to. Vic lay down in Martin's skiff, now empty. The Spreaders stayed with him, taking no precautions, believing they were Pures who had natural immunity.

"I'll nurse Vic," Penny said to Azura's group before they parted.

"Do you want the Hazmat suit?" Constance asked her.

"No need."

"You must have infected him," Molly said.

"You're the one who was all over his neck."

"I'm a Recovered, not an active case. I couldn't infect anyone, unlike you."

The two women hurled venomous looks at each other.

"Stay away from him, Molly. You could lose the baby," Constance said. "I told you to wear a mask. Maybe you'll listen to me now."

She pulled her daughter toward the lean-to.

"What about the water? We need the kids to carry it," Brenner said.

"I'm not exposing my daughter or her friends to any of you from now on," Azura said. "It's bad enough they were near Vic in the skiff and with Penny on the hill."

"If the virus infects anyone on this Island, the only thing that might save them is the red heifer cure. All that's left is adding spring water and herbs to the ashes. It would be insanity to stop now when we're so close."

"I'm not insane enough to let the girls near any of you. They can't carry water, anyway. They would spill it. Find another compromise."

With that, Azura and her group marched off. Brenner went to the skiff to talk to Vic.

"Hey, man. How're you doing?"

"I'm... *cough*... hanging in there... *cough*."

"Do you want one of us to take you to the mainland to an active case residence or do you want to stay here and try the red heifer cure?"

"Stay."

Brenner nodded.

"Penny will take care of you until it's ready."

"Don't make him talk. Help me turn him onto his stomach," Penny said.

After helping Penny, Brenner called a meeting of the Spreaders.

"We goofed. Three things were supposed to be added to the fire — cedar, red wool, and hyssop," he said.

"What's hyssop?"

"Some kind of herb that doesn't grow here, I bet. No cedar trees exist on the island, either. And does anyone have red wool with them?"

They shook their heads.

"We'll have to mix them or their substitutes in with the ashes."

"There's no cedar, but plenty of pine is on the hillside. Let's get pine cones and use rocks to break them into pieces."

"Who's good at recognizing edible plants? We need a few leaves."

"I'll go."

"You. Your shirt is red. See if you can tear off a piece."

"I'll rip off the pocket."

For the next hour, they gathered and prepared the three additions, throwing them into the pit with the rest.

"What about the spring water?"

"We can bring it in the two buckets and get the girls to dip their hands in the pit. That's the best we can do."

"It'll take all day to bring enough water to the pit."

"Let's get going."

The next day, while the Spreaders were still fetching water, Azura approached Brenner.

"Constance is going to row to the mainland to get supplies. The children are tired of fish. Do you need anything?"

"Food. More buckets with tops to store the concoction. A large ladle and funnel. Some kind of mesh for straining. Penny wants oxygen for Vic, just in case."

By the end of the day, there was enough water in the pit for a mixture of the consistency of soup.

"Get the girls. Tell them to dip their hands in. Everyone stand back."

Azura let Noam, Daisy, and Sandy to the edge of the pit and knelt with them, helping them.

"You've touched the mixture! Only the girls are supposed to."

"I don't want them falling in," Azura said.

"Icky."

"It smells bad."

When the girls returned to the outcropping, Brenner used an oar for stirring before scooping the concoction into the buckets with the ladle, strained first through the mesh. The procedure took a couple of hours.

"It's ready!"

The Spreaders gathered. Azura's group remained at a distance, observing. Brenner yelled his question.

"What's next, Rabbi?"

The Rabbi yelled back.

"Sprinkle some on yourselves."

"Why?"

"To remove contamination from being in contact with the carcass."

"You mean, like, germs?"

"The Israelites believed being around a cadaver made them impure. They didn't have knowledge of germs."

The Spreaders plunged their hands into the mixtures and flicked it at each other.

"Now what?" Brenner yelled.

"Drink some. But I wouldn't."

"Why not?"

"For a long list of reasons. The oar's been in the lake. You didn't purify the spring water. No one's washed their hands before dipping them. The ash is full of bone particles. The whole thing might be poisonous. And you made one compromise after another with the ritual."

The Spreaders conferred.

"What should we do?"

"Give a small amount to Vic and see what happens," Penny said.

"He might die anyway."

"We've nothing to lose."

"His fever seems high. We should bathe him in the lake."

"First, let's give him a little."

Penny ladled a small amount through the mesh several more times. Then she brought the ladle to the skiff, holding her hand under it to catch drips.

"Help me sit him up."

Two Spreaders rushed to her aid. Between gasps, Vic took a couple of swallows, after which they carried him to the lake and submerged his body. When his breath eased, they figured his temperature had lowered, and they put him back in the skiff. Penny would watch over him through the night, giving him the concoction at intervals.

Constance returned with the supplies, minus the oxygen, which she had no way of obtaining. Vic's breathing was labored. He slept between Penny's ministrations. She poured some of the mixture over him, hoping his skin would absorb it. Toward dawn, Azura came with a lantern to see how he was doing.

"It's hard to tell in this dim light, but I think he's doing better than last night."

"I thought it was my imagination. He's coughing less, and he seems cooler."

Azura kept her distance.

"You're doing a good job, Penny."

"I haven't had medical training. I'm doing my best to shove as much of the red heifer mixture down him that I can."

She smiled at Azura.

"Just keep Molly away from him."

"She's convinced they're together."

"He didn't even know her name. I don't think he's into her."

"I don't either. He's into you, Penny."

"Me? Ha! He's just a flirt. Or he was."

"No. I mean it. He's attracted to you. For real."

"I think he's into you, Azura."

The two women continued their friendly argument, not noticing that Vic had his bloodshot eyes open. He heard them from a great distance, as if he floated on a cloud. Perhaps he was dead and listening from Heaven. But if he was dead, he would not have such terrible pain in his muscles and joints. If he was dead, he would not be gasping. If he was dead, he would not care what they said about him. He did not care. It was the second day of an illness that often lasted weeks. When he had it before, he was too ill to listen to anyone, even the doctors. He lay in bed in the active case residence on his stomach with oxygen tubes spaghetti-ing into his nostrils, not knowing if it was day or night. This time, he waited for a snake to show up, unless it was a fever dream.

When it came, it was a python, lying in wait, now spiraling up his length, tightening itself around his chest, squeezing. He moaned each time it forced the air out, knowing it would soon be his last breath, that inhaling would become impossible. There was no fight left in him. It was time to submit. Just let go. Stop trying. Then he heard a thumping. When he turned his head a slight bit, he saw the red heifer running toward him, moo-ing, its massive head lowered. As soon as it reached the skiff, it leaned over and bit into the middle part of the snake. A pop followed by a loud hiss sounded as the python deflated, like bubble wrap that had been punctured. The heifer chewed the python piece it had bitten off before dipping its head to bite off another. Blood dripped from its mouth. Its enormous tongue waggled the snake meat from one side to another. Chunk by chunk, it freed Vic from the death grip, until he could take shallow breaths.

The python reacted by roaring and thrashing. It twisted around, jamming its head into Vic's mouth, collapsing the top half of its body, now severed from the bottom half, to fit inside its host's chest. The heifer, catching on, grabbed the end of the top half of it—just before it disappeared inside of Vic—and yanked. It pulled hard as its hooves scraped the earth, leaving ruts, while the python lashed at the heifer with its tail.

"You have to help," the heifer said in a strained voice.

"How?"

"Vomit it out."

"I can't. It's wrapped around everything inside me."

"Grab its tail and pull."

Vic, who was lying face down, reached around his back, fishing for the tail. The python whipped back and forth, keeping it out of Vic's reach.

"It's not working."

"Just grab any part you can with both hands and twist."

By pushing his hands beneath his buckling torso, he could grab the part lying flat against his stomach. Using what little energy he had, he twisted the way he would a wet towel. The snake gave a muffled howl inside him, causing Vic's body to shudder and buckle harder.

"Keep it up. We're gaining."

The heifer had its eyes shut tight, its nostrils flared, and its teeth clenched with effort. Vic noticed the teeth were fanged, like a big cat's. He could feel his own fingernails growing into long claws, ripping at the snake's skin as he twisted.

It was a slow progress and a long struggle, but little by little Vic felt the snake being withdrawn from him, from his genitals and his intestines, through his lungs, esophagus, and throat. The heifer grunted, throwing itself into a backward cartwheel in one sudden motion, causing the python's head to burst from Vic's mouth, its upper half flying back toward the heifer. When the heifer regained its footing, it reared and came down on the writhing snake with both front hooves, crushing it. The dying creature gave a loud shriek, then lay limp. Its bottom half fell away.

"We did it," the heifer said, panting.

Vic took his first joyous, effortless inhalation.

"I couldn't have done it without you," he said.

He reached out with his hand, and the heifer reached out a hoof. They shook. Then the heifer turned and lumbered away. Vic fell asleep.

CHAPTER 24
THE CURE

When everyone awakened to find Vic cooking fish for breakfast, they were astonished, believing the red heifer mixture worked. The Rabbi claimed it was a coincidence, since experts had not investigated the heifer and proclaimed it pure according to Jewish law. And the group had not observed the ritual in the manner commanded by God in the Bible. And even if it was, it would not work on Vic because he was not an Israelite or Jewish.

Vic insisted the mixture did not cure him. The second red heifer did. He showed the group the piece of snake skin he clawed off while twisting its midsection, the ruts in the ground made when the heifer raked the earth while pulling the snake, and the welts on his back from the lashing of its tail. The snake had been enormous—a python-like reptile.

"There's a second red heifer? Penny, you were with Vic all night. Did you see it?" Brenner asked.

"I fell asleep after a while, so I saw nothing."

The Spreader who brought the bribe spoke up.

"When I was in the settlement, I asked if any of the heifers escaped. They said 'no'."

"It's possible there's a colony of heifers on this side of the island," Vic said. "You said there were red heifers on the settlement side when the Spreaders first arrived. There could have been some on both sides."

Penny bit her lip.

"What if the coincidence is that the red heifers on this side bred pure ones through natural selection instead of through the intentional breeding we practiced in the settlement? If there's an advantage to being all-red, the reddest cows would reproduce more often. Over time, the white and black hairs would disappear."

"What advantage does its color make?" A Spreader asked.

"I don't know. But if there's a colony, we should look for it," Penny said. "A family of pythons might be somewhere nearby, too."

"Pythons are in India, not America," Brenner said.

"If you're wrong, that's dangerous for the children," Azura said, her voice high with alarm.

"Hold on," Brenner said. "We need to determine what cured Vic — the mixture, a second heifer, or some unknown factor. Unless there's a second heifer, he just had a fever dream."

"Maybe he never had COVID."

"I took a test. It came out positive."

"There have been false positives," the Rabbi said.

"It looked like COVID to me — the fever, the cough, the shortness of breath," Penny said.

"I say we rule out the second red heifer. Then one of us can go to the mainland for an antigen test to eliminate the theory that Vic never had COVID. The only cure left would be the mixture," Brenner said.

There were murmurs leaning toward approval of the plan.

The Spreaders broke into parties of two, each taking a section of the non-settlement half of the island to cover. They would return in several hours with their results, while Azura's group waited, keeping a close eye on the children. Vic had the energy to join the search. It was as if he had never been ill. Meanwhile, the children, who had been confined to one large room in The Pure House, were discovering the pleasures of being outdoors, of bugs, getting dirty, climbing rock structures, running, wading in creeks, collecting berries. They stopped complaining about the loss of their privileges. Within a few days, they were enjoying the freedom of a natural childhood. If they were in danger, they would have to be confined again in the outcropping.

When the Spreaders returned without having sighted a colony of heifers, one girl — Daisy — who overheard, spoke up.

"I saw a cow over there," she said, pointing.

"Me, too," said Sandy.

"I saw it, too," said Noam.

"When?" Asked Azura.

"That time when they put Vic in the lake."

Everyone looked in the direction the girls had pointed. No animal was visible. They decided the children were just being imaginative. Constance rowed back to the mainland for a personal antigen test, sold over-the-counter in pharmacies. She returned with news of the extensive search for Azura and the girls, with many checkpoints and blocked roads.

The antigen test distinguished between outbreaks. Although this was the second time Vic seemed to be an active case, the test revealed the virus had infected him twice. He had COVID, not another illness.

"No one can explain his cure," the Rabbi said.

"I can. It's the mixture," Brenner said.

He asked to talk to Penny in private. They walked a little way into the field.

"If there's no second herd, the buckets of mixture are all that exists. They're priceless. But if there is a herd, it diminishes the value of what we have," he said.

"Your point?"

"We don't have to continue looking for a herd. No one but the children and Vic have seen the second red cow. But if the story of giant snakes spreads, no one will want to search. We should control what the authorities and the media are told."

"Hold on. We can prove Vic had COVID. We can't prove the mixture cured him."

"There's the dated positive personal test and the dated positive antigen test. We can prove he had a twenty-four-hour infection. That's unheard of. And we can give experts a sample of the mixture. Let them analyze it. They'll discover it works."

"Or not."

"You and I should hide the buckets from the others tonight. Then get the tests and the sample to the mainland. If we divide the profit into two, we'll get more than by dividing it into seven."

"If the bosses believe we have a cure, they'll swarm the island and find the buckets."

"Not if we bury them. We have a shovel. I say we take a chance."

"We'll get in trouble for hiding Azura and the girls."

"We didn't kidnap them. Constance and Vic may get in trouble, not us."

"We withheld information."

"When we make a deal, we determine the price and whether they can arrest us for anything. Think it over. But hurry. We have to move fast before one of the others beats us to it, or if they decide to just give the mixture away, keeping us stranded on this island, with nothing."

When Penny returned to the group, Molly spoke to her.

"I appreciate you looking after Vic while he was ill, but I'm carrying his baby. I'll be able to prove it with a paternity test after it's born. He's my boyfriend, and I want you and Azura to stay away from him."

"Shouldn't Vic decide that?" Penny asked.

"He's the love of my life, and the father of my child. If you break us up, I'll kill you."

The threat startled Penny. Then it angered her. How dare a Recovered, who would most likely miscarry, threaten her? The next thing would be a demand to split the money in more ways by including Vic and Molly. Brenner was right. The smaller the split, the more control they'd have. If the authorities knew Molly had changed places with Azura, they'd arrest her and Constance. It would solve a problem. Penny had half a mind to reveal this during the negotiations.

She told Brenner she would help him bury the buckets. That night, they slipped away, found a spot, and spent the hours before dawn digging another pit. They buried all the mixture except for one jarful. It would be the sample they would give to the experts on the mainland.

The next morning, there was consternation when the others discovered only one bucket next to the original pit.

"Where are the others?"

"This side of the island is strange—a second red heifer, a python, and now the disappearance of the buckets," Brenner said.

"We didn't find a herd or a nest of pythons. You took the buckets, Brenner."

The Spreaders fought among themselves. Some believed Brenner, and others guessed he had hidden the buckets. Two stomped off toward the hill, intending to tell the others in the settlement what happened, then changed their minds and came back. Constance told Molly to get into the skiff. They would sneak off to the mainland before things got ugly.

Molly refused.

"I belong with Vic. I'm staying here."

The Rabbi picked that moment to demand his freedom.

"You kidnapped me to supervise the red heifer ceremony. I did what you asked. It was your choice not to listen. My congregation, what's left of it, needs me. Take me back!"

He turned to Azura.

"You and your daughter should come with me. Only a few of our members remain alive. Our numbers need to be rebuilt or our people will disappear."

"What about Sandy and Daisy?"

"I can shelter them with you in the synagogue."

"I'll take all of you back if you promise not to reveal my role or Molly's in your escape, Azura," Constance said.

Brenner stepped forward, aiming the gun used to shoot the heifer at Constance.

"Hold on, there. No one's going anywhere."

"Let them go," Penny said.

"I'll take care of this. I've got the gun, and I'm in charge. Molly, Azura, Rabbi—take the girls back to the lean-to and wait there."

"I'll go with them," Vic said.

"No, you don't. You're needed for evidence," Brenner said.

"Of what?"

"Of the cure. The mixture cured you."

157

"The second heifer cured me."

"Shut the fuck up. I'm not interested. Tie him up, someone."

A Spreader used the rope that had lassoed the heifer to bind Vic.

"What about me?" Constance asked.

"You're going to the mainland, since you're not classified as a Spreader. I'm giving you a jar of the mixture and Vic's two tests. Tell them we have a COVID cure and want to negotiate. If they invade the island, they won't find the mixture. It's disappeared."

"Why should I?"

"Because Molly'll stay here, and I'll kill her if you don't."

"They'll arrest me."

"Make sure they don't if you want to see your daughter again."

He gave Constance the two tests and the jar. She headed for the skiff.

"I'm of no further use to you. Send me back with her. I'm just another mouth to feed here," the Rabbi said.

"He's a senior. What if you Spreaders make him ill?" Azura asked.

"We're all safer here than on the mainland because we have the mixture."

"*Pfft.*" The Rabbi turned away, exasperated.

For the second time in two days, Constance directed the skiff toward the mainland. If only she had not given the gun back to Brenner after killing the heifer. At least she knew which authority in The Pure House would listen to her report and alert the bosses. If they considered her sane. No one except the Rabbi was likely to have heard of the miracle of the red heifer. How was she to make anyone believe a pure red heifer, bred on the Spreaders Island in secret, without a single black or white hair, cured someone with COVID in one day? She cringed at the idea of handing over a jar of suspicious, muddy-looking liquid for the microbiologists to study. They might laugh at her and dump the mixture before locking her up and throwing away the key.

But she had to save her daughter and her unborn grandchild. She had to be convincing.

The mainland was in sight. Suddenly, she did not think she could row any further. She lay down in the skiff, exhausted. The coughing began. She might have been the only one glad to be infected. When the skiff drifted to the shore, she would find the energy to take a personal test, hoping it would be positive. The authorities would find her. She would drink a sip from the jar in front of them. The next day, when she was no longer symptomatic, she would take an antigen test.

They would believe her. If it worked.

CHAPTER 25
THE SNAKE

From the entrance to its tribal warren, the guardian of the snakes raised its upper half enough to see but not be seen. It was irate. The four-legged beast, with the help of the two-legged creature, had slain one of the guardian's numbers. It was a humiliation to be vanquished by a being with no permanent fangs and another without strength.

The one without strength had ten companions. There were also three young for the tribal hunters to pick off before attending to the adults. A wrap just below their heads would stop their breath. It was a mistake to wrap the midsection of the one without strength before its top, where the air entered. The murdered snake was dumb as a toad. It entered the top opening of the one without strength, leaving its own vulnerable bottom half at the mercy of the four-legged beast. The strategic thing would have been to overwhelm the four-legged one before tackling the weak one.

The guardian snake observed a female take a hollow tree and cross the lake. Why it did not slither below the water was a mystery. She would be seen. Perhaps she wanted to be seen. The weak ones could be puzzling. They did some things in secret, like burying treasures while the others slept, and other things where all could see, like killing and burning the four-legged beast without a thought of the consequences when the other beasts saw. But those beasts were docile, so it might not have mattered. Their red color made them easy targets. The female with the fire stick did not even have to chase it when its color made it unable to hide.

Now a male had the fire stick. It made him the boss of the others, the ones with the young near the big rock and the ones who lingered in the field, making their squeaks and grunts loud enough to be heard and not bothering to camouflage themselves, as if there were no predators — like the snakes themselves — in wait for them.

It was an achievement to breed four-legged creatures in a color that anyone could see from a distance. All it took was the disposal of any young whose outer layer was a mixed hue until only the mono-colored ones remained. They reproduced more young in the same shade as themselves. The hunters in the tribe had no trouble locating the herd, which stood out on the flatland of grass like snakes in fresh snow.

Some of the two-legged creatures had skin colors never seen before on the island, which they shed almost every day, with new skin growing in an instant. Then the old skin reappeared again. The guardian paid more attention to the faces, which ranged from dark to light. Their three young had just such a range. The lightest would be harder to locate on the flatland, and the darkest would be harder on the hill. The one with the middle tone might be a suitable compromise. If the hunters disposed of the light-faced creature and the dark-faced, the mid-toned one would remain alive to breed. He would have to report this to the bosses of the tribe. They would decide.

The guardian watched for several hours until the sun touched the top of the hill. Then there was an uproar among the creatures. They ran to the shore. A large hollowed-out log approached. The creatures on the shore raced away, while others of their kind emerged from the log, wearing skin the shiny color of fish, even on their faces.

The guardian guessed these mainland creatures were the enemies of the island creatures. Many had fire sticks, and they took the fire stick from the islander boss. The oldest male stepped forward with his arms raised. After many grunts, hoots, squeals, shakes of his head, they escorted him to the hollow log.

Next, the fish-colored ones untied the weak two-legged creature who had lain in the lake and took him, too, to the log. He remained silent. Meanwhile, without touching him, they surrounded the boss of the islanders. There appeared to be an intense communication, with much gesturing of the upper limbs and loud grunts. This lasted until the fish-colored ones took out light sticks — not the kind that were dangerous — and illuminated the area. As far as the guardian was able to guess, the islander wanted something from the fish-colored ones, and the fish-colored ones wanted something from the islander. Neither would give what the other wanted.

When there did not seem to be a resolution, the fish-colored ones took two females and the three young to the log. This would be disappointing to the tribal bosses if they wanted a two-legged herd bred to their specifications. Unless that was not what they wanted at all. The guardian never predicted the desires of the bosses.

When the log departed, almost all the remaining islanders crossed the field, heading for the hill. The island boss and one female stayed behind. The guardian did not hear their grunts. From their gestures, he guessed they also had a dispute. After a short time, they followed the others.

It would be unusual for two-legged creatures to inhabit the snake tribe's side of the island, although sometimes they visited. Their place was on the mainland and on the other side of the hill. The tribal bosses would have to come up with a plan if another invasion occurred interfering with the goals of the tribe. If no young existed to ensure continued propagation, there was no reason for the hunters to be cautious. They would wrap around any of the two-legged ones without fire sticks for the tribe's nourishment until they extinguished them or made them unwilling to return.

The red four-legged beasts provided a constant source of nutrition for the snakes. Depending on how many of the young they hunted, they could increase or decrease the herd. The two-legged creatures were unnecessary and even detrimental. Because of them, one of the herd of beasts was killed, and not for food, although the islanders ate part of its carcass.

For no purpose the guardian imagined, they burned the beast, mixed its ashes with water, and stored the solution in containers. The two who remained after the others left, buried them. Only the weak one drank the mixture, and it allowed him to be upright again, as was the habit of his kind.

CAROLYN GEDULD

Now that the islanders had left, the snakes would dig the treasure up and examine it to determine if it might be of some use. If it caused them to regrow the limbs that had been stolen from them, according to an old legend, for angering the god of the creatures, it would be priceless.

The guardian had seen where they buried the treasure. He drew his head back into the warren. The bosses would want his report right away.

CHAPTER 26
THE RADIOLOGIST

When his skin goose-bumped and his stomach flipped, he never understood if it meant excitement, anxiety, or nausea. With the infection rampant, he imagined he had contracted COVID, although he did not have the usual symptoms. But many had symptoms that were not ordinary. That was one of the insidious things about the virus—it imitated other viruses. What could be the beginning of COVID might be a mere head cold.

In time, he became less of an alarmist, waiting the required hours after the start of a suspicious symptom for a personal test to be effective and the seconds to see the result. Red—go at once to the active case unit on the outskirts of town. Green—carry on as is. Over a year ago, the test had turned red, and within hours, he felt sick as a dog wishing to be put out of its misery. After a few weeks lying on his stomach, which he barely remembered, his status changed to Recovered, and he moved into his new beehive quarters until they transferred him to The Pure House after he took the job as staff radiologist. He accepted a more restricted life serving the Pures for the honor of working in proximity to the bosses. He used this when meeting women.

"Boss Franklin spoke to me the other day. He said I was doing a terrific job. I said I just did my duty."

That was not the truth. He had seen none of the bosses in the building. Even during the last week, when the disappearances turned everything upside down, none of the bosses appeared in the medical wing. Like almost everyone else in town, the Radiologist watched Boss Franklin's speech on a device.

"Some of our priceless treasure, a pregnant Pure and three Pure children, have been stolen from under our noses. This is an affront not only to our town, but to humankind, since without Pures, our species won't survive. I promise you this..."

Boss Franklin pointed a finger at the camera. The Radiologist flinched, as if the finger pointed at him.

"We will find the four precious females and round up those who abducted them. When we do, we shall prosecute to the fullest extent of the law. In the meantime, because of the threat to our well-being posed by opportunistic outlaws, I asked our council to pass more proactive measures to keep our streets safe from both disease and criminals."

The Radiologist shuddered. He had been a hair's breadth from being one of those prosecuted to the fullest extent. Obstetrics caught the switch from a Pure's ultrasound to a Recovered's right away, and it was the acceptance of the Radiologist's plea of innocence—he ignored his patient's externals—that saved him. He had only half-lied. Azura's face did not interest him.

Now that the recaptured Pure was back in the building in the Preliminary wing, waiting overnight with the three children to see if the virus had infected any of them before being reassigned to their former quarters or to an active case unit, she became his patient again. He would administer the rapid COVID test, followed up by the slower-acting, more specific one. He would perform the ultrasound to check on the health of the fetus and do an amniocentesis, if it seemed at all compromised. The three children would be tested twice as well.

He wondered how much to tell the Pure and if the right time to tell her was now. Everyone was in an uproar. Constance and her daughter were under arrest, although rumor had it that the Bitch made a miraculous recovery from COVID, and because of that, they locked her in the research wing. A man who had been wherever she had been—no one knew where—was confined with her. Did Constance have a secret boyfriend? Her daughter was not so lucky. They imprisoned her. Martin was also under suspicion, but the Radiologist did not know why. The team was fractured. As guilty as he was, he was the only one of the three to emerge unscathed.

In the late afternoon, Martin escorted the four females to the medical wing. Noam and the girls huddled around Azura. The rapid test only required each of them to spit on the end of the testing pen, but the slow test needed a blood draw. The Radiologist was not a phlebotomist and had to poke each girl more than once to get the sample. He was irritated by the unnecessary screaming of the girls. It was not as if he hurt them. The Pure annoyed him with her questions.

"Must you do it again?" And "Do you have to be so rough?"

No, this was not the time to tell her anything. Down the road, when she was under his control, he would teach her not to question him. But now he had to be patient. After all, she seemed upset by her capture when it was her abduction that should have upset her. Why would she want to leave The Pure House, where they treated her like a queen?

His daydreams returned, more elaborate than before. If someone kidnapped her once, someone could kidnap her again. He imagined the dungeon he would lock her in, with shackles on the walls and a gag in her mouth. He did not want to hear her damn protests. It pleased him to think of all he could do to her. He might put a bag over her head, although he would miss seeing the terror in her eyes. In his custody, she would learn to be a slave instead of a queen. When he finished with her, she would no longer be a Pure or a Recovered. She would be a piece of trash buried in a dump.

Like many Recovereds, he hated the Pures. They were despised for their privileged existence, supported by workers and The Pure House staff, unsullied by disease, and favored by the bosses. They never gasped for breath, raged with fever, or wept from muscle cramps. They did not lose everything they had during transfers to and from active case units. They did not use up their energy after two hours of work. The mass of Recovereds were the second-class citizens of the COVID-35 age. Older white ones, like the Radiologist, who had survived the illness, remembered the advantages they used to have and resented a different demographic having them now, defined by health status.

Microbiologists searched for a vaccine and better treatments for active cases. They, too, were hampered by two-hour shifts, after which "brain fog" robbed them of the ability to concentrate. The Radiologist wondered if his fantasies meant he should have pursued a more creative profession, although Recovereds were seldom creative. Few artists arose from that group.

The next day, the Radiologist ran the blood tests through the automated analyzer and the results agreed with the rapid tests. Two girls were negative for the virus, but Azura and her daughter tested positive. The two Pure girls had to be separated right away and kept in the Preliminary unit until more testing determined whether COVID had spread to them. But if Azura and Noam did not develop symptoms by the following day, they would be classified as Spreaders. The Radiologist's heart skipped a beat. He would never realize his dream if the Pure, now no longer a Pure, left The Pure House.

And who was he kidding? He had no way of building a dungeon. And the Preliminary unit crawled with security. There would be no further abductions.

Later, he heard there was quite a scene when they separated the Pure girls. They had grown close to Azura, who acted like a second mother to them, and they carried on when Martin removed them from her. The third girl, Noam, had become like a sister to the other two, and she also fussed when they parted. He could only imagine the screaming if the girl's face was tattooed.

Soon after that, he received a text from Martin.

Bringing the former Pure to you for testing of her fetus. It's an order from the bosses. Suit up.

The Radiologist put on the silver Hazmat outfit, but put the gloves aside. The former Pure was going to be transported to Spreader's Island, no matter what the state of the fetus. He would never see her again. If he was going to act, it would be during this examination.

He grabbed a pen and paper and wrote in block letters without revealing his identity.

I SWITCHED THE PURE EJACULATE WITH MY OWN DURING THE INSEMINATION. YOUR BABY WILL BE MY OFFSPRING. NEVER TELL.

He folded the paper into a tiny cube and thrust it in his pocket, then put on the Hazmat gloves. Later he would transfer the cube to the former Pure's pocket. The gloves hid the trembling of his hands while he did the ultrasound. His demeanor was professional. He never spoke to the former Pure except to say the fetus looked good. She said nothing. No observer could tell what either felt. The Radiologist delivered his third secret message. By now, the former Pure should have figured out they all came from him. Surely.

During the vaginal ultrasound, the Radiologist lifted his face shield and inhaled. He committed the scent of her cunt to memory. Her scent was her signature. He would recognize it years from now, even if they blindfolded him. One day, maybe his nose would guide him to her.

The Spreaders inhabited half of Spreader's Island. According to the satellite images he consulted, the uninhabited half was prairie. What if they met there one day? He fantasized about different circumstances. He would trap her in a dungeon he would dig there. She would come to him of her own accord, begging to be his slave. They would become a family with the baby, if he figured out a way of getting rid of the older child.

They were harmless daydreams. He did not even have a way to get to the island or to get her a message to meet him there. He did not have the courage to do more than he did. The notes always put him at risk. Security might find a way of tracing the notes to him. Then what? He knew what. Prison. Worse, if security thought he switched the ejaculate. But if there was ever to be a chance for him to have the Pure for himself, the note would help convince her.

A case from the research lab arrived. They often asked him to run samples from them through the analyzer. A folded paper was tucked between the vials. This time, someone sent a message to him! Constance.

SAVE MY DAUGHTER. TELL THE AUTHORITIES YOU SWITCHED THE PURE EJACULATE MEANT FOR AZURA WITH YOUR OWN. THEN YOU GAVE MY DAUGHTER YOUR EJACULATE BEAUSE YOU ARE IN LOVE WITH HER. MY

DAUGHTER WILL BE HAVING A PURE BABY, NOT AZURA. THEY WILL FREE HER.

Constance did not reveal her name or Molly's. She wrote more on the other side.

IF YOU DON'T, YOU KNOW WHAT I'LL TELL THE AUTHORITIES.

The Radiologist was tempted to tear up the paper and burn it. Unknown to Constance, what she wrote about switching the ejaculate was what he had written to the Pure. Then he had an idea. If he could not have the former Pure, he might have Constance's daughter instead. Did it matter which woman came under his control? Constance could be persuaded to make all the arrangements—get Molly released, get her to agree to be his, find a means for them to live on the uninhabited part of the island.

In either case, if Constance told the authorities he showed too much interest in his patient's genitalia or if he escaped with Molly, his job in The Pure House was finished. He wrote a note to go back to the lab with the empty vials and his analysis. Mentioning no names, he laid out his terms.

He imagined his life with this new woman, Molly. Her baby would not be his. She was a Recovered, likely to miscarry anyway. He would make her his slave, if he could not have his first choice—Azura.

CHAPTER 27
THE SNAKE

There were many changes happening on the half of the island owned by the snakes, all of which the guardian observed.

Hollowed logs kept returning with two-legged creatures carrying digging instruments and strange devices that they swept over the ground. They came and went, swarming over the grasses. Unknown to them, a male and female hid in the little cave in the outcropping. They had arrived in the night, after the other mainlanders had gone for the day. The female had a bump in the middle. Either she had swallowed a small beast or she was about to lay eggs. Sometimes she tried to run away, and the male dragged her back. He wanted to dominate her, as males should, but she was strong-willed, refusing to obey him. Unlike the other mainlanders, they took up residence and stayed.

The male, too, had a digging instrument. When he did not gnaw away the grasses first, the instrument could not budge the earth. The guardian guessed he wished to make a hole in the ground for some obscure purpose, but had to give up. He threw the instrument in a show of exasperation, a foolish gesture if he did not want to be discovered.

The snake did not understand the motives of the male and female, who isolated themselves rather than live with their tribe. But the mainlanders hunted for the buried treasure. The mixture seemed of value to them because it cured the weak one. To the snakes, it was treasure because it contained the ashes of a four-legged beast. It had yet to cause legs to be regrown on the snakes who ingested some of it.

There was dissension between those who thought the potion had a purpose and those who thought it was junk. Time would tell.

The mainland creatures were problematic because they might discover the herd. Hunter snakes steered the herd away from the areas of two-legged concentration. But stray two-legged creatures roamed away from the others. They must be the scouts, looking for places to dig for the treasure.

Some creatures with silver skin climbed over the hill and returned with the one who was once the boss of the islanders. They bound his hands behind his back, and two silver creatures held each of his arms. The former boss led them to the exact place where he had buried the treasure. The silver ones pulled him back a short distance. Then others used their instruments to tear away the grass and dig. There was consternation when they found nothing. The former boss made grunting noises and shook his head. The silver-skinned ones were rough with him, knocking him down. They all made loud, snarling sounds. Finally, they took the former boss back up the hill.

Those who remained stood on their back legs close together and made softer noises. They appeared to be conferring. The guardian guessed they discussed what to do next, where to dig, whether to stay or leave. They did not see the male and female peeking out at them from time to time, perhaps to see if they had left the area. The two must have broken some creature law to stay hidden like that.

The bosses of the tribe would soon announce their plan for ridding their domain of all two-legged creatures. It was not acceptable for them to be acting like they owned the place and for any to take up residence. And it would be a disaster if their devices discovered the tribe's underground warren. Who knew what would happen if the creatures found an entrance? Would they use their fire sticks to commit genocide?

The guardian heard what the bosses planned. Hunters would find creatures who strayed off by themselves. When a creature sat or lay down, as they sometimes did to rest, a hunter would attack, wrapping itself around the limbs and torso of its victim. Another snake winding itself around a leg would trip any who did not sit.

When the others saw that any of their fellows were missing, they would search and find the crushed carcass. They would not know what happened or how. Perhaps that would scare them off.

First, the hunters would go after the hidden male and female residents. The plan was elegant in its simplicity. The guardian stretched its head toward the sun with pleasure.

CHAPTER 28
AZURA

Spreaders Island had none of the luxuries of The Pure House, yet Azura would have freedom she had not experienced since leaving the forest. Penny met her and Noam on the shore and showed them around, after the officers — in Hazmat suits — transported them across the lake.

Her face was tattooed and her identity card had been stamped "Spreader." Noam, the first child Spreader, had her face striped with indelible marker. Tattooing would wait until she was older.

"There's beehive housing for twelve. That's all the bosses thought they would need. Counting you and your daughter, there'll be thirty-five of us. The mainland delivers materials for housing, but we have to do the construction ourselves."

Attached to the small beehive was a crudely built addition, used as a dormitory. The atmosphere was more relaxed than on the mainland. There were no Hazmat suits, no masks, no personal tests, no one coughing or needing long naps. Everyone seemed healthy and energetic.

"They call us Spreaders. As you can see, none of us are ill. We are the real Pures," Penny said.

"Where are the children?" Noam asked, standing close to her mother.

Penny squatted down.

"Guess what? You're the only child here. That makes you very special."

Azura's brow knitted.

"None of the women on the island can conceive. And we don't use birth control. That's another thing we hope a pure red heifer will do for us. Solve fertility problems."

Penny addressed Noam again.

"Want to see the cows?"

She led the newcomers past the residential area to a field. The settlement was as flat as the landscape on the uninhabited part of the island. Crops grew in this area.

"We raise as much of our own food as possible. Goods we can't produce ourselves come from the mainland."

Past the crops was a large enclosure. Several red cows were inside.

"Those are not pure. They have black or white hairs growing among the red. You may not see them from here. That's because they are ninety-eight percent red. We're getting close to a hundred percent. The bulls are in their own enclosures over there."

Penny pointed.

After the tour, Penny led them to the communal dining hall and kitchen built onto the beehive. The Spreaders removed one wall so the entire population, three times the expected size, could fit and dine together. Azura knew some residents — Penny, Brenner, and the others who had visited the uninhabited side. Those who they had not met introduced themselves. Noam was the center of attention.

"We don't have a school, but we have plenty of teachers," Brenner said.

"You can bunk next to me. We'll rearrange the cots so there'll be space for yours and Noam's," Penny said.

Later that night, after Noam was asleep, Penny said she had a secret.

"When Vic was ill, and we gave him the mixture, I drank some, too. It may not be like a vaccine, but it seems to be like a treatment."

She did not say she drank it just before she and Brenner buried the buckets.

"I missed my period. We don't have pregnancy tests here, but I sent to the mainland for one."

"Is Vic the father?"

"Vic? No, no. Vic's attractive, but nothing happened between us. The father's Brenner. He drank some, too, so his sperm count normalized. We're relaxed about sex, here. The women have synchronized menstrual cycles, and we hook up with whoever during ovulation. That's what we've noticed about our little colony. The women get interested in the middle of our cycle. The men, well, they're men. They're always turned on. I expect you'll synchronize with us in a few months. Nature will take care of it."

"Doesn't the fact that all the women here have fertility problems mean there is something wrong with their health?" Azura asked.

"It's more likely because of stress. They captured all of us, accused us of infecting others, marked our faces, and transported us here against our will. Then we had to learn to be self-sufficient after they supplied all our needs on the mainland. We lost jobs, careers, relationships, family. We think of ourselves as political prisoners who the bosses scapegoated because they want someone to be blamed for COVD, so they won't be. No wonder we have psychological problems affecting fertility."

Her argument seemed convincing. Azura worried that the stress would affect her pregnancy.

"You have a secret. Everyone knows about my pregnancy. But I've been under stress, too. I'm scared I'll miscarry."

Azura had not yet found the note. She reached into her pocket while undressing. The folded cube of paper was inside.

"What's that?"

"Another note. Someone has sent me several this way."

"What does it say?"

She stared at the block letters.

"Oh, no," she whispered.

Penny grabbed the paper and read it.

"Who wrote this!"

"It had to be the Radiologist. He was the only one who had the opportunity."

"The Radiologist at The Pure House?"

"Yes. He had access to my outfit during the exam. And to the semen."

Azura shivered. She had given little thought to the father of her baby, except for vague imaginings of a perfect Pure male, the kind who would be on a Romance novel cover. Sometimes, he resembled Vic, although she would not confess this to Penny. But the Radiologist! He was an old, fat pervert, who sniffed at her genitals while examining her. He disgusted her. And now she was having his baby?

"Get it out. Get it out."

Noam stirred. "Mommy?"

"Take it easy. There's no one here who can perform an abortion. You're in shock. Get some sleep, and see how you feel in the morning."

Azura did not sleep. What happened to her was a kind of rape. They coerced her into becoming pregnant, not permitted to choose her partner, and tricked into having the child of a man she detested. Now they forced her to live on an island with no possibility of the life she dreamed of when she left the forest. Not for Noam or her unborn daughter, either. Not even a school or other children to grow up with. Just the stupid red cow project. That's what her daughters would inherit — a bunch of cows.

How would she be able to love the baby growing inside her, against her will? The unwanted, ugly child of the Radiologist. Penny might have the baby of handsome Brenner. Noam resulted from a romantic night with Larry. An older, attractive man. No one to be ashamed of. She would give her unborn daughter to a woman on the island who could not conceive one of her own, who wanted a baby. Any baby.

But how could she not love the baby growing inside her? Half of her was Azura. Until now, she had loved her more than she loved herself. There was no turning off a bond that was already operating or to split her feeling into love and hate, although they were alternating at the moment.

She wept in Penny's arms. Her tears and anger were for all that had happened since she came to town, to The Pure House, and to both sides of Spreader's Island. Then she wept for all that had happened before that — the death of her mother, great grandmother, and her friends living in the forest, for the drought that was killing the forest, for the dust that choked the town, for the pandemics that were driving humans to extinction. Then, exhausted, she finally slept.

Her thoughts seemed to continue in her sleep. She knew she had a responsibility to humankind since she had conceived. She was a hope against extinction. But would extinction be bad or good? It would be bad for humans. Maybe it would be good for the forest and the planet. Or it might not matter. It depended. For Rabbi Sam, losing the Jewish people mattered. For others, losing whatever people they belonged to mattered. For the bosses, the town mattered. Unless it mattered just to serve them, unseen on the top floor of The Pure House.

What mattered to her was Noam and, if she got over the facts of her conception, her other, unborn daughter. She wanted her children with her, not separated from her while she endured endless pregnancies. That's what the bosses got wrong. Girls do not thrive if they lose their mothers, if they are raised without boys or fathers, if they are secluded and given toys instead of school and diverse playmates. Noam was becoming a spoiled brat before Azura had her abducted. Now, all the sudden changes confused her. But Azura had hope for her.

A figure floated into her sleep so covered in dust she did not see its face.

"Your baby is pure," it said.

"Who are you?" She asked.

"The red heifer."

It stood up on its two hind legs and morphed into the shape of a man. Although he was still dust-covered, she could tell it was Vic.

"Wait for me," he said, before disappearing into the dust.

When she awoke, a white film covered everything.

"It's from the mainland," Penny said. "When there is a wind blowing toward the island, it carries dust across the lake."

"I thought it was a dream."

"I don't like it, Mommy. It's icky. It was cleaner in The Pure House."

"There are superior HEPA-filters where the bosses live," Penny said.

"What should we do?"

"Wait for the wind to die down, then wash everything and ourselves," Penny said, coughing.

"This is awful." Azura tried whisking the dust off of her skin and Noam's, but more seemed to collect.

"We'd be lucky to be on this island if they did not force us to be. People in town live with dust all the time. It only coats the island now and again."

Noam stood up and stamped her foot.

"Take me back!"

"I can't do that."

"Why not?" She stamped again.

"The bosses won't let us back. We're Spreaders."

Noam raised her voice.

"I'm not a Spreader. I'm a Pure."

"Control your child. The others will expect that," Penny said.

"Noam, you sit down right now and behave, or no breakfast."

"I don't care. The food here is yucky food."

"We'll see what you say if I don't give you any. Remember the forest where you didn't have any food? That's what it will be like if you don't eat breakfast."

Noam sat down, twisting her lips into a scowl and flaring her nose, sulking for the benefit of her mother and host. The adults paid no attention.

"What will you do if you're pregnant?" Azura asked.

"Celebrate... and worry."

"Why worry?"

"There are no medical services here. We've rejected them to prove we're healthy. There's no one who knows how to deliver a baby. There's nothing set up—no diapers, no infant clothes."

"When we were on the other side of the island, the three girls did fine. As for childbirth, we'll have to help each other or send for someone in a Hazmat suit."

"Ha! Like the Radiologist?"

"Ugh. We'll do it ourselves."

"That's the island spirit."

Both women laughed, although their worries continued. Neither knew that the Radiologist and Molly were just over the hill and in great danger.

During the day, while Penny helped Azura decide what chores to do, Azura thought about Vic. He was an outrageous flirt, but she missed him. There was some significance in his appearing in her dream. He had said the baby is pure. That helped her accept it again, somewhat. The Radiologist had no claim on her or her baby. Her baby. Like many fathers, the Radiologist played a minor part. He contributed a single cell. She would contribute her body, her care, her years of nurturance. It would be hard work believing in the baby's purity, quelling the waves of revulsion whenever she thought of how it was created.

At that very moment, another pregnant woman, in a state of exhaustion and hysteria, was dragging herself over the hill, heading through the pines toward the settlement. That she had conceived without miscarrying was a rarity. She was a Recovered, about to endanger herself and her unborn child by coming into contact with Spreaders. She had no other choice.

CHAPTER 29
DYBBUK

Molly ripped off a sleeve and wound it around her nose and mouth as a mask. Then she made her way down the hill, grasping saplings and low branches to steady herself. The climb uphill had been draining for a Recovered. Downhill brought the fear of tumbling, falling, miscarrying. The image of the Radiologist kept flashing before her eyes.

By the time she dragged herself into the settlement, her panting breath had turned into sobs. She sank to her knees as members rushed toward her.

"Not too close," she gasped. "I'm a Recovered. I'm expecting."

She stretched out her arm, palm outward, in the universal signal for "Stop!"

The crowd halted. Brenner took a half-step forward.

"Who are you? What brings you here?"

"My name is Molly. The Radiologist from The Pure House brought me to the other side. I was kind of kidnapped by him. We set up camp there."

She paused, letting out a few sobs.

"This morning, I left our lean-to in order to fetch water, and when I returned…."

Everyone waited in silence, giving her time.

"He lay where I left him, but, like, crushed, as if a big truck — a semi or a bus — ran over him."

"Crushed?" Brenner asked. His puzzled eyes stared at her.

"I don't know how else to describe it. His chest was caved in, and there was blood, and... and...."

Unable to finish, she collapsed further and wept.

"Did a stone fall on him?" Someone asked.

Molly shook her head.

Azura spoke up.

"I know her. She's the daughter of Constance, a woman who worked in The Pure House until she became an active case. From what I heard, they locked Constance in the research lab, where she is being studied with another person, Vic. They both regained their health overnight."

"Vic is the father of my child," Molly gasped out.

"So she says," Penny murmured.

"My mother made an arrangement with the Radiologist to get me out of prison. It's a long story."

"Vic spent time on the other side of the island with Azura and Ncam. We were with him when he became infected," Brenner said, leaving out the part about red heifer concoction that cured him. "The authorities came and took Vic away. They almost arrested me, but did not want a so-called Spreader on the mainland."

He turned to the others.

"We need a party to go over the hill to see what happened to the Radiologist."

Five volunteers, all men, stepped forward.

"If you own something that can be used as a weapon, bring it."

They directed Molly to an empty shack several feet away from the communal dorm. Brenner led the five armed men toward the hill. Three hours later, they were on the other side of the island, standing in a circle above the Radiologist.

"What did that to him?" Group members asked.

There was nothing in the lean-to that could account for such devastation. Everything else — lantern, clothing, bedding — was undisturbed. The hairs on the back of Brenner's neck rose. Nothing he imagined offered an explanation.

"Let's separate and look around. Meet back here in an hour."

Sixty minutes later, Brenner and four men gathered at the lean-to.

"Where's Alf?"

They waited another half hour for the fifth man.

"This time, let's stay together and find him. He can't be far."

They walked in a widening circle, calling his name, looking for a sign that someone had passed through the prairie grass—broken or bent stems, trodden areas. The day was warm and hazy. Tiny dust particles from the mainland floated in the air. The men rubbed their eyes and coughed. They gripped their tools and knives.

"Where is he?"

"If he's standing, we should be able to see him."

"How could anyone just disappear?"

"It's like the heifer mixture. It disappeared, too."

"Do you think he went back over the hill?"

They kept walking, circling the lean-to at increasing distances, now in silence, each of them contemplating the mystery, no one admitting being shaken. They suspected they would find him in the same state as the Radiologist, but no one wanted to say so aloud. As long as they did not say it or find him, it was not true. He might be okay, playing a prank or lost or have fallen asleep.

Something red flickered in Brenner's peripheral vision.

"What's that?"

Everyone stopped and stood still. Brenner held his hand palm outward, as Molly had done hours earlier.

"Quiet!"

They all stood there, listening. They heard no sound. Perhaps the dust muffled any noise.

"Did any of you see something? Something reddish?" Brenner asked.

No one had.

"Let's spread out a little, keeping each other in sight."

They distanced about ten feet apart, each still visible in the haze, and continued searching.

"Alf! Alf!"

Penny texted Brenner.

Where R U? R U safe?

Alf gone, like the mixture. Spooky. Thought I saw something red.

Vic said there was a 2nd red heifer.

What ran through Brenner's mind was that he might have sighted the one they did not catch. If it was pure, they could make another mixture and hide it more carefully the next time. He would not tell the others. They needed to focus on finding Alf. Did a heifer harm him? Stomp on him? Those raised in the settlement were not aggressive. But they weighed hundreds of pounds. Accidents happen.

One of the men yelled. Brenner and the others raced to him.

"Look at the ground."

Something had flattened the grass, as if an object had been dragged through it, creating a pathway. The men followed. At the end of several yards, they found Alf in the same condition as the Radiologist. His chest and neck were crushed, as if a boulder had fallen on him. But there was no boulder, nothing nearby that would even break a fingernail.

Everyone was shaken, again. A couple vomited.

"What should we do?"

Brenner needed to restore calm.

"Bury them. There's a shovel near the lean-to."

The labor of digging two graves would keep the men from engaging in useless speculation, although Brenner could not control everyone's imagination. Demons lived on the island. Or aliens. They would pick them off one by one. Alf was either taken by surprise with no time to yell or whatever crushed him covered his mouth. What happened on this half of the island might happen on the settlement half. The important thing now was to stick together. Something crushed the two men when they were alone.

None of this would have happened if the bosses had not banished the so-called Spreaders to the island. Before COVID-35, the entire island was uninhabited except for birds, snakes, and rabbits. Now, something or someone murdered two people and stole the buried buckets of the mixture. This was not lost on any of them. After they buried the two bodies, the men voiced their fears.

"The bosses did this. They want to eliminate Spreaders. They have always scapegoated us."

"If we're the targets, what about the Radiologist? He's a Recovered?"

"That's just a cover-up."

"We should've reported the deaths. They'll blame us."

"You think there'd be an investigation? The mainlanders are too scared of being infected. They'd ignore us."

"If we're all murdered, they'd be pleased."

Brenner spoke.

"Let's put aside the motive for the murders and try to figure out how Alf and the Radiologist died."

There was a momentary silence.

"Some kind of death ray from the mainland?"

"A ray couldn't crush someone like that."

No one came up with an answer.

"When Penny and I were here with Azura and her daughter, Vic — the man who brought them over — was infected. He claimed a red heifer saved him. No one else saw it. I say we search for it. I don't know if it exists or how it connects to the murders, but I have a hunch there is a connection."

There was more discussion of where and how to look. No one objected. They would go as a group for their own protection. It was mid-afternoon. In an hour, they would have to start up the hill. No one wanted to spend the night on this side.

The search did not turn up any cattle. Back in the settlement, the men told the others what happened. Brenner called a meeting, and everyone gathered in the dining hall. Murmurs of shock and panic came with the account of the strange things that happened over the hill.

"We must come up with a way to defend ourselves," Brenner said.

"We need more guns from the mainland."

"Or a wall. Let's build a fortress around our settlement."

"A fence with barbed wire."

"Unless it's supernatural. You can't fight the supernatural."

"Post guards. A sentry at night."

The discussion continued, filled with wild ideas, until reality set in. They had no funds for weapons. The authorities only delivered necessities from the mainland, and they decided what the necessities were. There were no resources to build a fortress or to fence in the settlement. If they took turns guarding at night, it was the best they could do. The group decided there should be two sentries. Everyone would have a turn once every two weeks. They drew up a list and gave the only gun to the first two. Everyone else rushed to the sleeping quarters, feeling ill at ease, hoping nothing would invade from the other side.

Penny and Azura talked after Noam fell asleep.

"I'm worried about my daughter. I'll never forgive myself if she's harmed."

"Me, too. And I don't even know if I'm pregnant for sure."

"The three of us — you and I and Molly — should figure out how to get off the island."

"We'd have to go over the hill. The skiffs are hidden on the other side. If they're still there."

"At least one should be, I think."

"That would be dangerous. Something's evil over the hill. Anyway, what would we do on the mainland? If we're caught, they'll send us back. Anyone could recognize us with our facial tattoos.

"We'll figure that out later. Has anyone ever escaped?"

"We so-called Spreaders visit sometimes, wearing heavy make-up. Connections there get us things the authorities won't let us have."

"Like what?"

"Weed. Alcohol. Devices. But not to escape. There is nothing on the mainland for us. It would be different if they treated us like the Pures we are. Instead, we're shunned. We'd have no way to support ourselves."

They fell into a light sleep, startling awake with each night's noise. Azura remembered her mother telling her the tales her great grandmother told about *dybbuks*, evil spirits who possess the living. She and her mother regarded these as superstitions. But red heifer cures, disappearing buried buckets, and the crushing of the Radiologist and Alf would have seemed like superstitions, too — except they happened. Maybe *dybbuks* inhabited the other side of the hill.

There was no reason to think they were the *dybbuks* that Yiddish-speaking Jews of the nineteenth-century and before believed in. But some sort of evil thing was doing these strange and terrible things. Azura would call them *dybbuk*s as a kind of short-hand for whatever they were.

On the other hand, not every unexplained thing was evil. The mixture cured Vic and Constance. Penny's fertility problems may have been resolved. The red heifer mixture seemed ridiculous to her and Rabbi Sam, not like the way high priests rid the community of contamination in the Bible, but despite all the compromises, it worked. Was every gift accompanied by a sacrifice? Did every good have an evil counterpart? Or was that more superstition?

Azura had the disturbing sense that she would soon find out.

CHAPTER 30
THE INVASION

The next morning, the discovery of a sentry crushed to death horrified everyone. Azura held her hands over Noam's eyes, whispering "*Dybbuk*" under her breath.

"What did you say?" Penny asked.

"Nothing. I'm taking Noam back inside. I don't want her to see.'

Brenner ordered everyone to look around. Something had also crushed a heifer—not a pure one. It strayed to the far side of the pen, away from the other cattle. They found a hole in the fencing about a foot in height and unusual markings on the ground—wide stripes or slithers, such as snakes make. Smudges lay along both sides of the markings, like footprints or stumps without toes. If there had been toes, the Spreaders would have imagined an alligator, although they were too far north for that reptile. And alligators don't have stumps without webbed toes.

Unease heightened to panic in the settlement. COVID had been frightening, even though they thought they had immunity. It was a virus, and everyone knew more or less how viruses worked. People caught them from each other, either from contaminated air or from contaminated surfaces. The symptoms, like fevers and coughs, were recognized. Active cases could not function until the virus ran its course. Some died; most did not.

But these crushing deaths were foreign to the Spreaders, who suspected a connection between the markings and the killings. What made the marks? Some kind of large reptile? But no one had observed a reptile bigger than a garter snake on the island or on the mainland, as far as the authorities had made public.

Azura had a plan, which she revealed to Penny.

"Tonight, the four of us — you, I, Molly, and Noam — should sneak out and head for the other side. We'll take a skiff to the mainland, where we'll be safe. I've traveled in darkness before when I left the forest. I can lead the way. We'll all have to wear masks for the sake of Molly, even if you don't think it's necessary, Penny."

"But..."

"Masks or we don't go."

Azura glared at Penny, daring her to refuse.

"Not a word. If the others knew about the skiffs, they'd all run over the hill. I will not risk Noam being left behind. Our newborns might be in danger, too, when we deliver them."

"I'll tell Molly. Maybe it's crazy to go at night when whatever monster out there could catch us."

"As if we're less vulnerable in daylight. Anything strong enough to crush a heifer is strong enough to overpower us, day or night."

"That's not an encouraging thought."

"My plan is better than waiting here to be picked off."

"That's true."

Despite her brave talk, Azura shivered. Penny's coloring paled to near-white with a greenish undertone.

"Wear good shoes. Pack a few things. Take matches, a flashlight, a knife, and food. Although we'll try not to use the flashlights until we're in the skiff. We don't want to awaken anything."

Through the day, Brenner worked to keep the Spreaders calm by giving them tasks. Whatever could be used as a weapon was collected. Scouts were sent in a group to find more markings. Cattle were counted and recounted. The fence was repaired. A grave was dug for the sentry. The dead heifer was dragged away. Plans were made for the entire colony to stay together at all times.

The three women whispered about their escape plan whenever their paths crossed. The Spreaders would slumber lightly, if at all. Azura would pretend to feel ill around midnight, and the two other women would help her get to the small sick bay — a separate hut. They would take Noam with them to keep her from crying and disturbing others. Their packs would be hidden outside earlier in the day.

Once outside, they would head away from the sick bay and up the hill. They hoped no one from the settlement would follow them. Fear of whatever might be out there might keep the others inside.

At midnight, Azura moaned.

"Is she going into premature labor?" Someone asked.

"Molly and I will take care of her. It might be false labor," Penny said.

Penny took Azura's arm while Molly carried the sleeping Noam. Azura bent and staggered as if in pain. Once outside, she straightened. Noam awakened.

"I can't carry you or put you on my back. You're a big girl now. You can walk with the grown-ups."

Noam rubbed her eyes without crying or protesting. She held Azura's hand while the three masked women walked across the field toward the hill. The moon lit their way. The easy part stopped when they came to the first sapling as the ground rose, the beginning of the hill.

"I brought a rope," Penny said. "If we tie ourselves together around our waists, none of us will get lost."

Azura would take the lead, with Molly in the middle, and Penny in the rear. As the trees thickened, it became darker. The moon seldom penetrated.

"We'll have to use a flashlight. Just one. Mine," Azura said.

As they climbed, their apprehension increased. What if the monster that crushed the Radiologist and Alf saw or heard them? The sound of their footsteps and their panting breath seemed loud enough to attract it. Azura tightened her grip on Noam, who dragged, slowing them down.

"We'll have to take turns carrying her. It's easier if she rides on our backs," Azura whispered.

She squatted, and the girl climbed over the rope and onto her, just as she had when they left the forest. That was before her mother's pregnancy. Now Azura carried one daughter in front and another behind.

If only Vic showed up to help carry the child, as he had the other times she escaped with him. Where was he now? She scolded herself for thinking about him. He was nothing to her. Molly was having his child. They belonged together. She must put him out of her mind for good. But it was useless telling herself what she should or should not imagine. Her mind flew to a place of terror of the *dybbuk* or to a place of desire for Vic. As much as she tried to steer her thoughts in another direction—to the past or the future—some force took them where it wanted her to go. Unwelcome thoughts of the *dybbuk* stopped her in her tracks. She would have to settle for thoughts of Vic. Flirtatious Vic.

Her years in the forest taught her sure-footedness. The other two women had no such skill. They stumbled along, sometimes falling with a tiny shriek or a gasp, alerting anything nearby of their presence. Unseen beings scooted away, possums or raccoons. Azura whispered reassuring words. She knew the typical night sounds of the woods. She heard nothing unusual. Still, she had goosebumps.

If the *dybbuk* caught them and tried to crush them, the other two would have to fight it before it's squeezing killed them and the babies in their wombs. They had stolen kitchen knives for defense, the only weapons they had.

As they neared the top of the hill, a couple of hours into their journey, Molly began to cry.

"I can't go on. I'm too tired. Noam's too heavy for me to carry. We should have stayed in the settlement. I'm so scared."

Although Penny and Azura did not complain, they, too, were spent.

"We'll have to camp here and try to get some sleep. At least rest. We can continue to the other side at daylight," Azura said.

Feeling the space on the ground with sweeps of their hands, the women lay down, still tied together. They encircled the sleeping child. Molly's soft weeping kept the others awake. They remained too frightened and too uncomfortable to sleep, anyway.

How Azura missed the luxurious beds in The Pure House, even the rougher mat in the settlement. In her time in the forest, she made comfortable nests with leaves and grasses. The hard, uneven ground beneath her now would have prevented sleep if she had not been so exhausted and cold. She finally fell into a light doze.

In a dream, Vic came to her, although she could not see him in the dark. The noise of the breeze became his words, whispered into her ear.

"I'm the father of your baby. The Radiologist lied."

She laughed. What a joy to discover the baby's true father. It was the second time Vic came to her in a dream to reassure her about her baby.

"Will you stay with me?" She asked.

"Forever," he said.

The sky lit up. But, no, it was a giant TV, suspended overhead. A zigzag pattern appeared, then some static, which cleared after a few seconds. An enormous head revealed itself. It was Boss Franklyn. He looked straight at her with knowing eyes.

"All the children of the Pures come from me. I am the father of your baby," he said.

He smiled and clapped his hands, as if enjoying a performance. The clapping became louder, morphing into a sound like thunder.

Penny shook her.

"Wake up!"

She opened her eyes. It was light. The clapping noise continued. Then she realized what it was. A herd of red cows surrounded them, stomping with their hooves, a sound she mistook for clapping. Their mooing had the same tone as Boss Franklyn's speech in her dream.

Noam awoke and pointed. The cows formed a protective ring around them, lowering their kind heads to gaze at the child.

"Can I pet them?" Noam asked.

"The ones at the settlement enjoyed petting," Penny said.

Noam reached out a hesitant hand and stroked one on the side of its head.

"These must be from the unsettled side of the island. We know there were at least two heifers there. It seems there are several more. And they look pretty close to pure red, closer than any of ours."

"Who takes care of them?" Molly asked.

"Cattle are domesticated. But I guess they could survive on the grass at the bottom of the hill," Penny said. "I don't know. Brenner takes charge of animal care in the settlement, not me."

"Would it be crazy to think the cows guarded us from the *dyb*..., the monster?" Azura asked.

"Even if they were that smart, why should they?" Penny asked.

Azura had no answer. She thought of her father's hallucinogenic rites. He believed in communication with animals. Perhaps he was right.

The women got to their feet, and the cows lumbered to a pathway, turning their bobbing heads to see if the women followed. They crested the hill and led the women to a spring of fresh water, letting the humans drink first. Then they took the lead again, winding their way down the hill. The women grasped saplings as they descended to avoid slipping. Noam scampered ahead with her new "friends."

When they reached the field, the cattle appeared to lose interest in the women, busying themselves with grazing, then dispersing. The women were on their own again. They were less frightened in the daylight, although still not at ease. But they could scan the area for danger. They removed the rope from their waists and left it in the field. If anything came after them, they would scatter, each in a different direction. That was the new plan.

They were hungry, but stopping to eat was unsafe. They gave Noam bread to eat while they made their way to the lake. While they searched, they stayed together. At last, they found a skiff. It took all three women to push it off the shore.

As the skiff drifted away from the island, the women relaxed. Molly and Penny handled the oars while Azura sat in front with Noam. They all turned to give the island anxious looks, dreading the sight of something swimming after them. No monster could be seen. Ahead of them lay another kind of danger — the mainland. If they were caught escaping from Spreaders Island, they would be arrested and sent back. The skiff would be destroyed. Somehow, they had to dock unseen. Then figure out how to survive.

CHAPTER 31
THE MAINLAND

The further they rowed from the island, the more obscure the mainland became. It was as if they encountered a thick fog.

"It's a dust storm," Penny said.

Now the masks protected them from both the virus, the visibility of Azura and Penny's tattoos, and the sooty air. Their eyes teared from irritation.

"This is a bad day. The dust count must be higher than usual," Penny said.

"It may hide us from the authorities," Molly said.

They rowed on in silence until Azura told the others about her dream, omitting the part about Vic.

"Last night I dreamed that Boss Franklyn said he was the father of my baby."

"I wouldn't put it past any of the bosses to have that kind of ego."

"That's not how it works, according to my mother. There were only a few male Pures, and the authorities froze their semen. It's said they escaped or became infected and died. The semen they left behind is still being used to impregnate Pure women," Molly said.

"I hope you're right," Azura said.

"Of course, Vic is the father of mine. I'm sure. Will you both help me find him? He's my soul-mate."

"He might be locked in a research lab, like your mother, while they try to find out what cured him," Penny said. "But I have news. The pregnancy test arrived yesterday. It's positive."

"You're just like us, now," Molly said.

As the fog became denser, they became disoriented and had to stop rowing. The mainland might have been in any direction. They drifted in the current, hoping they would not land back on the island.

"I still have my Recovered identification card," Molly said. "It won't be a problem for me to return to my cell. I could even squeeze you all in if you weren't Spreaders."

"We can't infect you," Penny said in an exasperated tone.

"I can't take the chance. We'd be in close quarters, in each other's faces. I have my baby to consider."

"Why don't you go to your cell, and Penny and I will go somewhere else? If the authorities spotted us, they'll look for three women and a child. It'll be safer with two," Azura said.

"But I'll need you to help find Vic."

"We'll send him to you if we find him."

Just then, there was a bump. The skiff docked on the mainland or back on the island. Sounds of traffic told them which. After helping to pull the skiff onto the bank, Molly took off, walking toward the noise of honking as vehicles navigated the fog. Visibility was only a few feet.

"If we can find our way to The Pure House and sneak in, my dad can help us," Penny said.

"Martin?"

"Yes. Martin. My dad."

After giving Noam the last of the food, Azura hoisted her onto her back. They began walking. Whenever they encountered someone, they lowered their heads and asked them to point toward the river. Some were not sure. They were lost in the fog, too. Others seemed to know. If there was an alert for them, the masks hid their identities. No one asked for their cards or their names. The officers they passed were too busy preventing looting to bother with them. Brenner might not have reported them missing.

Everywhere, people commented on the dust.

"Hasn't been this bad since '36."

"I'm looking for Beehive 457. Am I near it?"

"Is public transport running?"

When they heard running water, the women knew they had reached the river. Finding the bridge the next task. They slid their hands along rail lining the edge of the river walk until they came to an opening. Guards wearing face shields stopped them without asking for their identification cards, perhaps because the dust coated the shields, making reading difficult. They did ask what their business they had in The Pure House.

"We're staff," Azura said.

"Is that a child?" A guard asked.

"I found her wandering around. She has to be from The Pure House. I'm bringing her back."

The guard accepted her astonishing story and waved them through. The bridge and the park leading to The Pure House were equipped with fog lights, making it easier to navigate. Azura led Penny to the staff entrance.

People came and went, covering their faces with masks and scarves. Another guard stationed there let everyone through without comment. They relaxed rules in the storm. Inside the staff entrance was the bottom of the same staircase Azura had used before. People stared at Noam, but no one questioned them.

"I'll text my father," Penny said.

The reply came after a few seconds.

U here? Wait for me in my cell. #286. Code to unlock is 4431.

He did not realize he would find Azura and Noam with Penny when he returned from his shift.

Bring make up, food and drink. Lots. Haven't eaten since yesterday, Penny texted. *And BTW, I'm pregnant. See? I'm no Spreader.*

No reply came.

#286 was on the second floor. As usual, no one asked the women where they were going or why, even if they saw their striped faces. They soon found Martin's cell, an upper unit, accessed by a ladder. Penny climbed first and coded herself in. Noam and Azura followed. The space inside was just large enough for all three. A twin size cot and a bureau took up the entire width. Azura sat her daughter at the bottom of the cot, where a TV was mounted. They allowed the child to watch muted cartoons. Penny and Azura, lying next to each other on their sides to take up less space, whispered to each other.

"The dust gave us an advantage," Azura said, drawing a deep breath.

HEPA filters in The Pure House cleansed the air. The bosses and the Pures would have no difficulty breathing without masks.

"My father will have to figure out where we can hide."

Their wait could not be long. If Martin had just begun his shift, it would be two hours. Less if he had begun earlier.

About an hour later, the lock clicked and the door opened. Martin's head appeared in the frame. He stood on the ladder. There was no room for him to enter. He, too, spoke in a whisper.

"What the...? Why are you off the island? And with the former Pure and her child!"

"It's a long story, Dad. We were in danger there. We're in danger here. Help us. We need a place to hide."

"Did you bring food? Noam is hungry," Azura said.

He passed a bag from the dining hall to her. She opened it and gave her daughter a sandwich. She gave another to Penny.

"Just stay put. I'll be back," Martin said. "*Geez.* Spreaders in the Pure House. They'll have my head if you're found."

The door closed. Another wait began.

"My father will figure something out. You'll see."

Penny's voice was confident. She dozed off, but Azura remained too anxious to do the same. Where would they go? Any place Martin found would be temporary. Neither the mainland nor the island were safe. Should they go back to the forest? What would they do there for food? Now that she no longer had to fear the *dybbuk*, a thousand other worries plagued her. The worst was that the authorities would find her and Noam and send them back to the home of the monster, where death by crushing awaited them. She wondered if the *dybbuk* had killed other Spreaders since she left.

Her thoughts drifted to Vic. He saved her in the past. She owed it to him to return the favor and bring him to Molly. If he was in the research lab, she should try to free him.

Martin returned and poked his head in, whispering.

"One of the Preliminary suites isn't in use. We can hope another Pure doesn't show up. I'll give you the number and key code. Don't let anyone see the child. Use the make up, and wait there until I think of something else. And don't sleep in the bed. It's got to look fresh."

"Did you read my text?"

"Yes."

"And?"

"We'll discuss your situation later."

After Martin left, the two women applied the makeup and, with Noam, crept out of the cell when the hallway was empty. Pretending to be staff, they used the back stairs to go up to the Preliminary floor, then walked to the room Martin indicated with the boldness of those who had reason to be there. As usual, no one stopped them.

Noam was the happiest of the three.

"Mommy! Mommy! I remember the Pure House. I liked this room with the bed and the bathtub. But I liked the Children's Quarters better. My friends are there. Can I play with them?"

"Not yet."

"I'm a Pure again, right? I belong here again."

"No. You and I are Spreaders. That's a secret. Don't tell, or they'll make us leave."

Noam's eyebrows lowered.

"I am too a Pure. I won't be a Spreader. They're yucky. Boss Franklyn said so."

"Maybe he did."

Two hours later, just before beginning his next shift, Martin, wearing a mask, brought more food. Before she could stop herself, Azura made a demand.

"Noam and I won't leave here without Vic. I'm not sure where he is—a research lab or prison. Just figure it out and bring him to us."

She did not know she would say these words until they had left off her tongue.

"He's not my concern. Even if he was, how am I supposed to free him from wherever he is?"

"How you do it is not *my* concern. Bring him here or when the authorities find me, I'll tell them you helped us."

Martin raised his voice, although anything above a whisper was a risk.

"My concern is my pregnant daughter. Anything I do for you or your daughter is extra. If I get her to safety, I don't care what happens to me."

"Dad, smooth sailing is best, remember? That's what you taught me. Let's not take chances. Try to find Vic."

"Funny how you only remember what I taught you now. Not when you insisted Spreaders weren't contagious or when you left the island."

The only thing that kept him from slamming the door on the way out was fear of getting caught.

Penny turned to Azura.

"Are you in love with Vic? Is that why you want him here?"

"No. I mean... I don't know how I feel. He's been in a couple of dreams I had, telling me my baby is a Pure and that the Radiologist isn't the baby's father."

"Did anyone ever tell you dreams contain wishes?"

Azura lowered her head so Penny wouldn't see her blush. She wished her baby would not catch the virus from her, and she also wished the Radiologist lied. Did that mean she loved the message or the messenger?

That night, they made a bed for Noam on the sofa, while Penny and Azura tried to sleep on the floor. At least it was rug-covered. Azura continued to sort out her feelings for Vic. She did not want to care for him. Molly had a claim on him, and Azura was honor-bound to step aside. Or was she? Vic may have been drunk when Molly's baby was conceived, and he did not admit to being the father of her child. Wouldn't a Recovered have a low sperm count? There would have to be a DNA test after the child's birth.

If the test proved Vic was not the father, what then? They were friends, nothing more. She did not know if he had feelings for her. She wouldn't let herself have feelings for him, would she? Through the night, she went back and forth, her thoughts winding round her like a snake wrapped around a mouse.

CHAPTER 32
MARTIN

His daughter pregnant? Martin froze in place when he saw Penny's text. It stunned him. His heart raced, ready to rip itself from his chest. Without thinking, his hand rose to hold the thumping organ in place. His breath came in gasps.

Although it was a temptation to reply to the text seconds after receiving it, he had enough sense to wait. Impulsivity could get him in trouble with his daughter, whose condition might be delicate. He did not want to cause a miscarriage.

What he bordered on doing was yelling at her for risking so much. In his head, he shouted.

"You're a Spreader, God damn it! You've never accepted that, and now you've gone and done real damage to yourself. The virus will infect the baby, if it even survives the pregnancy. You didn't think of that, did you? And don't you fucking dare say you and it are Pures. Because deep down you know you aren't!"

He had to get his breath under control. He was in Security, wandering the halls at the moment, needing to drain off his emotions. Although he was not on the schedule, he went to the gym. He sparred with a boxing bag for as long as his energy lasted. No one would suspect he did anything but work out, as his job required him to do.

If the authorities or anyone found out that he put three Spreaders in a Preliminary suite, they would arrest, try, and sentence him to prison. No mitigating circumstance would excuse placing anyone in danger in The Pure House, especially the Pures. Spreaders spread infection through their own arrogance and carelessness. Experts said the virus was airborne, but if surfaces carried the contagion, they would contaminate the entire Preliminary suite, if not the whole Preliminary wing. Perhaps virus-laden exhalations escaped the HEPA filters and drifted through the entire establishment. What then?

Martin imagined the staff succumbing one-by-one, not able to leave their cells or failing to show for their shifts, giving themselves away with coughing and moans. The Pures could become active cases, miscarrying. They would wind up as Recovereds, tossed out of The Pure House like wadded-up trash. He shuddered, wondering what the bosses would do when the disease hit them. He hoped the penthouse had extra filters.

Slugging the boxing bag hard and fast, Martin perspired, panting this time from exertion, while worrying about Penny. If they captured her, she would be punished. Something worse than being sent back to the island, although that, too. She and her baby—his grandchild— needed protection.

While holding his head under the shower, letting the spray wash away sweat, shock, anger, and panic, his thoughts turned over. Spreaders were infertile. That had been well established. No Spreader had become pregnant. The males had no sperm count, and the women did not ovulate viable ova. The soap slipped out of his hands. Another stunning idea entered his head.

What if Penny was right all along? What if she wasn't a Spreader? She always claimed to be a Pure who they mislabeled. Pregnancy proved her right. The authorities would have to agree. He shook his head. All this time, he doubted her, his own daughter. He had been a terrible father. He had to make it up to her, help her.

Then another thought popped into his mind, making him smile. He was going to be a grandfather! The wonder of it almost knocked him over. He placed a palm on the shower stall wall to steady himself, picturing himself holding a swaddled newborn—a granddaughter or a grandson! His chest swelled. He never let himself hope for one. If alcohol were not bad for pregnant women, he would sneak champagne into the suite to celebrate with Penny. Maybe just a sip.

But a competing worry interrupted his glee. How would Penny get medical attention and help to deliver her baby? She was a fugitive. The boxing bag and the shower had resolved his panic. Now it returned. Suddenly, he was running on empty. He would have to go to his cell and sleep until his next shift. Later, he would think about his concerns.

In his cell, he fell right to sleep. The stress proved to be his friend in that way. Two hours later, he awoke. In two more hours, it would be time for his shift. He should try to fall back to sleep in order to have the stamina for work. But his worries returned. His hope and exhilaration faded.

Of course, Penny was a Spreader. They had tested her before sending her to the island, after several of her contacts became active cases. The test came back positive. False results never happened. They retested her. The authorities did not want to send anyone who was not a Spreader to the island, where others would infect them.

Her pregnancy was unexplained. Rumors circulated about strange happenings on the island. They confined the Bitch and another person, probably Vic, in the Research Lab. There was speculation that the two had travelled to the island, been infected, then recovered on their own within days, without treatment, an unheard-of occurrence. Active cases waited for the virus to run its course or kill them. Medication eased some symptoms without reducing the length of illness, which lasted weeks.

Martin thought of his late wife, Ethel, a victim of COVID-19, the forerunner of COVID-30, still circulating even though the later illness had overtaken it, twice as contagious and able to evade the earlier vaccines. She had fallen ill just after Penny's birth and contracted COVID-30 in the active case unit. The two viruses killed her. He caught COVID-30 himself when visiting Ethel. Penny spent her childhood in a Recovered Children's Unit before being sent to the island when she was still an adolescent. They forced him to stop his regular visits when she left the mainland.

Could whatever cured the Bitch have enabled Penny to become pregnant? Was Penny still a Spreader? It occurred to Martin that the two lab prisoners had been there for some time. Perhaps the researchers shared their findings with them. Even if no one told them, they could have overheard. There were no prison cells in the lab.

Although they might be confined to exam areas, they might have learned what cured them.

An idea popped into Martin's head. He could free the prisoners, give them masks, although Hazmat suits would be better, take them to the Preliminary unit, then figure out where to take everyone next. Once they were all away from The Pure House and in some sanctuary that Martin would have to find, Penny might benefit from whatever cured the prisoners. His grandchild might survive after all. His hope returned. It was a long shot, but any plan he would come up with would also be a long shot.

Everyone in Security had ways of getting access codes that would unlock any door. If the fire alarm sounded, for instance, there would be no time to get authorization. The codes were all on his device in a secure file. He checked to see if the codes included Research Lab. There it was — in the file under "R."

He did not think any of the researchers worked at night, but lab cleaners might. Just in case, he would say the authorities had sent him to pick up the prisoners for questioning. If that did not work, he would have to use the subduing device he carried. He would threaten to use it on the Bitch if she gave him any flack. There would be no time for niceties.

He ended his next shift, depleted, as usual. He stopped in the dining hall to pick up a takeout, stuffing his pockets with rolls and cookies for the child. No one said anything, although others in the line must have seen. They were too depleted themselves to ask why he needed extra food. Then he returned to his cell and set the alarm on his wrist device for midnight. He clicked on vibrate. Any sound might wake the others. He fell into a light sleep.

The vibration startled him awake. For a second, he did not know why it went off. Then he remembered his mission. It was risky to leave his cell. Someone could ask why he climbed down the ladder in the middle of the night.

"A job," he would say.

They would assume there was trouble somewhere in the building and that the head of Security sent for him. He had been called to manage disturbances in the night. Sometimes, the virus attacked the brains of new active cases, not yet diagnosed, which caused incidents and altercations. It always alerted Security. His neighbors would be curious, but not surprised.

No obstacles came up between his cell and the back stairway. Staff were going up and down, carrying vacuum cleaners and linens, going about their business. He passed someone from Security, who just nodded, asking nothing. That took his breath away for a moment. Finally, he reached the Research Lab. The lights were off in the hallway. The researchers were back in their cells.

Martin typed the code into the lock and heard the familiar click. Inside, it was dark, except for the blue light of computer monitors analyzing data through the night. He used the flashlight on his device to look around. No one was in the main room. Several doors led to other rooms for obscure additional purposes.

He opened the door next to the entrance. A terrible odor greeted him, along with rustling sounds. Shining his light, he saw cages filled with rodents. Hundreds of red eyes stared at him.

"What are you doing here?" They seemed to ask.

Horrified, he closed the door. Would other rooms contain caged pigs or chimpanzees? But the next two rooms only held stacks of boxes. He opened one. Test tubes for blood samples.

The next door was labeled "Exam Room." It was unlocked. He opened it a crack. It was much darker than the previous rooms. He angled the flashlight inside, opening the door wider. A round stool. A chart on the wall filled with numbers. A vital signs machine. A metal exam table with a white paper cover. On a cot, the Bitch lay asleep. He said her name twice. She blinked, pulling the blanket up to her chin.

"Who is it? Martin? Is that you?"

Explaining would come later, in the Preliminary suite.

"Get dressed, please. I'm taking you to the authorities for questioning."

Without waiting for a response, he closed the door and stood for a moment at the door. A light appeared beneath the room where Constance had been sleeping.

Against the wall of the next room, another exam room, was a cot containing a man risen on his elbow, holding a hand up against the light.

"What the fuck?"

Martin thought fast. This must be the other person besides the Bitch who recovered from the virus. He would say what he said to her.

"Your name, sir?"

"Vic, for God's sake."

"Security. Get dressed, please. The authorities want you for questioning."

"Again? In the middle of the night? Why?"

"They don't tell me. I've awakened the other individual."

"Constance?"

"Yes. Do you want me to turn on the light or leave the door open?"

"Just leave it open."

Now that Martin had a moment to consider, he realized the two had awakened the way healthy people do, the way he had years ago, before COVID-30, within seconds, without the lingering effects of exhaustion, without needing several minutes to transition from sleep.

Vic emerged, buttoning jeans.

"What's this about?"

Martin shrugged. If the authorities requested he bring someone for an interview, they never told him why.

"Can you turn on the main light, at least?"

The research room was still dark. Martin found the switch. Constance came out of the room she slept in, dressed, with circles under her eyes. She glared at him in silence.

"They've instructed me to take you by the back stairway," Martin said. "Wear these masks."

"That's not procedure, is it?" Constance asked, putting hers on.

"It's the way I was told to take you. Follow me, please."

He would avoid questions if he took the lead, allowing them to follow, knowing they would all the way to the Preliminary unit.

"Wait. Slow down! Something's wrong. You're going the wrong way. They don't conduct interviews on the upper floors," Constance said.

Martin did not turn around or stop. He felt for the jar he grabbed from a table in the lab and put in his pocket.

It was labeled "Sample."

CHAPTER 33
ABBY

Martin, Constance and Vic joined Azura, Penny and Noam in the Preliminary Suite. It was the middle of the night, and everyone spoke in hushed tones to avoid awakening the child, who slept on a sofa in an adjoining bedroom. The most emotional reunion was between father and daughter, who embraced each other as soon as they were all inside.

"Are you really pregnant?" Martin asked.

"Yes, Dad. I am. It's certain. I took a test right before I left the island."

"But how?"

"The usual way. With my boyfriend, Brenner."

"Spreaders can't get pregnant."

"Remember, I told you we were trying to breed a pure red heifer? Turns out there was one on the uninhabited side of the Island. It must have escaped from our herd. We followed the directions in the Bible and made a broth concoction from it and a few other ingredients. Brenner and I drank some, and it made us able to conceive."

"That's the explanation?"

Martin furrowed a skeptical brow.

"Vic and Constance drank, too, and it cured them of the virus."

Martin gaped at them both. Cow juice cured the Bitch?

"I bet you don't find any virus in any of us."

"She's right," Vic said. "There are no antibodies in my system or Constance's. The researchers told us. We can get the virus if we are exposed, like anyone. That's why we have to keep wearing the masks."

"All of us — except Martin, Azura, and Noam — are Pures now," Constance said in a dream-like tone.

"That's the best news. I'm not a Spreader, Dad. My baby will be healthy."

"I won't be a Recovered for long," Martin said, fishing the jar out of his pocket.

"It's the sample!" Vic said.

Martin gulped down a swig, then screwed the cap back on.

"I swiped it from the research lab."

Constance reached for the jar.

"That's all that's left. The rest disappeared. There were barrels of it. I need some for my daughter. Molly. She's pregnant, too," she said.

"No, you don't. I'm in charge of it."

Martin put the jar in an inner pocket of his coat. The Bitch was no longer his supervisor.

"If the researchers identify us as Pures, there will be a frantic hunt. Especially if the sample is missing," Vic said. "They'll search every corner of The Pure House. Also, they'll put a price on our heads if they think we made it to town."

The mood of the group darkened. It would be difficult to keep five adults and a child undetected. There was no food in the Preliminary Suite except for the few items Martin snuck from the dining hall. They would have to leave.

"If you give me a portion of the sample, I'll go to Molly's cell. I assume that's where she is, right?"

Azura and Penny nodded.

"That will be one less adult. You'll be safer that way."

They searched the Suite for another jar. Several bottles were in the bathroom containing shampoo, lotion, varicus soaps, and creams. Constance emptied the smallest and rinsed it out. Martin poured in a tiny amount.

"Give some to Azura and Noam so they don't get sick," Vic said.

Martin passed the jar to them. Noam scrunched up her face at the taste. Azura hoped her children, born and unborn, would be protected.

"We can't use our devices to communicate. The authorities might trace the signal to us. So I'm taking off now. This might be goodbye," Constance said.

Before leaving, she turned to Vic.

"Molly says you're the father. You should come with me."

"I've no memory of having sex with your daughter. I'm not saying I didn't. If I did, I was wasted, in a blackout."

"What will you do if you are? Will you take responsibility?"

"I'll catch up with Molly after the delivery and take a paternity test."

Constance gave him a hard stare.

"There's a lot of 'ifs.' If they haven't caught you. If you're still alive. If you're still in town and not in prison."

"Take it or leave it."

With an exasperated huff, Constance left. Her daughter's "soul mate" was abandoning her. He was leaving Constance with the fallout.

"We need to have a plan before Noam wakes up. She'll be hungry and will fuss. That might alert the authorities."

"What are our choices?" Martin asked.

"Not the island," Penny said. "There's a monster that's been killing the people in the settlement and some cattle. That's why we left."

"What kind of monster?"

"Nobody's seen it."

"There's no such thing as monsters. If there're homicides on the island, the killer is human."

"Dad, it crushed people to death. No human would be able to do that."

"Hmm," Martin said, not believing what he did not see with his own eyes. "Okay. The island is out for whatever reason. That leaves the forest or somewhere in town."

"The forest is dying. There's no food," Azura said.

"That narrows our choices to the town," Martin said.

Just then, there was a click at the door.

"Turn the lights out," Vic whispered.

Everyone hid, scurrying behind furniture and into closets. The door opened, and the lights came on again. A young woman about Azura's age entered with a vacuum and a pail of cleaning sprays. She stood still, scanning the room, and closed the door behind her. Penny coughed. The woman looked in her direction, then plugged in the vacuum, turned it on, and announced to the room.

"I know you're there. I'm just here to do my job, not to report intruders."

The others emerged. There was nothing else to do.

"Abby?" Vic asked. "It's me, Vic."

"You know each other?" Azura asked.

Another of his girlfriends? She looked familiar.

"I've seen you before," Azura said. "When I arrived, they took me to a medical exam room. You were there, too. You told me to get out while I could."

"Yes. I remember you. There was a note under the coffee pot that I left for you. When I can, I try to save the new Pures."

"How do you know Vic?"

"From when he lived here."

Azura turned to Vic, confusion in her eyes.

"You lived here?"

Martin interrupted.

"There's no time for chatter. We have to decide what to do."

"We need a place in town to hide," Vic said to Abby.

"I only have my cell. I could squeeze one of you in for a short time."

She looked at Vic. Was she flirting with him?

"We must find a sanctuary that can hold all of us."

"Me, too?" Abby said.

"There are already four of us and a child," Martin said.

"Abby can come," Vic said. "One more won't make a difference. Besides, she helped me once, and I owe her."

Azura tried not to object. Vic and Abby must have been together in the past. They must still care for each other. Maybe he did not want to be with Molly, but he and Abby had a history. Besides, Abby tried to help her, too.

"Sure," Azura said. "You can come with us. Martin has a potion you must drink first. It's for your protection and ours."

With a second's hesitation and then a shrug, she took a sip from the jar Martin offered.

"Ugh! Tastes awful. Hope you didn't poison me. I'll have to continue cleaning while you decide where we'll go. If I don't finish my shift, they'll come looking for me."

Paying no attention to the others huddled together to hear each other over the vacuum noise, Abby continued to clean.

It's not like I care for Vic, Azura thought. He's like a lot of young men, full of himself. I care for him as a friend, that's all. I'll soon have two children to raise with no time for boyfriends.

Right before she cleaned the bathroom, Abby turned off the vacuum. Without turning around, she spoke.

"There are always the churches. People hide in them, sometimes."

Then she turned on the machine again.

A call came from the bedroom.

"Mommy! Mommy!"

Azura rushed in. Noam was on the floor, sitting up. Her blanket was crumpled. The floor was a hard bed, even for a child.

"Did the vacuum wake you up?"

"I'm hungry."

Azura went to Martin, who gave her the cookies. She returned to the bedroom with them.

"Here you are. Do you want a glass of water?"

"No. I want to go to the Children's Quarters. They have the fizzy brown drink there."

"Coke."

"That's what I want. Coke. And to see my friends."

"It's still night. They'll be asleep."

"Can I see them when I wake up?"

"I'm not sure. You go back to sleep, and we'll see."

When she came out of the bedroom, Vic was standing apart from the others.

"Have you decided anything?"

"Not yet."

"Why didn't you go with Constance?"

"I have no feelings for Molly."

He smiled at her. What for?

"It doesn't matter if she's going to have your baby."

"I don't want to be stuck with her unless the baby's mine. Even then. That may sound hard, but if she's not my responsibility, there's no reason for me to be with her."

"I suppose there's always Abby," Azura said, walking away.

She caught herself having the terrible thought that if the authorities arrested them, they would separate Vic from all the women in his life. A smile spread on her face. Then it occurred to her that only a jealous person has such an awful thought. She would not allow it to enter her mind again. Besides, if they were arrested, they would separate Noam and her. When the baby was born, she'd be separated from her, too.

Abby came out of the bathroom, and Azura slipped in, closing the door. She turned on the faucet, looking in the mirror above the sink. Her skin was very pale. How pathetic she was. She slapped her face, hoping the others would not hear the hard crack. Then she slapped the other side. That was for her thoughts about a man she did not have, who she did not even want.

When she returned to the living room, the four adults had split into two groupings. Near the door, Penny and Martin were deep into a conversation Azura understood in part.

"You never had faith in me," Penny said.

Martin's shoulders slumped.

On the other side of the room, Vic was helping Abby, lifting chairs so she could vacuum beneath them, handing her items from the pail. She could not hear what they were saying.

How Azura wished she could slap everyone as hard as she slapped her own face. Why were they discussing their relationship issues while they were still in danger? They had to get out of the Preliminary Suite before dawn, or others would see them leaving the building. Plans had to be made. A place had to be chosen in town and a method of getting there. Soon, the researchers would show up for their shift and discover the sample missing, along with their two research subjects. All hell would break loose.

In one fluid movement, she walked to the wall and unplugged the vacuum. She spoke in a stage whisper. They all listened.

"Enough! We must decide where to go right now. Abby, you said something about churches."

"They say some are sanctuaries for people trying to escape, especially Pures. Not all the churches agree that mothers and babies should be parted, and many don't agree with women having babies outside of marriage. The bosses don't mess with churches. It would make people rise up, if they did."

"Does anyone here go to a church or know a minister?" Penny asked.

For a long moment, there was silence. Then Azura spoke up.

"Rabbi Sam said he would let us stay in the synagogue. He meant me, Noam, and her two friends. But I'm sure he would help all of us."

"Brenner kidnapped the Rabbi to take the role of the high priest when we slaughtered the heifer. He might not be too happy with us."

"Sam was my mother's friend when they both lived in a cooperative in the forest. He would do anything for me. Can anyone think of another place to go?"

After another period of silence, they decided they should go to the synagogue. They would split into three pairs — Martin and Penny, Vic and Abby, Azura and Noam. Each pair would leave the Suite at a different time and go to the sanctuary by a different route. Because Martin had the sample, their only leverage if arrested, he and Penny would leave first. Azura and Noam would follow, while it was still dark. Vic and Abby would wait for dawn.

CHAPTER 34
RABBI SAM

It had not been easy for a man in his seventies to be yanked about, kidnapped, handcuffed, forced to stay on the island, returned, then questioned several times by the authorities. Often, he placed a hand on his wrist, checking his pulse. He surpassed his allotted four-score-and-ten and did not expect to beat the nine-hundred-sixty-nine years Methuselah lived or the nine-hundred-sixty for Noah. According to the *Torah*.

He was a Reform rabbi, not a believer in a literal interpretation of the Bible, which was a creation of exiled rabbis after Babylonians destroyed the First Temple in Jerusalem. It was a metaphorical guide for the Jewish diaspora, a moral compass to be used until the building of the Third Temple, after the second was also destroyed, and the arrival of the *Messiah*. Not that he imagined that would happen, not in his lifetime or the next or the one after that.

The world was full of crazies who believed otherwise, that God wrote the *Torah*, that every word in it is the literal truth. They believed the patriarchs lived hundreds of years. Take *Exodus*. It was plausible that a heroic leader like Moses helped free Jews from bondage in Egypt. But the twelve plagues? A metaphor for the power of *Eloheim*, the Jewish God, when used to defeat the Pharaoh, the Egyptian God, unnamed but probably Amenhotep II. *Exodus* is, at heart, a simple tale, teaching the love of God for his people, proven when He frees them from slavery.

The Rabbi was an educated man, adept at reading between the lines, knowledgeable about Biblical history, able to read the *Torah* in classical Hebrew and Aramaic, sophisticated, enjoying textual explications with Jewish scholars and other rabbis, a studier of academic articles in academic publications. How proud he was to be a rabbi in the modern era, the age of science.

Pride had been his failing years ago, during the first year of COVID-19, when he took a hike in the forest by himself, a foolhardy act, he couldn't recall what he had been thinking, and in his arrogance became lost, in need of rescue by a group living there off the grid. That's where he met the love of his life, Eva, mother of Azura and the leader of the group. Of course, she turned down his offer of marriage. He was much older, shorter, rounder, no match for her beauty. They remained friends until he returned to town to be with his congregation, where he knew he belonged.

After that, a new humility awakened in him, and with it, like a buried treasure awaiting excavation, the old memories and beliefs from childhood. His grandfather, Papa Sol of blessed memory, a rabbi before him, made him a wooden Noah's Ark, with rough sets of animals, lions, horses, elephants. Back then, he believed the flood happened, until he got older and discovered doubt. The adolescent Sam, taking geology and physics classes, determined that the early verses of Genesis were myth, not reality. But his grandfather's teachings were cemented within him. The creation of the world in six days, the "big bang," the Garden of Eden, and evolutionary theory co-existed in his mind.

The verses about the red heifer lay in the intersection of his divided brain. His thoughts ricocheted around his head ever since his kidnapping. The ancients needed a ritual to rid the community of moral contamination. Communities sinned then and now. They start unnecessary wars, worship idols or money, forget to feed the hungry. Maybe they used a red heifer hundreds of years ago, or maybe it was a metaphor for purity. Something that was not part of daily life with its pollution and poisons, something rare that gave the ritual its power. That's what the red heifer was. A power-giver.

The Rabbi smiled. He had the subject for his next sermon! He snapped open his laptop, opening a new document.

"*D 'Var Torah*: Red Heifer."

Before writing the sermon, he would make tea. He left his office and headed for the synagogue kitchen. No one was in the building at this late hour. It was then that he heard the whoosh of the furnace ignite and, within it, the sound of Papa Sol's voice.

Sometimes, a red heifer is a red heifer. I'll make you two for the Ark.

The Rabbi whirled around.

"Papa Sol?"

Nothing was there but the same old, dated kitchen, once used before the virus for *onegs* and luncheons after weddings and *bar/bat mitzvoth*, with its wooden table, industrial double oven, and large capacity sink.

Was Papa Sol sending him a message from beyond the grave, or was this just an old man's delusion? The red heifer could be a metaphor, his grandfather might mean, but it treated the virus that infected the young man who kidnapped him. And the authorities had an interest in the lost containers. It was possible that some element of the heifer concoction contained a cure. It could be like aspirin. No one knew how it worked, but it did. The red heifer might be a red heifer in this case, even if they did not perform the ritual according to Biblical standards.

There was a question for scientists, not Biblical scholars — could they repeat the cure using another heifer from the island? And there was a question for the authorities — where were the missing containers? What would happen if they found them, and everyone in the town became uncontaminated? What if any woman could become pregnant? Would the bosses still be bosses?

The Rabbi returned to his office with his tea. He buried his first idea for a sermon under his second idea, which he owed to Papa Sol. Or a delusion. He would begin by describing his relationship with his grandfather, the Noah's Ark, his early literal beliefs and his later metaphorical ones, then his return to the possibility — just a possibility — of literalness. The red heifer would be his example. What if it did cure disease? What if God's plagues did overwhelm Pharaoh?

There was another whoosh.

Noah built an Ark — or there's just the toy I made for you. Or Noah built an Ark — and there's the toy I made for you. Which?

215

There was nothing to be seen. The Rabbi raised his hand to his chest. Papa Sol haunted him. Before the island, he had confidence in his opinions. He thought the Spreaders were being ridiculous when they tried to breed a pure red heifer. He called them idiots when they did not do the ritual as proscribed. But the concoction worked. He was the fool. His grandfather taught him another lesson in humility.

Now he had a third idea for a sermon. We should read the *Torah* with an open mind. All interpretations were valid and welcome. They are all *Torah*. There is no one truth. There are multiple truths. Thousands. Millions. The red heifer was an example. A symbol of God's power or a cure or both or something else. It did not matter. He would choose an "and," not an "or."

"Thank you, Papa Sol," he said.

He put down his tea and set the tab for his first paragraph on his document. He stared at the white space beneath the heading. A moment later, the synagogue doorbell chimed. The Rabbi sighed. In the old days, an administrative assistant would have answered and asked the visitor to wait. It might be a congregant with a need for pastoral counseling. Since emerging from the forest, he had become warm and accomplished at this part of his duties.

But his third idea threatened to melt back into his second or first if he did not quickly capture it in the document. It lolled on the tip of his tongue, not yet saddled in his brain. Would Papa Sol's ghost remind him if he forgot? He sighed again, closing the laptop, donning a mask, and making his way to the entrance.

"Yes, who is it?" He asked through the heavy oaken door.

"It's me," a female voice answered.

Most often, a woman requested his counsel. A grieving widow or the mother of a bride unsure of her daughter's choice of husband. His congregation consisted of senior women, now that the virus had killed off the men and robbed younger workers of the energy for services. But the voice sounded young.

"Who is 'me'?"

"Azura. It's Azura."

Azura? He had not seen Eva's daughter since their time on the island. He cracked the door a few inches. There she stood, as lovely as her mother. Her daughter Noam, named after the granddaughter of Eve in Genesis, leaned against her. There were faint stripes on their faces. Had they become Spreaders? He was glad to be wearing a mask.

He opened the door enough to let them in.

"Did Martin and Penny arrive yet?" she asked, removing the child's coat.

"There are only the three of us in the building."

"They should have come ahead of us. They left first."

He raised his hand to his chest. What was she talking about?

"Vic and Abby will be right behind us. There. I heard a knock. It must be them."

Without asking his permission, she opened the door. Four adults, two men and two women, stood on the doorstep. Azura motioned them in.

"We hid around the side," Martin said. "We were afraid no one would allow us in without you, Azura."

"Our religion requires us to welcome the stranger," the Rabbi said. He could not keep the tremor from his voice. These people would want sanctuary. His obligation was to offer it. Later, he would wonder if this central tenet of Judaism should be literal or metaphorical or both. If it was literal, he took a substantial risk. At his age, prison would finish him.

Years ago, before he fell in love with Eva, he would have found a way to refuse sanctuary, then done the scholarship to justify his refusal. The forest had turned him into a *mensch,* a good man. He remained as fearful as ever, but he had gained compassion. Papa Sol would be proud of him.

Azura introduced her friends. He recognized Vic, the young man who kidnapped him, and Penny from the island.

"Come into the kitchen. I just made some tea. There's milk for Noam."

"Is there Coke?"

"We can look."

He took the child's hand. A sweet warmth arose in him from her tiny palm in his. He had to help her. If Eva had accepted his proposal, she would be his granddaughter.

When everyone settled in the kitchen, Azura told the Rabbi about her return to The Pure House, testing positive and becoming a Spreader, hiding in the Preliminary Unit, and escaping with the others. Abby had suggested a house of faith for a sanctuary. She knew he would take them in.

The Rabbi tried to suppress a guilty smile. She knew before he knew.

Martin took the jar from his pocket and placed it on the open table. An inch of murky liquid remained.

"It's the red heifer concoction. It cured two people and removed all traces of the virus from the rest of us. For your kindness, Rabbi, please take a mouthful," Martin said.

Martin offered payment. For a long moment, the Rabbi eyed the concoction, remembering his sarcasm while it was being assembled. Now he shook. Right before him, on the synagogue kitchen table, was the "or" and the "and," waiting for his final decision, either a scoffing remark or wide-eyed wonder at the miracle from God. The purest of "pure" in a dirty-looking jar part-filled with filthy-looking broth. Yet, it defended against the virus, Martin said. He would give his eyeteeth, as they say, to never be an active case again.

The furnace ignited.

Four-score-and-ten is the most God promises.

He inhaled, pushing the jar back toward Martin.

"No. There are many who need this. You should not waste it on an old man. I'll accept whatever time remains for me. I'm content to be in God's hands."

Martin nodded, putting the jar back in his pocket.

Everyone was silent, respecting the Rabbi's sacrifice. Azura stepped forward to hug him, knowing she would not infect him.

Later, while the visitors slept, he returned to his computer. He had a sermon to write.

CHAPTER 35
AZURA

She and her friends were safe for the moment, assuming the authorities would not raid a synagogue. Assuming the authorities did not know they were there. Anyone in town could be a spy. Someone could have reported them if her child was spotted, or the stripes on her and Penny's face, arousing suspicions. Members of the congregation who saw them at the door would realize they did not belong.

Her rapid breathing slowed. They were in a house of worship, in the presence of the *Torah*, a scroll enclosed in an Ark in the front of the sanctuary. Rabbi Sam offered protection to all of them, even though only she and Noam were Jewish. They found shelter, but it was temporary. Figuring out where to go next had to be considered soon.

They slept wherever they found a soft spot — the sofa in the Rabbi's office, on floor pillows in the Religious School room, on rugs and carpets. There were no beds.

The next morning, they gathered in the kitchen to drink coffee. The Rabbi showed up with bagels and muffins. He had to be worried about how to feed them all. He solved the breakfast problem, at least.

Azura peered at all of them for signs of stress or illness. The Rabbi was the most vulnerable. Bags swelled under his eyes. Anxiety must have kept him up all night. The authorities would be hard on him if they found he had offered sanctuary to two pregnant women and a child. Martin, accustomed to being awakened at night for security tasks, drank coffee and smiled at Penny. She glowed both from a pregnancy blush and the improved relationship with her father. Noam danced around the synagogue with a child's energy. Abby was alert. They assigned her an early shift at work, and she was within her two-hour period of wakefulness.

The one who surprised her was Vic. She had to admit he looked handsome. What had changed about him? Then she realized he incubated the virus on the island, then became an active case before drinking the concoction. Now his skin color was normal, and he seemed toned. His posture had straightened. She stared at a healthy man. That's what made him handsome. Very few Recovereds had the robust appearance good health gave, and until now, she had never seen a male Pure.

It was just an objective appraisal, she told herself. She would not allow herself to be attracted to a man who liked another woman— Abby. Even though he had taken a seat next to her at the kitchen table, far from the end where Abby sat, Azura had seen the way he helped Abby clean the Preliminary Suite. She had seen the way he looked at Abby. It was clear they were becoming a couple, if they weren't already. Had they slept together? Azura had no idea where either of them spent the night.

Azura was in her second trimester and showing. Her midsection bulged. No man would be interested in a woman in her state, pregnant, fat, ungainly, stripe-faced, burdened with a difficult and demanding child nearing school age with no school in sight. She imagined the tantrums from home-schooling. Her daughter would resist her. There would be no energy for romance.

Vic handed her the bagel tray. She took one and then passed it to Martin, turning her back on Vic. She would not encourage him, only to be rejected.

"What are your ideas about where we should go next?" She asked Martin.

He chewed while considering, turning the fork he held in her direction, a gesture meaning he would soon say what was on his mind.

"I've been thinking. We should split up again. I'm going to take care of Penny. She's my responsibility. I'll use what's in the jar and the money I saved for bribes. I'm sorry I can't take the rest of you. My only duty is to my daughter."

Everyone at the table heard.

"Okay. But you should split what's left in the jar with us," Vic said.

"There's very little. Penny and I will need all of it."

Vic stood.

"C'mon, man. Don't be an asshole. We all need some for the same reason you do."

"Fuck off! I'm doing what's best for my daughter."

Martin stood, facing Vic across the table.

"And the rest of us can go to hell?" Vic asked.

"Possession is nine-tenths of the law."

"The other tenth is that you stole the sample from the lab. Share the loot, Martin."

"You and who else will make me?"

They raised their voices. The women kept trying to restore calm.

"Take it easy, guys."

"Dad! Your blood pressure!"

"Hey! Knock it off, you two!"

The Rabbi removed his slipper and banged it on the table, like a gavel.

"Everyone sit!"

The conviction in his voice caught the attention of the two men. They sat, hoping he would not revoke his offer of sanctuary.

"You've been through a lot, and it's frayed your tempers. We'll settle this in a way befitting the House of God," Rabbi Sam said.

"Sorry about my language, Rabbi," Vic said.

"Me, too," Martin said.

"Let's all have another cup of coffee and a serious talk," the Rabbi said, moving to the coffee pot to brew more.

Everyone relaxed. After a period of silence, Penny spoke up.

"Dad, I know you want to make up for your years of doubting me. Your idea of us splitting from the rest so you can concentrate on caring for me is a good idea. But hogging the concoction for ourselves isn't. I wouldn't be able to stand the guilt if Azura and Noam—a pregnant woman and a child—didn't have the same chance we had. You wouldn't either. Besides, we have your money to get us to safety."

Martin's expression softened.

"If we split the heifer broth six ways, there'd be too little for any of us to have a chance. But we can divide it in half. Half for the two of us and half for the others. That's fair enough, since Abby isn't pregnant, and she and Vic have no children."

Azura noticed the words "she and Vic." Penny as much as said Vic and Abby were a couple.

"An excellent solution," the Rabbi said. Later, he might consult Jewish texts to see if his words had validity. For now, stopping the hostility was crucial.

"I'm okay with that," Vic said. "Are you?"

He stared at his opponent. Martin grunted.

The Rabbi opened cabinets until he found a small container. Martin poured half the contents of the jar into it and handed it to Vic. He grunted again. Fairness, in this case, was against his better judgment. The lives of his daughter and grandchild were at stake.

"When I went to the bakery this morning, I stopped at the pharmacy, too," the Rabbi said.

He took a bag that had been under his seat and dumped the contents on the table. Hair dye in different shades fell out. Also, glasses with clear lenses and more make-up.

"You should disguise yourselves. Wearing masks will help. I'll go to the thrift shop for clothing," he said.

They all chose dyes. Abby cut off Vic's ponytail. The red color would have to go. They gave Noam a short haircut, scrubbed her face clean, and dressed her as a boy, despite her vigorous objections.

"I'm not a boy! I'm a Pure girl."

"It's just pretend," Azura said.

Her own blond curls would be dyed black and straightened. The most complicated transformation was of Martin into Martina, Penny's mother. It was the only disguise that might conceal the identity of the muscular security agent with the shaved head. He wore a thrift-shop dress for a large woman, a scarf tied around his scalp, and glasses. An oversized shirt hid Penny's tiny first-trimester bulge. Azura still looked pregnant, but she did not resemble the delicate blond who had lived in The Pure House.

When they finished, they looked at each other with grim satisfaction. Make-up and masks hid the stripes. If there were posters or APB photos, none of them would resemble the images. They hoped no one would ask them for their ID cards.

The authorities evicted people living in apartment buildings in town when they constructed the beehive housing. Many of the old residences still stood intact. Some had running water. Martin remembered where they were. On occasion, they put him on a special security team that hunted in them for someone who escaped. By now, other teams would have searched for him and his friends there.

"If you give me a piece of paper, Rabbi, I'll write down half the locations. That way, we won't all show up at the same ones. I'll take Penny to one near the train station. I'll bribe the guards there to let us on the train. We can hide in northern Michigan or Wisconsin until the baby is born."

"Then where will you go?" Abby asked.

"Don't know. We'll figure it out."

The plan was for Martin and Penny to leave that night, and for the others to leave the next evening. The Rabbi urged them to stay longer. He seemed relieved when they refused.

"We all need to leave town as soon as possible, changing locations every couple of days until we do. It's our only chance," Vic said. "Either Abby or I can shop for supplies for our group. When our money runs out, we'll have to shoplift. I'm pretty good at that."

"How come?" Azura asked.

"This is not the first time I've been on the run."

"Here. Take this." The Rabbi reached in his pocket and produced a few bills.

"We'll go now," Martin said, handing Penny a plaid thrift-shop coat.

"Ugh! This is ugly. Anyone who thinks I'd wear this on purpose deserves to be shot."

"No one who knows you would think a woman wearing this coat is you," Azura said.

"Although I look better than Martina, my new mother."

"Enough! Let's go," Martin said.

After quick hugs all around, they were out the door. Azura wondered if she would ever see them again. So many losses! Her friends in the forest—all gone. She would not be seeing those she met since leaving the forest. Constance and Molly, Brenner and the Spreaders, Noam's friends. Soon Rabbi Sam. The one she did not miss was the Radiologist. She was not sorry he was dead, even if he turned out to be her baby's father after all.

The extra night in the synagogue gave her the chance for a private talk with the Rabbi.

"I'm so confused. My thoughts go to dark places."

"It's difficult in dark times to avoid dark thoughts," he said.

"Like the red heifer. On the island, I agreed with you that the concoction was superstitious nonsense. But it has turned out to be a cure for the virus and infertility. It wasn't nonsense. It was a miracle."

"I'm not sure I'd use the word 'miracle', but I am reconsidering my own previous attitude."

"And whatever crushed some islanders. I've been thinking it was a *dybbuk*."

"That's a name for a monster, a metaphor. Whatever killed them was evil. Call it what you want."

"There's more. The first person crushed was the Radiologist. He molested me and told me he was the father of my child. That might not be true. I hate him. I'm glad he's dead… if someone had to die. Is that a transgression, Rabbi?"

"The commandment is Thou Shalt Not Kill. It's not Thou Shalt Not Have Thoughts of Gladness for a Killing. We don't have complete control over our thoughts, especially if someone molested us."

Azura hesitated.

"My thoughts about Vic are messing with me. I don't want to think about him at all. Every time he seems to be with another woman, I get jealous."

Tears bubbled on her lower lid.

"Perhaps you're attracted to him."

"I don't want to be."

"That's another thing you don't control. Who attracts you."

"What should I do, Rabbi?"

"Start by admitting what is true to yourself, no matter how difficult or painful. I've had to do that about the red heifer cure."

"Then what?"

"Once you admit it, you'll know what to do."

CHAPTER 36
BRENNER

The authorities brought Brenner to The Pure House for testing after rounds of questioning led to his confession that he drank some of the heifer concoction. Tests revealed no markers of the virus in his system and that his sperm count and quality were normal. They exchanged his Spreader id card for one stamped "Pure" and instructed the medical workers and interviewers to wear Hazmat suits around him. He refused their offer to remove the tattoos from his face.

They placed him in the Preliminary Unit. To his surprise, there were no guards posted outside his room at night. No one even locked the door. Perhaps when he could not or would not reveal what happened to the missing containers, the authorities stopped caring about him. They might also be uninterested if they had stored enough frozen semen for their needs at an earlier time. One Pure man's semen could impregnate hundreds of women. Female Pures, able to carry a baby to full term, were the rare ones.

He obliged the authorities by leaving the building. No one tried to stop him. As he walked through town, wearing a simple mask to protect himself and cover his stripes, he noticed signs of unrest. People talked, not even in whispers, out in the streets, not fearing being reported. Rumors spread about unsolved murders on the island, pregnant Pures escaping from The Pure House, a secret cure for COVID. The bosses were losing their grip. Were they still in control?

Now that Brenner had an identity card marked "Pure," they had also issued him a credit card. Spreaders were not allowed cards or cash for fear they would use them to escape the island. He found

CAROLYN GEDULD

PeoplesMart, the only store now that it had absorbed the lesser chains and left no Mom-and-Pops. No one stopped him from entering or making his purchases—security equipment. He would have bought guns, if they required no background check.

A skiff was still where he expected it to be. He loaded it with boxes from PeoplesMart. Even though he denied ever being a Spreader, he was stronger now. He rowed to the island after walking several miles carrying the supplies, then climbing the hill to the settlement side, without becoming tired.

Before reaching the community housing, he tore off his mask. He did not care if they labeled him a Spreader again, as long as he did not have to become an active case first. He would be careful. But the Spreaders had to trust him. He had to appear to be one of them. They were his people, and he would lead them in the fight for their lives, against whatever wanted to kill them.

One thing remained obvious—it was not the virus. Viruses do not crush people.

A warm greeting waited for him. The population had grown to thirty-eight with the arrival of Azura, Noam, and Molly. With the murders of Alf and the other guards, the escape of the three pregnant women and the child, and the arrest of Brenner, their numbers plummeted to thirty—thirty-one, now that their leader returned.

He showed them his purchases. Cameras with motion detectors. Night vision goggles. Alarms. They spent the day setting up the equipment and testing it. Determining what attacked them and their cattle would strengthen their defenses.

For several days, the cameras recorded nothing unusual. It seemed as if the monster knew it was being monitored. If any humans were involved, as the authorities thought, they could be members of the community, even one of those who put the equipment together. Brenner knew members might turn against each other. He kept reminding everyone that the first murder of the Radiologist happened on the other side of the island, when everyone in the community was accounted for, asleep in the dorm.

The authorities expected the Spreaders to solve the homicides themselves. Recovered officers would not risk becoming active cases by conducting investigations that included interviewing Spreaders on the island. This supported the idea, prevalent in the community, that the authorities were willing to let Spreaders die. It solved a problem for the bosses.

Finally, a guard reported a heifer killed. Everyone rushed to the monitor.

The camera in the cattle pen would have recorded significant images, among many worthless ones. Something crushed a heifer to death. Signs of its last agony were clear from its cadaver – popped out eyes, blood from all orifices, flexed tongue, swollen neck, caved in rib cage. The animal had visible white and black hairs. Why choose one so far from purity?

"It's, like, a warning. Something wants us to stop the breeding program."

This was speculation. No one figured out why.

"The bosses want to keep the virus going. If there's a cure, there's no reason for the whole setup they organized, ranking people by health status, keeping The Pure House separate, luxuries for them and a few Pures, toil for everyone else in town, keeping us on the island."

"If the bosses are arranging the murders, why choose impure heifers? You'd think they'd kill the ones further along."

"Not if it's meant to scare us from continuing to breed. Then it doesn't matter which they kill."

"They think we hid the containers. The crushed cadavers might be to show us what will happen if we hold out."

"Let's look at the images," Brenner said.

He unpacked the monitor he brought. He attached a cable to the camera and pressed "Play." A grainy image of the pen appeared on the screen, triggered by the movement of the cattle, shifting and changing places through the night. It did not cover the whole pen. The camera range only covered a large section. He changed the speed to "2X," hoping to find a recording of the killing.

"This is it!" Brenner said.

Everyone closed in behind him, the one's in the back craning their necks.

"Fuck! It's off camera."

The animal's kicking legs were visible. Its grotesque, suffering head bobbed in and out of view. But its body and whatever crushed it stayed off-camera.

"It knows we're recording. That's why it chose a heifer at the edge of the camera's range. Its black hairs had nothing to do with it."

The recording was useless. Brenner and a group went to inspect the cadaver. The surrounding soil was disturbed in a familiar way — snake-like slithers with toeless stumps.

"I'll be damned. What is it?"

"My guess is a reptile, or someone impersonating one," Brenner said.

It was hard to give up the notion of human involvement.

"C'mon. You mean a person put on a snake suit and killed a six-hundred pound beast?"

Brenner shrugged. He wanted the community to think it was impossible for one of them to be the murderer. He stated the idea for it to be rejected.

"Then it's some sort of animal, living on the other side and visiting us "

"It's not killing for food. No part of the heifer has been eaten."

"What animal kills but doesn't eat its prey?"

Speculation deepened the mystery. They lost a quarter of their stock. The predator had killed six heifers, always ones that strayed to the edge of the pen. Each time, it had ripped the fencing from the bottom, then crawled in through a hole it made from the ground upward.

The settlers measured the slither marks.

"It's one long reptile. Six feet, I bet. Ten, twelve inches wide."

"Nothing like that lives here. Climate change may be drying the island, but it isn't a desert yet. The town is arid and dusty. We're still green, here. We don't get snakes that big."

"And what about the stumps? A snake with legs?"

"The fuck!"

One of them examined the prints made in mud.

"Look over here," she said. She had been a veterinarian before the pandemic.

They rushed over, forming a rough circle around her.

"The stumps aren't shaped like hooves or paws. See? The ends are uneven, and there are little points. Here, here, and here."

"Like rudimentary toes," Brenner said. "What's your best guess?"

"A snake growing limbs," she said.

They looked at each other, saying nothing. Brenner felt the hairs on the back of his neck rise.

"An intelligent snake growing limbs," the veterinarian added.

"An intelligent snake? There're dumb as rocks. No such creature exists."

"It does now," she said. "Maybe."

She was not a zoologist. Like most in her profession, she treated domestic animals. But she could tell a reptile from a mammal. She needed to see the creature, to be sure.

One of the younger men stepped up.

"Is it, like, an alien? From, like, another planet?"

The alien theory had traction among the younger Spreaders.

"Its markings are reptilian. The question is, what kind of reptile," the veterinarian said.

"Aliens might be reptiles," the young man said.

"I wouldn't know about that."

She turned her attention to the mud print, making notes on her device.

Brenner walked away. He had two things on his mind—the creature and Penny. He needed to keep his focus, but thoughts of Penny kept drifting into his head. They had become lovers during their time on the other side of the island. Right before his arrest, she told him she missed her period. She tried to get a pregnancy test mailed to her from the mainland, along with other pharmaceuticals for the settlement. The authorities allowed these postings.

He never found out if the shipment included the test or if it did, the results. But she drank some of the concoction. She might be fertile. He might become a father.

A father! He! Never had he envisioned what he thought was impossible. He and the others were healthy, not Spreaders. Yet, there were no children on the island before Azura brought Noam and her two friends. They were imports. No child was born on the island. The settlers did not talk about this. None of them wanted to admit to anything that might mean they were Spreaders.

He tried to crush all thoughts of Penny. But they were sneaky, like the reptile, poking through the barriers he set up in his mind, coming at him from holes in the bottom. Then he would fantasize. A family. He, Penny, and a son or daughter. Perhaps more than one.

First, he would help the settlement kill the reptile. Then he would find Penny. They would run away and raise their children, now that they were healthy. He did not know where they could go. Somewhere. Not in the town. Somewhere else. They would figure it out together, like a married couple. Why not? He would marry her, then they would run away.

Yes, he would marry her, if she would have him. He did not think he was the type to ever marry. But the possibility of fatherhood changed him. He stood, looking out beyond the heifer pen, beyond the field, beyond the hill, to a place he imagined—a modest house, children around a Christmas tree opening gifts. A stupid, corny vision. After years on the island, it's what he wanted now. The stupid, corny vision.

"Brenner! Over here."

They were calling him. He snapped back to reality. He and the Spreaders were in a dangerous situation, and they could only depend on themselves. What weapons did they have? One gun. A few bullets. A couple of machetes. Pitchforks and shovels. Security equipment.

The reptile stalked at night. Guards were vulnerable when they circled the perimeter of the settlement alone. Cattle were vulnerable when they left the herd for the edges of the pen. All of them would have to guard the heifers at night with their weapons and catch some sleep during the day. When any of them saw the creature, all of them would gang up on it, beating it to death with their farm implements.

When Brenner finished telling the others the plan, he began coughing.

CHAPTER 37
AZURA

In the week after leaving the synagogue, Azura, Noam, Vic, and Abby changed shelters in abandoned residences three times.

"This is terrible for Noam. Her mood is tanking. Nightmares awaken her. She cries a lot, and I'm afraid she'll get sick. She's not eating, complaining her stomach hurts," Azura said

"We've got to stop moving all the time."

There was silence while they thought.

"We can stay in each place longer, only switching twice a week," Abby said.

"We need a permanent place. A regular house or apartment, where Noam can go outside and play with other children. Not hide-outs with the windows covered."

"She can return to The Pure House," Vic said.

"Never!"

"There aren't a lot of choices." Vic spoke in a soft tone.

"I'm not a child. Don't talk to me as if I'm a child."

Azura whirled away from him and stomped off to the next room. That was the one thing they had an abundance of—rooms, different apartments, a selection of floors. Even so, they kept gathering in the same place. In their frustration with their situation, they tried not to turn on each other. But Azura turned on Abby.

Abby, in particular, irritated her. The way she held her coffee mug in both hands, her constant cleaning, the sounds she made at night in their shared sleeping quarters all annoyed Azura, although she could not say why. She just did not like Abby. It was that simple.

Yet, Abby was always nice to her. There was no reason to be offended. A few times, when Azura snapped at her, she knew it was wrong.

She fantasized ways Abby might leave. She might decide to go it alone. If she met someone she knew while shopping for supplies, she might go with that person. If the authorities found her, they'd arrest her. Azura shook her head. Another horrendous thought! What kind of person has a thought like that? Would she come up with ways to kill Abby next?

For the rest of the day, she forced herself to be nicer to her roommate. Although she knew it was ridiculous, she feared Abby would read her mind.

Vic annoyed her, too. The way he watched Abby, always jumping on chances to help her. They did all the heavy work together — dragging mattresses into the bedroom for the night, pushing heavy furniture against doors as barricades. They would not involve a pregnant woman.

"I don't want to be responsible if you miscarry. You just rest," Abby said.

Azura ground her teeth, even though she realized Abby was right. She had already become attached to the baby, stroking her bulge and humming to it. No matter who the father turned out to be, she didn't want to lose her baby.

Her irritation with Abby had to do with Vic. The Rabbi's word floated back to her.

"Perhaps you're attracted to him."

His advice had been to be honest with herself, even if honesty was painful. Being attracted to someone who did not like you was painful. Between adults, nothing hurt more. That was the reason for her jealousy of Molly, Penny, and now Abby. She thought he liked them.

But if she thought about it, Penny loved Brenner, and Vic told her he was not into Molly. Only Abby was a threat. A threat to what?

She stamped her foot in aggravation.

The honest answer was that Abby threatened any relationship that might develop between Vic and herself.

"There! I'm saying it. I don't want Abby to have Vic because I want him. Satisfied?" She shouted at the walls in a room far from her friends.

Honesty hurt like hell, as the Rabbi said it would.

"Once you admit it, you'll know what to do."

Her choices were obvious. Push away all thoughts of Vic and Abby or tell the truth to Vic.

She allowed herself only ten minutes to pine over her choices, knowing she would wind up obsessing for hours, days, neglecting her daughter. If she acted like the adult she insisted she was, choosing to talk was the best option. She waited until Vic was by himself.

"Hey," she said.

"Hey."

This was going to be awkward.

"I've been a bitch, and I want to talk to you about it, okay?"

"Okay."

He took a sip from his water bottle, hiding an amused smile. She often seemed to amuse him.

"First, I'm sorry."

"We're all grouchy, living this way."

"Me most of all, it seems. At Abby."

Her hands clasped together, looking harmless.

"I've noticed."

"Yes, well..." She cleared her throat. "This is hard to talk about."

"Try taking a deep breath."

She inhaled.

"I haven't been kind to Abby because I'm jealous of her."

There. She said it. She exhaled.

"Go on." He did not hide his smile.

"Do I have to?"

"If you want me to understand."

"Okay. Promise not to laugh at me?"

"I'll do my best."

"I'm jealous of your relationship with her."

Vic's eyebrows arched.

"In the past, she helped me. Remember, I told you I was a rebel when we met? She's the one who hooked me up with the other rebels. We both belong."

The discussion twisted to politics, leaving the part about relationships paused.

"We'd like to see the bosses booted out and democracy restored. We're against health labels and beehive housing. It works as a temporary measure for the homeless, but humans need more space to be human."

"What about the virus? And babies? And climate change?"

"Whoa! That's several discussions worth. Let's just say we don't believe humans will die out, just be reduced in number. Recovereds can still have babies. It's difficult for them, but it happens. No one should force a woman to become pregnant or force her to give up her children."

"I agree so far, but what if the virus makes all women infertile?"

Vic stopped smiling. He looked at her with serious eyes.

"Then humanity will vanish from the earth, which might not be a bad thing. Humans mess things up. Another species might evolve to do better."

"What other species?"

"Who knows? Insects. A virus. Plants."

Now she smiled.

"Plants can't build things."

"Only because they haven't developed fingers."

"Are you teasing me?"

His smile had not returned.

"Nope. Not me."

She stared at him.

"If we can get back to our original topic, I'll ask you straight. Are you and Abby a couple?"

She felt her face redden. Her question was out on the table.

"Just friends."

His amused smile returned. Without masks, which they no longer wore after drinking the concoction, his expression was visible.

She bit her lip. She wanted to ask what type of friends. How close? Friends who had sex? Or a polyamorous couple? In relationships, each question led to another. What she most wanted to know were the ones she feared the most to ask — did he find her attractive? Was he falling in love with her? Did he love her?

It would have to wait. Her nerves frayed. This was not a time for her to receive his rejection, or hear him say they were "just friends." She was not ready. Besides, she heard Noam calling her. She took that as the excuse to avoid the rest of the conversation.

"Another time," she said.

She admitted her jealousy. Now Vic knew she had feelings for him. She had no idea if he had feelings for her.

That evening, the three adults conferred about a plan.

"If we had a vehicle, we could drive it close to a check-point and ditch it. That would lop several miles off our journey. We could bypass the check-point on foot if we detoured around it at night. Once we reach the other side, we'd have to get another vehicle," Vic said.

"Or count on our disguises to get us through check-points," Abby said.

"My ID has a Pure stamp. Noam's, too. They didn't re-stamp them Spreader yet. We escaped before they had a chance. Besides, where would we get a vehicle? Or vehicles?" Azura asked.

"Steal them," Vic said.

"You've done that?"

"Rebels have illegal skills."

"I'll make some calls," Abby said. "There'll be two vehicles waiting at designated spots before and after the check-point going out of town toward the forest, if I'm successful."

Azura stifled her amazement. Since coming to town, the authorities, then Vic, protected her. Abby and Vic had connections she did not realize existed. If she and her children survived, it would be because of the two of them.

"I can't call from here. There might be a tracer on my phone. I'll leave and take a bus to another part of town. Vic, you remember where the designated spots for the vehicles are, right?"

"I do," he said. "From last time."

Last time? Azura wondered what that meant.

Abby put on her coat and gathered her belongings. They might not see her again.

"Wait, Abby. Can we speak in private for a minute before you go?"

"Sure."

The two women walked to a different room.

"What's going on?" Abby asked.

"I've been bitchy to you, and I want to apologize."

"No need."

"You see—I imagined you and Vic had been a couple, and I became jealous."

"Hmm."

"I asked him, and he said you two were just friends."

"So you decided to apologize only when you learned we didn't happen to be a couple?"

Azura sighed.

"I feel terrible. I've been so selfish. Pregnant women are supposed to be turned off, but it's not always true."

"I'm guessing your hormones are all over the place."

"That's possible, but I'm not trying to make excuses. I haven't behaved well toward you, and I'm sorry."

"It's already forgotten."

"So, you and Vic are just friends?"

Abby groaned. The conversation went in circles.

"Sit down," she said.

They both sat.

"Look. Remember how I left a note under the coffee pot when I worked on cleaning staff in The Pure House?"

"Yes."

"The rebels assigned me there. Very few of us could get that close to Preliminary Pures. It was high risk. I gave warnings, and if they were heeded, helped the Preliminary Pure escape."

"I didn't heed your warning. It was beyond my understanding."

"That was common."

"You couldn't help me escape."

237

"No. They passed the assignment to Vic. He forced you into the broom closet to get your attention."

"I'll never forget."

"But he had no way of getting you out before they inseminated you."

There was so much to process. Vic and Abby were both assigned to the job of freeing her. She lacked awareness of their purpose in her life. Now there was a price on her head and Vic's, and Abby was helping both of them escape. And she did not answer Azura's question about whether she and Vic were just friends. Could Azura ask it a third time? She did not dare.

On an impulse, she threw her arms around Abby.

"You've been a good friend to me and my daughter."

"Good luck. I hope you find safety and a nice house with a yard for Noam."

"You'll be in my thoughts."

The women released each other. Abby rose to go.

"One more thing," Azura said.

"Yes? Make it quick."

"Where did you help Vic escape from the first time?"

"From The Pure House."

Azura reeled back.

"From The Pure House?"

"Yes. Vic was the only one left of the original Pure males."

CHAPTER 38
NOAM

My name is Noam, and I am a Pure girl.

I used to live in The Pure House with my friends, Daisy and Sandy. They are Pures, too. I don't like playing with girls who aren't Pures like me. Sometimes I like Sandy better, and sometimes I like Daisy better. When they only like each other, it makes me cry. The Recovered caretakers make them like me again.

My mommy did a bad thing. She made me leave The Pure House and hide. It's a secret. She doesn't want me to be found and taken back to The Pure House. But that's what I want.

What do I like about The Pure House? It's pretty. There's no dust. In the places I live in now, there's so much dust, I can write my name on the furniture. I know how to write my name. N-O-A-M. The caretakers taught me. My name is the easiest because there's only four letters. Sandy and Daisy have five.

Even the glass on the windows is dusty, so I can draw things on it. I wet my finger with my tongue first, then I draw The Pure House with everyone I like next to it, making the children smaller than the grown-ups, like in real life. I draw a tree because there are gardens where we can play. Drawing is what I'm very good at.

Another reason I like The Pure House is the food. Where I live now, there isn't enough. Mommy gives me the most because I'm growing, she says. I eat bananas and peanut butter sandwiches here. That's not what I'm used to. I ate cheese and apples and oatmeal and raisins. If I ate all the healthy things, I could have ice cream and cookies. I drank coke, not plain old water.

Before Mommy took me away, I had a real bed. It was a princess bed with white curtains. Now I sleep on the floor, on a mattress or on a dusty sofa. When I lie down, the dust tickles my nose, and I cough. There are no stuffed animals for me to cuddle with if I wake up in the night. There are no toys in the places we stay. Once I found a doll that someone left behind, but it was dirty and missing an arm. The dolls in The Pure House are prettier. They have clean clothes the caretakers wash and iron. If they break, we get new ones.

I miss Uncle Frank the most. He brought me lots of presents. One time, he took me to the zoo. Just me. Not Daisy or Sandy. He said where we were going was a surprise, and that I should hold his hand all the time we were there. I could call him "Daddy" if anyone talked to us. No one did, but I called him "Daddy" anyway. I was the only child there. The ones I liked best were the monkeys. They were funny.

I wish Uncle Frank was my daddy.

When I'm a big girl, I'll run away from Mommy and go back to The Pure House. I'll see my friends again. When I grow up, I'll have many, many babies. I've already picked out names. The first baby will be Amanda. The second will be... let's see, Dorothy. No, that's the third baby. The second will be Candy. Candy is a good name because it's the same as candy.

I'm being a bad girl with Mommy. I cry and kick when she does something I don't like. If I'm bad enough, she'll take me back. She never says so, but that's what I think. Then she'll be a good mommy again, and I'll love her.

She says, "Don't you want to be with me?"

If I don't want her to look sad, I say "Yes," but when I'm mad at her, I say "No."

Because I don't belong with Mommy anymore. I don't belong in town or in any of these icky places she hides me in.

I belong in The Pure House.

CHAPTER 39
AZURA

Abby's contacts hid the first vehicle in a spot close to the derelict apartment house that was her friends' latest sanctuary. They seemed safer now that they were just two adults and a child — a man, a woman, and their son. Children were unusual in town, but the authorities were not searching for a boy. They ignored boys, anyway. Girls were the valuable ones.

That reversed the way society operated for centuries. Since the dawn of civilization, people have prized their boy babies over girl babies. When ultrasound came along, some aborted female fetuses. After the virus emerged, women hoped for girl babies. As the fertility of the world's population declined, the potential of girls to become mothers increased their value. The bosses rose in power to conserve the social order in which men kept their worth, and fertile women had babies regardless of whether they wanted them.

When they discovered the link between fertility and health status, the greater worth of Pure girls and women became a punishment rather than a reward. The authorities isolated them, pampered them, and turned them into breeding machines, the envied and despised prisoners of their ovaries.

Vic explained this to her while they walked to the designated spot. The soles of their shoes snapped from the stickiness of the road whenever they lifted their feet. Azura listened, wondering what they would do if Abby's contacts did not deliver the vehicles. She felt too anxious to take in all his words. Her fears dominated her mind. She imagined the authorities descending on them, Vic shouting to her to run, shots fired.

But that did not happen. Vic took her arm to steady her. The sulking child held her other hand. Noam hated wearing clothing meant for boys. She had to be scolded and bribed.

"Act like boys act," Vic said. "Pretend to be braver than you feel. And quieter. Most boys don't talk much."

Was that true? What mattered is if Noam believed it long enough for them to reach the second car. If Azura said it, Noam would not have listened and done the opposite to spite her mother. But she had some respect for Vic. She could not predict what he would do if she disobeyed. She marched along with her lips pressed hard together in a show of exaggerated compliance.

Abby's contacts parked the first vehicle a few blocks away on the street. Azura imagined something well hidden, but it stood there in plain view — an older, gas fueled Subaru from the days when they still sold Outbacks. The keys were on the driver's seat, as if a careless owner had left in haste, late for an appointment. It had half a tank of old-fashioned gasoline, enough to get them near to the checkpoint. Paper towels and glass cleaner were on the passenger seat for cleaning the dust and grime off the windshield.

They settled in, with Noam in the back, complaining now that she thought passersby would not pay attention.

"I hate it when people think I'm a boy."

"Remember. No talking!" Vic said.

Noam quieted, giving him a hateful look, which he saw in the rearview mirror. He smiled at Azura, who smiled back, grateful to have another adult to help deal with the exasperating child. They drove out of town on the same road that Azura and Noam used to leave the forest, more than a year earlier. It did not have a checkpoint then because no Pures had escaped.

When they neared the checkpoint, Vic pulled into a small clearing. They piled out, and he threw the keys onto the driver's seat, leaving the Subaru as they found it, in plain view.

"Abby's contacts will pick up the car later tonight and take it back. If the plan works, the authorities won't suspect we've come this far," Vic said.

"Now what?" Azura asked.

"We hike about three miles through the cornfields, circling around the checkpoint."

He looked down at Noam, who scowled up at him.

"Want a ride?"

"How?"

"On my back."

He squatted, and the child climbed on. Azura remembered carrying Noam from the forest and again when escaping from Spreader's Island. Noam had been a year younger the first time and slept all the way. It would be much harder to carry her now. Another reason to be grateful to Vic. Although she did not like being obliged to him.

Hiking through cornfields was difficult. It was still hot even though it neared sundown. Dust swirled around, settling on everything. Visibility was diminished. Vic gave Azura a flashlight.

"One for me?" Noam asked.

"Okay."

He pulled a penlight from his pocket and handed it to her over his shoulder.

"I can have corn for dinner," she said.

"This isn't sweet corn. It doesn't taste good. But it grows high, higher than me, over six feet. It'll hide us while we hike."

"There's sweet corn near the road. We ate some when we left the forest," Azura said.

She was already panting and sneezing from the dust. Both she and Vic carried bottles of water. She drank a mouthful. It would take more than an hour to reach the second vehicle. The water had to be rationed. She concentrated on putting one foot in front of the other, parting the stalks with her hands, maneuvering between rows. They walked for half an hour.

"Now's the time to stay quiet. We should be about parallel with the checkpoint," Vic said.

"Did you hear that? No talking," Azura whispered to Noam.

The child pressed her lips together again.

They walked another twenty minutes. A sudden rustling sound made them pause. Had they been discovered? Azura took a frantic breath, then coughed.

"It's just a doe," Vic said. "Deer nest in cornfields. If there's no fawn, we'll be okay."

He put Noam down.

"Wait here. I'll look and make sure the doe ran off."

It was dusk now. Vic hurried down the row, flashlight beaming ahead of him. A few minutes later, he returned and squatted for the child.

"Coast is clear," he whispered.

But in those few minutes without him, Azura knew that if he disappeared, she would have to protect her daughter and her unborn child herself. The thought terrified her. Then another thought came to her from her time in the forest.

"I could if I had to."

A cornfield was less dense than some parts of the forest. Deer and other creatures nested in thickets, startled during her wanderings and searches for food when she lived among them. She knew how to handle herself in the wild. All she had to do was remember. Life in the town spoiled her. Her forest skills would return. She still had the book she and her mother consulted, "Roots of the Woods." Martin had removed her belongings from the locker in The Pure House where they had been stored, and he had returned them to her.

As the sun sank, it cooled off. Finally, they reached the second vehicle—a Honda sedan—just as Azura gave the last of the water to Noam. As with the Subaru, Abby's contacts left the keys in the driver's seat, the gas tank half full, and windshield cleaning supplies on the passenger seat. Water, sandwiches, cookies, and a can of coke were in the rear.

"I'll drive this time," Azura said.

As she inserted the key, she smiled at the simple action, her command of a vehicle many times her size and weight, doing what she made it do with the pressure of her right foot and maneuvers with her hands to turn the steering wheel.

"Mommy, I don't like this car. I like fancy cars."

"There'll be no more fancy. How would you like to learn to climb trees?"

"Not very much."

"I'll teach you, anyway."

Vic was looking in the passenger side mirror. He turned around to see out the back window.

"What is it?" Azura said.

"Not sure. There are lights in the distance. I can't tell how close they are with this low visibility. It might be someone from town traveling or it might be the authorities."

"Is your seatbelt on?"

"Yes."

"I'm going to outrun it."

She raised her voice for Noam.

"Don't be scared. We're going to go fast for a little while."

She pressed the accelerator, keeping her eye on the lights behind her. The car speeded up, taking the curves at a dizzying angle. I can do this, she kept saying to herself.

"Where are we supposed to leave the car?"

"In the next town. Twenty miles north," Vic said.

That's too far, she thought. If the authorities were chasing them, they would have faster vehicles. She did not hear a siren. That was something.

"I'm going to pull into the first entrance to the forest. We can shelter there until it is safe enough to be on the road again. I'm turning off the car lights and driving in the dark."

"You're the driver," Vic said, with one hand on the dash.

"Don't be scared," she called to the back, again.

At a clearing familiar to her, found more by her instinct than by her sight, leading to an unused lane hidden from the main road, she turned the wheel and entered the forest. The lane was rutted, and Noam cried from the shaking. Azura kept going, taking the Honda deeper in. Fires had thinned the forest, and she did not want the authorities to spot the car while driving by, even in the dust.

When she figured they had gone far enough, she braked.

"The safest thing is to spend the night in the car. Noam can stretch out in the back. We're stuck sitting up, Vic."

"I've been through worse," he said.

She went around to the back to tuck her daughter in. There were blankets in the trunk for the three of them, along with other supplies, including a bottle of wine and cork screw.

"Abby," Azura thought.

She handed the bottle and corkscrew to Vic, then finished putting Noam to sleep. She was willing to leave the job of opening wine bottles to a man. It was more romantic that way. The way she had driven thrilled her, and being thrilled put her in a romantic mood. An attractive man was going to spend the night with her, although sitting up.

When they were both in the front seat, Vic tilted his head at her.

"I didn't know you could drive like a bat out of hell."

"That was the old me, the one who survived in the forest with a child, not the so-called Pure who never lifted a finger."

"Is the old you taking over now, or was that temporary?"

"I hope it's permanent."

They passed the wine back and forth. She took tiny sips. Alcohol was not good for the fetus.

"What's the best plan?" She asked.

"I say we try to get the car to the next town so Abby's contacts will have it for the next escapees."

"Sounds good. And after that?"

"Our choices are town or forest."

"You mean the town we drive to?"

"Yes. Or the forest that's nearby."

"What if they're not good?"

"We can keep going. Until we find a place."

She noticed he said "we."

One day, she would be in her third trimester. That was an uncomfortable time, with many trips to the bathroom, contractions, hard kicks from the baby, and no restful way to sit or lie down. She would go into labor at some point. It would not be a good time to travel or be unsettled.

She would have to stay in a town to find help to deliver the baby. When Noam was born, a community of women were in the forest to help. They were gone now. If she had stayed in The Pure House, she would have received excellent medical attention before they took the baby from her. Now she had to take more risks, find a woman who had experience delivering babies, or chance going to a local hospital that might alert the authorities back in the town she was fleeing.

Vic might just take her to the next town, then go back to Abby for more assignments, or stay with her until she had the help she needed. If what Abby said was true, and Vic was one of the original Pures whose semen was frozen, could he be the father of her baby? Did she dare to hope? She had to find out his intentions.

"Are you planning to dump me soon, or stick around until I'm in a safe place for my baby to be born?"

He gave her a puzzled look. Her tough way of talking was new.

"I won't leave a lady in distress."

He was making a joke of it.

"What about when the distress ends?"

He shifted in the passenger seat to face her, staring at her for several seconds.

Then his lips curled into his most amused smile.

CHAPTER 40
THE SNAKE

The guardian watched from his new post on the side of the island where the weak two-legged ones lived with their red four-legged creatures. He waited for an opportunity to report a straggler to the hunters. It had infuriated the bosses when the two-legged ones slaughtered another of the tribe. They issued new orders. It was war, and the bosses meant to gain control of both sides of the island.

To start, they determined to crush the leader, who had gone to the mainland and returned, inciting his clan to attack the tribe with sticks. Only one was a fire stick, the most menacing kind. Then the leader became weaker, barking and gasping for air. The others lay him in a dwelling. While they did their chores, the one caring for him fell asleep. Such perfect timing might not happen often. The guard immediately summoned a hunter, who carried out the mission without a hitch.

The two-legged ones defended themselves by staying together with their sticks beside them, ready to be used. They reduced the size of the pen for the red four-legged creatures so they would huddle together, too. The hunters waited for a two-legged one to stray off to get water or other supplies. Even if he ran, the hunters could move with lightning speed, catching him before he returned to the group.

In this way, they planned to rid the island of the last seven or eight weak ones, then take charge of the four-legged creatures. The entire island would belong to the tribe.

The guardian took pleasure in scratching his sides with the pointy parts at the end of his stumps. Whenever he drank some of the treasure, his stumps and their ends grew. It was beyond imagination to think what the tribe could do when their stumps were as long as those of the two-legged ones, with extensions that could manipulate stones and other small objects. Crushing would no longer be their only way of mastering their environment. They could build structures, go greater distances, remove all obstacles.

The bosses wanted to rename the island "Eden." The elders said that was what it was called before loss of limbs disabled the tribe, and they could no longer be in mastery of their surroundings. They competed with the other inhabitants of the island—those that flew, those that moved on land—for dominance. Now that was settled.

Once they defeated the last of the two-legged ones, the bosses had ambitious plans. They had their eyes on the mainland. The hunters could use hollowed logs to travel across the waters, or simply swim. Although it would take more time because of the larger population there, the tribe could conquer it, plundering stores of fire sticks, using their new extensions to operate them.

And after that? The bosses had visions they did not share with the guardian. One thing he knew—their tribe had ways to make more treasure when the containers were empty. They would kill the reddest four-legged creature of the herd, then burn it and mix its ashes with spring water and ferns, as they had seen it done by the two-legged ones.

It would be for cleansing the land of the tribe's enemies.

ABOUT THE AUTHOR

Carolyn Geduld is a mental health professional, raised in New York City, but residing all of her adulthood in Bloomington, Indiana. All of her life, she has read, written, listened to, and told stories. She is the author of *Take Me Out The Back*, *Who Shall Live*, and *The Struggle*.

NOTE FROM THE AUTHOR

Word-of-mouth is crucial for any author to succeed. If you enjoyed *Who Shall Die*, please leave a review online—anywhere you are able. Even if it's just a sentence or two. It would make all the difference and would be very much appreciated.

Thanks!
Carolyn Geduld

We hope you enjoyed reading this title from:

BLACK ROSE
writing™

www.blackrosewriting.com

Subscribe to our mailing list – *The Rosevine* – and receive **FREE** books, daily deals, and stay current with news about upcoming releases and our hottest authors.
Scan the QR code below to sign up.

Already a subscriber? Please accept a sincere thank you for being a fan of Black Rose Writing authors.

View other Black Rose Writing titles at
www.blackrosewriting.com/books and use promo code
PRINT to receive a **20% discount** when purchasing.